Alex scrambled to the edge of the ridge and looked down. 50 metres, at least. Not a cliff, but certainly a class four scramble. It would not be an easy down-climb, especially with his overweight pack.

He hesitated. This was not a good idea. By rights it should be SAR out on the mountain right now, not him. If it hadn't been for that creep at the wedding. All of his training and courses screamed in his mind: Safety first. Always.

He shook his head. Too late to turn back now. Zoe was out there somewhere. And Tyler and the others. He needed to find them and make sure they were safe. He turned around and slowly began climbing down, placing each hand and foot carefully. A rock shifted beneath his foot and tumbled down to the glacier below. "Rock!" Alex called, then snorted. Not that there was anyone below him to warn. No one even knew he was there, except Mac. "If you don't hear from me in two days," he'd told Mac, "then call out SAR and tell them where our base camp was. And if any creeps come nosing, you don't know anything." Mac had laughed.

Two days would be a long time to wait if he had a fall.

THE DOOR

Leane Winger

1. Edition, 2021
Copyright © 2021 by Leane Winger
All rights reserved.

ISBN 978-1-7777664-0-5

Published by Leane Winger, Saanichton BC, Canada
leane.n.winger@gmail.com
leanewinger.com

Cover art © Leane Winger
Cover design by Aiden Walker

For my Nan

who in the weeks before she died expressed regret

that she still didn't know what was behind the door

but refused to let me give her any spoilers

And for Jesse

who was there for every step of the journey

A Glossary of Mountaineering and Climbing Terms:

Anchor: One or more pieces of gear affixed in a way that provides a secure attachment point for a rope.

Backup: Additional protection designed to hold the rope if the anchor fails.

Belay: To protect a climber from falling too far by controlling the movement of the rope.

Belay device: A tool used to increase the braking force on the rope when belaying.

Carabiner: A metal loop with a spring-loaded opening on one side, used to connect or clip things together.

Clipping in: The process of attaching to a belay line or anchor for protection.

Cordelette: A multi-purpose loop of thin rope.

Crampon: A set of metal spikes that strap onto the bottom of a boot to provide increased traction when walking on ice or snow.

Crevasse: A deep fissure or crack in a glacier.

Dyno: Short for a dynamic move in climbing, usually involving a jump when both hands and feet temporarily leave the rock face.

Glissade: The act of voluntarily sliding down a steep slope of snow.

Harness: A nylon webbing device worn around the waist and thighs, used to attach the rope, anchor, belay device, etc. securely to the person.

Ice axe: A safety and balancing tool used for ice climbing and mountaineering with a sharp pick on its head and a point on the end of its shaft.

Ice screw: A metal, tubular screw twisted into the ice to provide protection when climbing steep ice.

Nut: A wedge-shaped piece of metal attached to a cord which can be fitted into cracks in the rock and clipped to the rope to provide protection while climbing.

Piton: A thin, wedge-like piece of metal that can be pounded into a rock face and clipped to the rope to provide protection while climbing.

Protection: Any device used to secure a climbing rope to rock, snow, or ice to minimize the consequences of a fall.

Prusik: A sliding knot that holds because of friction when under stress, but slides when the stress or weight is removed.

Rack: The set of equipment used for a climb.

Rappel: To descend a cliff by lowering oneself on a fixed rope using a friction device.

Self-arrest: The act of planting the pick of an ice axe into the snow to stop a slide down the mountain in the event of a slip.

Wicket: A thin pole with a reflector or reflective flag attached to one end.

Chapter 1

"Falling!"

The voice echoed across the glacier as Alex threw himself down onto the icy surface, burying the pick of his mountaineering axe deep into the ice. Several moments passed, with nothing but the hissing of the wind in his ears. The rope tied into his harness remained slack. "Is everyone okay?" he called back over his shoulder.

"Okay!" came Zoe's voice from behind him.

"I'm okay," Jani called from further away.

"Yeah!" Tyler called.

There was a short silence.

"Mostly okay!" Jae called from furthest away.

Relaxing his grip on the axe, Alex lifted his head and looked back down the steep glacier at the rest of his rope team. Zoe lay prone on the ice behind him, her axe embedded in the glacier in the same self-arrest position that he had taken. Behind her, Jani and Tyler were the same.

Jae, last on the rope team, was still upright, but only half of him was visible above the ice. A snow bridge must have collapsed under him, dropping him into the crevasse below. Thankfully it was a narrow crevasse—he had fallen up to his thighs, but the fissure was not wide enough for him to fall any further. His face showed surprise, not pain.

Alex smiled with relief and stood up carefully. His dark brown skin tingled as melting snow trickled down his neck. "Dammit, Jae!" he called over the heads of the rest of the rope team, "I told you not to fall in any crevasses!"

"Well excuse me!" Jae called back. "I'll be sure to remember that next time!"

Next to Alex on the rope team, Zoe got back to her feet cautiously. "You would think it would be an easy thing to remember," she muttered.

Alex smiled at his sister. Her dark skin only showed between her mountaineering goggles and bright red jacket. They were close friends, Alex and his sister. Only a year and a half apart in age, they were both attending the same university and loved many of the same things, including mountaineering.

Alex turned and looked up the glacier toward the peak looming above them. The early morning light glimmered on the snow. "Alright, let's keep going," he called back to the others. "You need help out of that crevasse, Jae?"

"Uhh ..." his arms flailed for a while. "Yeah, that might be nice."

"It might be easier if you put your camera down."

"I'm not putting my camera down!"

"Fine! But if you fell in that crevasse because you were trying to get a picture on a snow bridge, I will confiscate that camera!"

The mountaineers carefully backtracked down the steep glacier, the spiked crampons on their boots digging into the icy snow. Tyler was next to Jae on the rope team, and with his help, Jae was able to pull himself out of the narrow fissure.

Back on his feet, Jae gingerly shook each leg, then adjusted his pack.

"All good?" Alex called.

"Good to go!"

Alex turned to continue the trek up the glacier. Kick in a foothold, step. Kick in a foothold, step. The wind had picked up during the delay; what had been a clear view of the summit was now partially obscured with blowing snow.

"Alex?" Jani's voice was hard to hear through the gusting wind.

Alex stopped. "Yeah?"

"What do you think of those clouds to the south? The really dark ones?"

Alex squinted in the indicated direction. Shadows on the horizon. He'd noticed them before, but now they clearly weren't a distant mountain range. "Yeah, we should keep an eye on those. They don't look too close, so we'll keep going for now."

The friends continued their trek up the mountain, but Alex couldn't help glancing over his shoulder with a sinking feeling in his gut. The wind was blowing stronger all the time—blowing the storm clouds right toward them. He stopped.

"What do you say, Zoe?" he called back to his sister. "Are they getting closer?"

Zoe just nodded.

"What's that?" Jani called, cupping her hand around her ear.

"Storm coming!" Alex had to yell to be heard above the wind. "Tyler?"

"How far to the summit?" Tyler shouted back.

"Maybe two kilometres?"

"Just two kilometers?" Jae shouted from his place at the end of the rope team. "Come on, we can make it! Right, Tyler?"

Alex's heart sank. An unfamiliar mountain, and a storm approaching. They'd be idiots to keep going.

Tyler shook his head.

"I'm calling it," Alex called down the slope to the others. "We don't want to get caught up here."

A mixture of disappointment and relief showed on his friends' faces. One by one, they turned away from Alex to face down the mountain. Now the last of the group, Alex watched his friends begin the descent down the mountain, their heads bowed into the wind.

Alex followed. The pace was slow and careful down the steep incline. Too slow. The dark clouds on the horizon drew steadily nearer, billowing larger and larger before them. Didn't Jae see that? Why wasn't he setting a faster pace? Alex bit his tongue. Shouting wouldn't do any good—the wind was even stronger now. His words would barely make it to Zoe, never mind Jae at the front of the rope team.

Step by step, they continued their descent, as the oncoming storm stretched to engulf the entire southern sky. Then, with a rumble like thunder, the storm swept up the mountain toward them. Jae disappeared in a wall of white obscurity. Then Tyler. Jani. Zoe.

The storm broke over Alex with a force that made him stagger backwards. Shrieking winds and blinding snow engulfed his senses. Crouching against the force of the wind, Alex peered into the grey tumult surrounding him, attempting to shield his face from the sting of the snow. The rope stretching between himself and Zoe swayed and tugged wildly in the wind. Was that patch of darker grey Zoe's figure in the distance, or just his imagination? He stepped forward. The whirling snow made it difficult to see the crude steps they had kicked into the glacier surface only a short while before.

After a few dozen steps, Alex had not reached Zoe. That meant the others were still moving forward. Good. They had to make it down, and the quickest way would be to retrace their steps before the snow covered their boot tracks.

Alex stumbled on, following the rope stretched out in front of him, trying not to let it get too taut or slack. Step after careful step. Don't slip. Don't fall. As long as Jae could see well enough to follow their tracks, they would be fine.

Finally, the gusting wind did not seem as strong. The stinging snow was not as painful. Shadowy shapes moved in Alex's vision and began to solidify into recognisable figures. The others had stopped and were just ahead of him, huddled together penguin-like against the cold. Alex hurried to catch up.

"Is everyone alright?" he asked as he joined the huddle.

There were silent nods of affirmation.

"That wind was brutal." Jae rubbed his face gingerly. "At least it's not so bad now. If it stops soon enough do you think we'll be able to—"

"No. It's already past our turnaround time. We wouldn't make it, even if the storm stopped right now, which it hasn't." Alex put a hand on Tyler's shoulder. "I'm sorry. I know you really wanted to—"

"Eh," Tyler shrugged it off. "There's always another day."

"But—"

"We're behind a ridge." Zoe was staring at the snowy slopes around them with a look of deep suspicion. "We shouldn't be behind a ridge that would offer us this much shelter."

Alex glanced around. Zoe was right. Beyond, the wind still whistled fiercely.

"Are we lost?" Jani's voice was a little too loud.

"Not necessarily lost," Alex spoke carefully, "but we might be off track. Let's see what the GPS says."

Tyler unzipped a pocket and pulled out the group's GPS. He fiddled with it for a moment, then frowned. "It won't turn on. Those were new batteries too." He sighed and reached into a different pocket, pulling out a bag of replacement batteries. Tucking his gloves under his arm, he popped off the GPS's battery pack.

Alex pulled out a bag of trail mix and offered it around. Might as well take the chance to eat.

"Alex, look at this." Tyler leaned over, the GPS in his outstretched hand.

Alex handed the trail mix off to Zoe and moved to Tyler's side. The screen on the GPS was flashing an error symbol. Then it went black. Tyler tried turning it on again. Nothing happened.

"Different batteries?" Alex suggested doubtfully. They tried again, but the same thing happened.

"I've never seen that error screen before," Tyler muttered. "Trust the GPS to crap out at a time like this."

Alex glanced around the group. He trusted Tyler and Jani to keep an even head—they were students in the same outdoor leadership program that he was and had trained just as hard—but even so he could tell that they were worried.

Jani's family was from India, but she had lived her whole life in Canada, growing up not far from where all of them were attending university in Monksford. Tyler had grown up only a few streets away from Jani, and they'd known each other since they were kids.

The rest of the friends had met at university. Jae's family came to Canada from South Korea when he was young, and he'd grown up in Vancouver. Alex and Zoe came from rural Ontario. Their mother was Kenyan by birth, but their father's family had lived in Ontario for generations.

In the two years since Alex had come to British Columbia, he'd never seen a storm this bad, and he'd gotten out into the mountains whenever he could. He had the training to deal with high-risk situations, but even so he knew that their position was not good. They had to get off the mountain or find shelter soon. From helmets and goggles to down coats and Gore-Tex, they were dressed in the best mountaineering gear they had, but even that wouldn't be enough to keep them warm in this kind of weather for long. Jae was already stamping his feet and blowing on his gloved fingers. He often joked that he had tropical blood—anything below fifteen degrees Celsius, and he was freezing. By the bite of the wind, Alex guessed it was more like fifteen below zero. Blowing snow still obscured any significant features of the landscape. Easing his pack off his shoulders, Alex pulled out their trip plan and turned to the topographical map. "Any guesses where we are?"

Zoe looked over his shoulder. "If we veered west, we might be behind that ridge." She pointed to the map. "Or that ridge. If we veered east we would have fallen off that cliff before now. Unless we're all the way down there. It depends on how long we've been off track."

Alex glanced at Jae. "How long ago did you stop following our tracks?"

"I never stopped following our tracks. Not intentionally, anyway. How should I know how long it's been?"

"How long since you stopped being sure you were following our tracks?"

"I don't know. I thought I was still following them, okay?"

"You won't believe this," Tyler gestured to the compass that he had pulled out of another pocket. The needle was slowly spinning.

"Are you serious?" Alex protested.

"In a roundabout way." Tyler gave a wry grin.

Alex shook his head and sighed. "Okay. I guess we'll just head down the mountain, and hopefully things will clear up soon so we can figure out where we are."

Jani frowned. "But we read about a restricted area on the west side of the mountain, remember? What if we end up there by accident?"

"We could hardly be held responsible for that, given the circumstances." Alex assured her. "Anyway, we do have some shelter on this side of the ridge, and I don't want to give that up. Our first priority is to get down off this mountain without freezing to death. Once the storm lets up we can worry about getting back on track and finding our base camp."

The others just nodded. Jae set off right away down the snowy slope, and one by one the others followed.

Alex returned the trip plan to his pack and followed last, still going over the map in his mind. There was another significant glacier down the west side of the mountain—was that what they were travelling on now? He hadn't seen any crevasses yet. It was hard to say just how much distance they had been able to cover, but at least they were steadily dropping elevation. As long as they kept moving, the blowing snow did not seem quite as bitterly cold.

A sickening crack echoed through the silence, jolting Alex out of his thoughts. The snow beneath Jae's feet had given way, dropping him down into darkness below.

"Fall—" Jae's voice echoed across the snow as Alex turned and threw himself to the ground, digging his axe into the snow. There was another shout in the distance and then a sharp jerk as the rope went taught. His axe held firm.

"Who's still up?" Alex called.

"I'm here!" Zoe replied.

"I'm alright!" Jani called breathlessly.

Silence.

Glancing over his shoulder, Alex could see Zoe and Jani, but where Tyler and Jae should have been was a gaping chasm.

Damn.

"Jani, dig in! Let me know when you're secure."

"Secure!"

Cautiously, Alex got to his feet. "Zoe, you'd better stay down for now, in case Jani slips. I'll set up the anchor."

Carefully, Alex made his way past Zoe to where Jani waited in self-arrest, about six metres from the edge of the crevasse. Working as quickly as he could, Alex set up an anchor, tying it to the rope with a prusik hitch, just a short distance down from Jani.

"There. Let's ease off a bit and see how that holds."

Carefully, Jani moved just enough to transfer the weight of Tyler and Jae to the anchor instead of her harness. Alex watched the anchor carefully. "It's holding."

"Good." Zoe stood up, "Jani, you be our backup for now. I'll set up the second anchor."

While Zoe set up a t-slot anchor with her axe, Alex took a moment to look around. The crevasse that stretched out before them could easily swallow a bus. How much more of it still lay hidden beneath the snow? They would have to make a significant detour, just to make sure no one fell in again. At least the storm seemed to be letting up.

"Ready," Zoe said, clipping a carabiner into the new anchor. Together they made sure that both anchors were sharing the load equally. Slowly, Jani rolled to her side and sat up. Alex could tell that she was worried.

"You two wait here," he said, attaching another sling to the rope and clipping it to his harness, "I'll see if I can talk to Tyler and Jae."

Carefully, Alex walked towards the edge of the crevasse, sliding the prusik along the rope. Before each step, he probed the ground in front of him with the shaft of his axe to see if it would hold. On the brink of the crevasse, he leaned over as far as he dared. "Tyler! Jae! Are you alright?"

"Yeah," Tyler's voice echoed through the chasm.

"Are you hurt?"

"No. I'm fine."

"Good. How about Jae?"

"He's okay too."

Alex breathed a sigh of relief. "They're alright!" he called over his shoulder. Turning back to the crevasse, he called to Tyler, "What's the situation like down there?"

"Well, Jae's upset because he dropped his camera."

"I don't care about his camera. How's the ice? Do you have free movement?"

"Yeah. The ice looks really good. Should be pretty easy to climb. We've got our prusiks, but it will be easy enough to find a handhold if we need it."

"Great. You both think you can manage the climb?"

"Yeah. Um ..." Tyler hesitated, "Jae says he wants to go down after his camera."

"Jae!" Alex yelled down into the crevasse. "Are you *nuts*?"

Jae's muffled voice echoed from deep in the crevasse, "I'm not leaving my camera behind!"

"It's lost, Jae! Get over it!"

"But I can see it! It's not that far to the bottom!"

"Really?"

"Yeah," Tyler confirmed, "I can see the bottom. It looks like bedrock down there."

"Huh. That's strange."

"It's actually really cool down here," Tyler added. "Lots of ice formations and things. Do you think we could explore a bit before we move on?"

"Tyler, you're crazy. We're lost on a mountain in a storm, with two of our party hanging down the side of a crevasse, and you want to go exploring. Why am I not surprised?"

"Okay, okay. I'll come up. What about Jae? I think the tail of the rope might reach far enough."

Alex sighed. "Okay. Jae! As long as you have enough rope, you can try to reach your camera. But if it takes too long I'm going to call you back. I'm not risking anyone getting hypothermia."

"Roger!"

"What's going on?" Jani's voice called from behind Alex.

Alex turned. "They're both fine. Jae lost his camera and wants to go down after it."

"Is that safe?"

"He says he's not far from the bottom of the crevasse. As long as he's attached to the rope he'll be safe enough."

"What about Tyler?"

"He's going to climb up."

"Should he wait on the rope until Jae is finished?"

"Not a bad idea. We should really get something under the rope so it doesn't dig into the ice. We'll do that while we're waiting."

Jani nodded. "On it."

Alex waited by the edge of the crevasse. He couldn't see Tyler or Jae, but at least he'd hear if something happened.

Minutes dragged by.

"Got it!" Jae's voice echoed up from the depths of the crevasse.

Alex let out his breath. "Good! Tyler, you climbing up? We're ready for you!"

Tyler didn't reply. Alex could hear Jae and Tyler talking to each other, but their words were muffled. "What's going on?"

"I'm going down after him!" Tyler called.

"Tyler! What are you ... what's going on?" Alex leaned as far over the ledge as he dared. He could just see Jae moving cautiously along the bottom of the crevasse—no longer attached to the rope. What an idiot! And Tyler said he was going after him—

"Tyler! Don't do it! You'll get yourself killed!"

Silence.

Well, crap. Alex turned back toward Zoe and Jani. They were both staring at him. "I don't know what's going on down there, but Jae has unclipped, and I think Tyler has too," Alex explained quickly. "I'm going down there to find out what's going on. I'll radio you as soon as I know."

Alex grabbed the belay device off his gear loop and quickly set up what he needed for the rappel. Leaning backwards over the edge, he stepped down into the crevasse.

Silence engulfed him. The air was still and piercingly cold. Quickly, Alex rappelled to the bottom, then paused to get his bearings. The icy walls of the crevasse stretched above him, glimmering with grey-blue light. There was no sign of Jae or Tyler.

The slack in the rope only let him move a couple of metres. Wait—was that something over there? Just out of sight?

"Tyler! Jae!"

"Alex?" Jae's voice echoed in the distance. "You've got to come see this."

Something strange about Jae's voice made Alex pause, both curious and annoyed. What had they found? The rock beneath his feet seemed solid enough, and both Tyler and Jae had gone that way already. Anyway, it seemed like they wouldn't come back unless he fetched them personally.

Cringing inside, Alex untied himself from the rope and hurried towards his friends.

Rounding a corner, Alex found Tyler and Jae staring at a massive wall of rock, dark and imposing against the glacial ice surrounding it. And there, in the uncannily sheer face of rock, was a door.

Alex's heart thumped in his chest. The door was large—much taller than a person—and covered with strange geometric designs. It glimmered strangely in the icy light of a thousand crystalline ice formations. It was an unworldly sight.

"What's *that*?"

Alex turned to find the source of the voice behind them. "Jani! What are you doing down here?"

"I tried radioing you, but I couldn't get the radio to work. I was worried. What's that?"

As if Jani's arrival had broken some kind of spell, the others looked at each other in amazement.

"Some kind of doorway," Jae said, unhelpfully.

"A doorway to *adventure*! That's what that is!" Tyler hurried over to the door, poking at it and pushing it.

"Tyler!" Jani exclaimed, hurrying after him.

Alex's mind was spinning. What was a door doing here—under a *glacier*, of all places? How did it *get* here?

"This is really well made!" Tyler called, his nose centimetres from the door. "All these patterns are as sharp and clear as anything. And it's *solid*! This is one heavy duty door! Also, I can't get it open."

Alex's eyes moved back and forth along the door's elaborate designs. What did those symbols mean? Were they some kind of language? They didn't remind him of any of the ancient civilizations he'd learned about in school. And who would make a door under a glacier? The ice would move and you would never find it again. Could it be ... that this door had been here since *before* the glacier?

"It's iron. Or some kind of metal." Tyler continued his observations. "And it looks like each side was cast as a single piece. There aren't any hammer marks or anything."

Beside Alex, Jae was fumbling with his camera. Dropping to one knee, he started taking pictures of the door.

In the distance, the shrill note of a whistle pierced the air. It took a moment for Alex to register it properly. Was that Zoe?

Tearing himself away from the sight of the door, Alex hurried back along the crevasse to where the rope hung limp. He could just see Zoe's head, silhouetted against the sky.

"What is it, Zoe?"

"There you are! The wind has shifted and it's growing stronger. We should leave as soon as possible."

"Copy that! I'll go get the others." Alex hurried back to where the door stood, imposing and mysterious. This time he did not let himself be distracted. "Come on, guys! The storm is getting worse—we need to get out of here!"

Tyler turned to face him, disappointment clouding his eyes. "Yeah. You're right. Come on, Jani." Tyler and Jani stumbled away from the door and hurried past Alex.

Alex strode over to Jae, who was trying to get a close-up photo of some of the designs carved into the door. "Come on, Jae!"

Jae continued fiddling with his camera.

"Jae! Earth to Jae! We need to go!"

"But Alex, this could be the find of the century! Of the millennium!"

"And if we don't make it out of here alive, no one will ever know we found it! Come on!"

Finally Jae looked over at Alex and sighed. "Alright."

Together they hurried along the crevasse to where Tyler was standing by the rope. Jani was already most of the way up.

Alex watched as she hesitated at the lip of the crevasse. "Are you going to manage it, Jani?"

"Yeah," Jani panted, bracing herself. Then she pushed herself up, reaching over the lip. A couple moments of scrambling, and she disappeared from view.

Alex immediately tied in his protection and began to follow Jani up the rope. As he reached the lip, he realized why Jani had hesitated. The wind whistled past him furiously, taking his breath away. Digging his crampons into the icy wall before him, he steadied himself and stood up into the wind. The sting of the snow made his eyes water. He reached, pulled, scrambled to get his knees over the edge. Finally he made it, crawled a few paces further, and slowly got to his feet.

It only took a quick glance around to confirm Zoe's report. The storm was closing in again, and the visibility was rapidly dropping.

"Zoe!" he called to his sister, "let's give the others a pull. Help them up faster."

Zoe nodded.

"I'll watch the edge," Jani offered, moving toward the crevasse without waiting for a reply.

Alex quickly set up a three to one haul system.

"Ready when you are," Zoe said, waiting by the anchor to feed the rope through the prusik.

Jani secured herself at the brink of the crevasse. "Jae's ready!" she called back to Alex and Zoe.

With everyone working together, Jae was quickly up and out of the crevasse.

"Gosh!" Jae exclaimed as he staggered over to Alex and Zoe, "That wind is something else!"

Alex nodded. "Let's get Tyler up!" he called.

Quickly they fed the rope back down into the crevasse. Alex noticed that Jae's lips were turning blue. He was about to say something, but Jani called from the crevasse edge, "He's ready!"

"Alright, pull!"

Together, Alex and Jae pulled, while Zoe and Jani took care of safety and backups. Tyler's head was just starting to show above the lip of the crevasse, when he gave a sharp yell.

Alex stopped pulling. "What's wrong?"

"He says never mind. Just get him out of here," Jani relayed to the others.

As quickly as they could, they got Tyler over the edge and out of the crevasse. He staggered as he got to his feet, and Jani was immediately by his side. He put his arm over her shoulder and limped as they walked slowly toward the others.

"What happened?" Alex asked as he got Tyler sitting down a safe distance from the crevasse.

"My crampons got caught in the ice and my ankle twisted."

"Dang. Your right ankle?"

"Yeah."

"Okay, sit down and I'll have a look at it. Everyone else, start getting ready to go."

Alex gave Tyler's ankle a quick range of motion test and a weight bearing test. "We've got to get going, before Jae gets hypothermia," he said quietly. "Do you think you can walk alright?"

"Sure," Tyler said grinning, "I've had worse."

As quickly as they could, the friends roped up again. This time Alex was first. Then Jae, Jani, Tyler, and Zoe taking up the rear. The wind whistled past them, driving the blowing snow into their faces. Alex tried to set a slow pace so that Tyler wouldn't have to strain himself too much. At least some progress forward was better than none.

Cautiously, they gave the crevasse a wide berth, continuing their way down the glacier. Soon they were brought up short by another crevasse. Carefully, Alex navigated around it. Then there was another crevasse. And another. Half an hour and seven crevasses later, Alex motioned the others up to confer together.

"Holy freaking crevasses!" Tyler called as he came within earshot. "This is brutal!"

"Yeah," Alex agreed. "We really can't afford another fall like we had before. I'm wondering, since we're clearly not being sheltered by a ridge anymore, should we try heading parallel to the crevasses and see if we can get off this glacier?"

Zoe shrugged. "It's worth a shot."

Jani and Jae didn't say anything. They both looked exhausted.

Without waiting, Alex started off again. This time, instead of circling the crevasse, He led them parallel to it, and kept going in that direction. They passed one more crevasse, but after that the crevasses seemed to stop. They plodded on, with nothing but whiteness around them and icy snow under their feet. Then—something dark against the snow.

"Hey!" Alex called, "It's a boulder!"

"That's a nice boulder!" Tyler called back.

Alex couldn't help grinning. Soon there were more boulders poking up through the snow.

"Does this mean we're off the glacier?" Jani asked.

"I think so," Alex said, relieved. They may still be lost in a storm on a mountain, but at least they didn't have to be worried about falling down another crevasse.

Soon they found themselves on a rocky outcrop. Looking around, Alex realized he could see farther now. "We're on a ridge," he told the others. "Look. If we follow this down, we should make it alright. How are you holding up, Tyler?"

"Oh, I've been better, but I'm managing."

"Well, as long as you're okay, we'll press on."

Quickly, they unroped themselves, and Alex took Tyler's pack, wearing it on his front. With only a short break, they set off down the ridge. Gradually, the falling snow turned to slush, and then to rain.

"It looks like we're dropping below the storm," Jani said, "Do you think we're about the same elevation as our base camp now?"

"Could be," Alex said. "Man, I wish our GPS was still working."

A couple of minutes later, Tyler gave a shout. "Hey! Guess what! Our GPS is working again!"

Alex stopped and looked back. "What?"

"Yeah, I thought I'd just check it and see if I could figure out what was wrong with it, but it turned on, no problem at all!"

"Alright! Let's have a look!"

The friends all gathered around the GPS.

"Whoa—how did we end up way over *there*?" Jae said, pointing to the screen.

Tyler grinned. "You've got to admit, that's pretty impressive."

Alex zoomed the image in to show the elevation markers. "You're right, Jani, we are at the same elevation as our base camp." He zoomed the image out again, "We're just five kilometers too far north-west."

"Five kilometres?" Jae's eyes got big.

"Yeah. We're in for a long haul, it seems. But at least we know where we're going now."

The kilometres dragged by as they trudged through snow pack and scrambled across boulder fields, barraged by the relentless rain. Tyler's limp got steadily worse. Jani and Jae started stumbling.

Finally they rounded an outcropping of rock and found themselves in their rain-drenched campsite.

"Glory, hallelujah!" Tyler cried as he sank to the ground at the foot of his tent. A moment later he added, "That's a puddle I just sat in."

Alex gave a tired smile. "Let's get your foot elevated and have a look at it."

Jani set her pack on the ground and started pulling out her camp stove.

"Can we sleep now?" Jae asked.

"For a bit, if you want," Alex replied, "but we should only stay an hour or two. Unless we *want* to spend another night on the mountain after that ordeal."

"No, not really."

"Just let me know if you're starting to feel chilled."

"Alright." Jae crawled into his tent.

Carefully, Alex pulled Tyler's boot off and started icing his ankle. No one talked much. They were all too tired and lost in thought. Alex couldn't stop thinking about the mysterious door they had found. Who made it? How old was it? And most intriguing of all—what lay hidden behind it?

"Hot chocolate, anyone?"

Alex shook himself out of his reflections. "Jani, you're the best," he said, accepting one of the steaming cups she held out to them.

"You bet she is," grinned Tyler, "that's why I'm dating her."

Zoe had the other stove out and was re-hydrating the dried chili they had brought along. A warm meal helped everyone's spirits, but even so, their short rest passed all too quickly. As the grey light faded, they turned on their headlamps and packed up their tents, dividing Tyler's pack between them. Jani helped Tyler wrap his ankle and get his boot back on.

"That nap was not long enough," Jae mused to no one in particular.

Night had fully fallen by the time they set out on the winding trail down the mountain. Subdued and silent, they trudged on, switchback after switchback, the tramp of their boots a dull, hypnotic beat. Columns of pine trees marched past the glow of their headlamps like a ghostly army, shrouded in the endless sound of falling rain.

Alex blinked out of his half-waking dream to see that the path had turned onto an old logging road. They rounded a bend, and there was the car.

With aching backs and aching feet, they eased their packs into the back of the car and pulled off their boots. Alex sighed with relief. But even as his friends piled into the car for the long drive home, Alex couldn't resist a long glance back at the mountain, looming black against the starless sky.

Chapter 2

"I'm going back there."

Alex looked up from his laptop and grinned. "I know, Tyler, you've said that five times now."

Tyler fidgeted with the papers and maps scattered around him on the couch. His blond hair hung messily around his shoulders, a half-eaten bowl of mac and cheese sat forgotten on the coffee table. It wasn't an unusual sight; Alex and Tyler had been roommates for two years of university now, and they had gotten to know each other pretty well. When something new caught Tyler's imagination, there was no distracting him.

Zoe was curled up in her usual spot on the other couch, her black curly hair tied up in a high ponytail. Although she technically had a room in dorms, she was over at her brother's apartment so much she practically lived there. Alex and Zoe had a lot more in common than the dark skin and curly hair they had inherited from their Kenyan mother. They both loved a good puzzle, and Alex didn't have to look at the way she was hunched over her laptop to know that she was deep in research, trying to figure out who could have made the door, and what its purpose might have been.

Jani's voice called from the kitchen, "Do you guys *ever* wash your dishes?"

"When we need a dish, we wash it," Tyler explained without looking up from his papers.

Jani stuck her head out from the kitchen just long enough to roll her eyes at him. Her long, dark braid whipped out behind her as she ducked back around the corner.

Alex closed his laptop. "Can I help you, Jani?"

"I'm alright," Jani answered quickly. "I'm just trying to find a plate to serve these samosas on before Tyler and Zoe die from malnutrition."

Alex grinned. "I'm pretty sure they would die if you weren't around to feed them."

"That's not true," Tyler protested. "Pizza has all the important food groups."

"You guys have pizza?" Jae stepped in through the open screen door and slid it shut behind him. Friends were always coming and going from unit 412, and everyone knew there was no need to knock.

"Not pizza. Samosas," Alex explained, gesturing to Jani who was just emerging from the kitchen. She held up the loaded plate.

"Even better!" Jae grinned. "Jani's family makes the best samosas ever." He glanced at the papers scattered across the couch. "Studying maps already?"

"I'm going back to that door," Tyler replied in a matter-of-fact voice.

"Of course you are," Jae retorted, "and I'm going too."

Alex exchanged a glance with Tyler.

"Samosas?" Jani offered.

Everyone gathered around the table, except for Zoe, who would not budge from her spot on the couch.

"Have you been able to get your camera working, Jae?" Alex asked as he moved a pile of textbooks off one of the chairs.

"It's completely busted," Jae frowned. "That's actually why I'm here. Do you think you could look at it, Tyler? I was using my old film camera, but the latch mechanism is broken and I can't get the film out."

Tyler shrugged. "Sure, I can have a look."

"Like, right now? I need those pictures asap."

"What's the rush?"

"My column for the university newspaper is due in half an hour."

"It's due today?" Alex raised his eyebrows. "Why didn't you submit it *before* our trip?"

"Because I was planning to submit a collection of photos *from* our trip. I'm glad I waited. Now I have the most exciting news story I've ever written—but no one will believe it's real if I can't include a picture of the door with it."

"You're broadcasting the news about this door to the *whole school*?!"

"Why not? This will generate interest in my column if nothing else will. Anyway, my article doesn't give any particulars about where it was, so we don't need to worry about competition. When we go back I'll document the whole expedition and I can make an entire series on it. Everyone will love it!"

"I'm not interested in everyone loving it," grumbled Tyler, "I just want to find out more about that door."

"So let's get this camera open," Jae concluded with a cocky grin. "I know we all want to see those pictures I got."

No one could disagree, so Tyler took the camera back to his couch and began pulling it apart. Jae hovered over him nervously.

"If we're going back to that door, we should go as soon as we can," Alex mused out loud. "That crevasse field was rough, and it's just going to get worse the farther we get into the mountaineering season."

"We should go this weekend, if the weather permits it," Zoe agreed.

Alex looked around at the others. Jae nodded. Tyler pulled a tool kit out from under the table. "Jani and I don't have any plans."

"But you do, Alex," Zoe interjected. "Our cousin's wedding."

Alex's heart sank. "That's right. We have a wedding this weekend."

Zoe shook her head. "*You* have a wedding this weekend. I'm not going. Weddings are way too crowded, and knowing our cousin, it will be much too loud for me."

Alex nodded. Zoe had been diagnosed with autism when she was in high school, and she'd learned to be a good judge of what she could handle and what she couldn't. "Fair enough. But I have to go, I told him I'd give a speech at the reception. And it's in Ontario, so I can't just ditch early so we can head up the mountain. How about the next weekend?"

Jae looked up. "I have a journalists' convention that weekend."

"The *next* weekend?"

"Tyler is coming with me and my family to visit my grandparents in India." Jani smiled apologetically. "We'll be gone for three weeks."

Alex sighed. "And after that the glacier may be completely impassable."

"So we should go this weekend," Jae concluded.

"But I'm gone this weekend."

"That doesn't mean the rest of us can't go."

"But what about next weekend?" Alex looked at Tyler and Zoe. He knew they wouldn't want to go without him.

"Hey!" Jae protested. "I'm the journalist, you can't leave me behind!"

"So skip your convention if this trip is so important to you!"

"Alex—" Jani interjected timidly. "I checked the weather forecast. It's supposed to be clear through the weekend, but after that the weather turns unstable again. If we wait, we'll be risking storms like we got caught in yesterday."

"So this weekend is the best time to go," Jae concluded. "Sorry, man."

Alex held back a snort. Yeah right, Jae was sorry. But if the weather forecast was right, this weekend might be the only opportunity for a return trip to the mountain. His heart sank, but he wasn't going to try to talk his friends out of it. There was no point in all of them missing out on the adventure, just because he had to.

"I've got it." Tyler held up the roll of film, safely extricated from the camera.

"Great!" Jae grabbed it and headed for the door. "I'll be back to work on our plans after I've submitted the article. Be sure to pick up a copy of the newspaper when it comes out this weekend!"

Alex turned away, silently cursing his luck. He listened as Jae's footsteps receded into silence.

"It's a good thing Jae was using an old film camera," Tyler mused.

"Why?" Jani asked, tidying up the table.

"I've turned the GPS and the radios inside out. Can't find anything wrong with them."

Alex frowned. "Then why did they stop working?" Tyler shrugged. "Maybe because we were close to that door."

Jani's eyes widened.

Zoe looked up for the first time that afternoon. "Really? Was something interfering with the electrical current?"

Tyler nodded. "Maybe. We can't know for sure till we go back and try a few tests. But we can't count on anything electrical to be working—lights, watches, communications—anything. Or a compass for that matter."

Jani frowned. "But then we can't use a SPOT device to call for help if we run into trouble."

Alex looked over at Jani, who quickly glanced away. "Jani, are you okay with this? You don't need to go if you don't want to."

"I'm fine," she answered quickly. "We just need to think things through carefully."

"Of course," Alex agreed. "But—"

"We can still use the SPOT," Tyler interjected, "as long as we're far enough away from the door. For everything else we can just go old school: propane lanterns, mechanical clocks. It will be fun!" He turned to Zoe. "Do you think we'll figure out how to get in?"

"If the symbols on the door are some kind of language or code, I can figure it out. Did they look anything like cuneiform?" She tipped the screen on her laptop to show an example.

Tyler shook his head. "It was more pictorial, or like a design."

"Hieroglyphs?"

"More geometric than hieroglyphs."

Alex just listened as Zoe and Tyler debated the possible origins of the door. He didn't have much heart to join the conversation.

Late that evening as Zoe was leaving, Alex stepped outside with her for a moment.

"You'll make sure they don't do anything stupid?"

"Of course. I wouldn't let anyone do something stupid, especially on a mountain."

Alex smiled at his sister. "I know. I'll expect updates every step of the way, as long as the technology works."

"Of course. It's always best practice to keep someone informed of where you are. You know that."

Alex nodded. He knew that. And he knew that Zoe wouldn't make any foolish decisions. But he still felt uneasy.

Or maybe he was just disappointed to be left behind.

Chapter 3

Alex slipped through the door, away from the loud dance music and flashing coloured lights. He needed a break from the overstimulation, and anyway, he wanted to check his phone for updates from Zoe. He hadn't heard anything since a message early that morning, saying that they were leaving base camp. If their suspicions were right about their electronic malfunctions, he wouldn't hear anything until Zoe and the others returned to base camp Sunday evening; but still, he wanted to check.

"Alex Wieland?"

Alex looked up from his phone to see a middle-aged man with a pleasant, approachable face walking confidently towards him. He slid his phone back into his pocket. "That's my name."

"Good." The man flashed a friendly smile and held out his hand. "I hear that you can help me with a few questions."

Alex shook the offered hand. "That depends on what the questions are." Something seemed strange about the man, but he couldn't quite place it.

"I am looking for information regarding a few people." The man flicked a piece of lint off his well-cut suit and pulled a notepad from his pocket. "Specifically, I want to know the location of Jae-Seong Kim, Tyler Harrison, Janilee Misra, and Zoe Wieland." He looked up from his notepad. "I believe she is your sister."

Alex was taken aback. "How do you know them? And why do you want to know where they are?"

The man pulled out a newspaper. "According to a very interesting article in the Monksford University Newspaper, you and four others were navigating a glacier when you discovered a most singular door, hidden beneath the glacier."

Alex's eyes widened. "How the heck did you get your hands on that paper? It came out this morning on the other side of the country!"

"We have agents in many locations," the man replied with a hint of pride in his voice, "and information can be gathered very quickly when necessary."

Alex gave the man a sharp glance. "Who is 'we'? Were you even invited to this wedding at all?"

The man brushed off the question. "I represent the Historical Acquisitions Agency. We have been tracking unusual electromagnetic occurrences in the Cariboo Mountains for quite a while, and your finding is of great interest to us. Naturally, I would appreciate whatever information you can give me. Which glacier were you traversing at the time?"

"We were lost in a storm and our GPS stopped working," Alex said cautiously, "we had no idea where we were."

"But clearly you must have some idea of where you were, because your friends have attempted to return." A corner of his mouth twitched upwards.

Alex grabbed the newspaper from the stranger and quickly glanced at the article. It wasn't much to speak of. Two blurry photographs and a short narration of the events surrounding their discovery of the door, written with Jae's flair for the dramatic. But it didn't say anything about their intention to return. It didn't even include their names! He handed the newspaper back with a frown. "What makes you think they've tried going back?"

"Since the events narrated in this article, the four other mountaineers in question have become untraceable, and you flew across the country. It is not hard to deduce that the others have returned to the mountain, while you were unable to join them because of a prior commitment to attend your cousin's wedding." He tilted his head as if listening to the music filtering down the corridor, an insufferable smile lingering on his face. "Is that not correct?"

Alex's face hardened. "Look here. I don't know who you think you are, but this is completely unacceptable. As your 'research' has doubtless informed you, my friends and I are outdoors enthusiasts, who take every opportunity to get out into the wilderness, so the fact that my friends are currently untraceable means nothing, and to tell you anything about their location would be a serious breach of privacy. As for myself, I have no interest in speaking to someone who has so blatantly been violating the privacy of myself and my friends, even to the point of intruding upon a wedding that you were not invited to. I want you to leave. Now."

The stranger arched his eyebrows, but the smile did not leave his face. "I see." He pulled a business card from his wallet. "If something were to happen to ... change your mind, feel free to call me. I might be able to help." With a curt nod, he turned on his heels and walked away.

Alex restrained his urge to throw the business card at the stranger's head. Who the heck did he think he was? And what was the Historical Acquisitions Agency, anyway? Alex repressed a smirk as he wondered if they called themselves the HAA, for short. But this stranger had been anything but humorous. How had he gotten so much information—even to show up to a stranger's wedding! There was something very wrong about this. After making sure the intruder had left the building, Alex grudgingly returned to the celebrations. He had lost any interest in dancing.

It was midnight before he was able to leave. Returning to the hotel room where he was staying, Alex locked the door behind him, sat down at the desk, and opened his laptop. It was time for him to do some research of his own.

Two hours later, Alex had to give up. He could not find anything on the internet about a Historical Acquisitions Agency. The business card was simple and black, with the name of the agency and a phone number. Nothing else. He tried searching the number, but it was unlisted, with an unusual area code that he couldn't identify. Frustrated and worn out, Alex collapsed into bed and slept fitfully.

The next morning as he was waiting for his flight back to Monksford, Alex continued to think about what the strange man had said. *If something were to change your mind.* It almost sounded like a threat. He shook himself. This was all so preposterous. Why should anyone take a couple of blurry photographs in a university newspaper so seriously?

Alex pulled out the business card and looked it over again. Was there anything else on it at all? Something that might give him more helpful information? Turning it over, he noticed that it was slightly thicker than a usual business card. Looking closer at the back, he could see the faint outline of some kind of microchip embedded in the card. What could that be? Some kind of data chip? But for what kind of data? Was it a tracking device?

Alex jumped as the com system blared an announcement through the speakers above his head. His flight was beginning to board. What should he do? He didn't want to give anyone the possibility of tracking him. A janitorial worker wheeled a cleaning cart past him. Quickly, Alex dropped the business card into the trash bin. That should throw off the Society of the Creepy Creeps for a little while. He hurried to board his plane. This whole business surrounding the door was becoming more and more alarming.

Chapter 4

The apartment was dark and quiet when Alex arrived home late Sunday afternoon—just the way it should be—but Alex still looked around for signs that someone had been snooping. He noted a dark car with tinted windows in the visitor parking spot near their patio. Could that be—Alex shook himself. Since when had he become so paranoid? Since finding a mysterious door under a glacier and being questioned by a creepy stranger who knew too much. Alex gave a dry laugh. And locked the door behind him.

Everything inside the apartment was as it should be, apart from the emptiness and silence of his friends' absence. He made himself supper with his phone on the counter beside him so he would know as soon as Zoe messaged him. Everything would be alright as soon as they got back. Together they could decide what to do about the stranger and the Historical Acquisitions Agency.

Settling on the couch, Alex reached for his cup, but his hand found nothing there. He looked up. Strange. He always left his cup there, and he was sure that he didn't put it away before he left for his flight Friday evening. He went to look in the kitchen, but it wasn't in the dishwasher. It wasn't in the cupboard. He went back into the living room. There was his cup. Not in its usual spot, but where Tyler's cup usually went.

The hair on the back of Alex's neck began to tingle. This was wrong. He was sure he wouldn't have left his cup in Tyler's spot, and he was the last one to leave the house. Quickly, Alex checked all of the doors and windows. They were locked. He looked in every corner and closet. No sign of any intruders. Alex forced himself to sit down and eat his supper, but he didn't feel hungry. If only he could get a message from Zoe. Then he wouldn't feel so restless.

Six o'clock. The targeted time for the expedition's return to base camp. No message. Maybe they were running late, Alex told himself, but he went to his closet and pulled out his backpack.

Seven o'clock. Still no reason to worry, but Alex started laying his climbing gear out across his bed, just in case.

Eight o'clock. Sometimes things run late, Alex assured himself, but he started rooting through the cupboards to see what trip food was still lying around.

At nine o'clock there was still no word from Zoe. Alex paced the apartment. If the others didn't return, what would he do? Call Search and Rescue? The last thing he wanted to do was give their expedition more publicity. And what if the delay was somehow *caused* by the Historical Acquisitions Agency? That would be entirely outside of SAR's jurisdiction. No, if his friends needed to be found, he would have to go himself. And the fewer people who knew about it the better.

Alex cringed inside. Glacier travel. He couldn't do that by himself. He hadn't studied mountaineering for two years to go and do something stupid like that. Quickly he pulled up the map on his computer. He had helped Tyler and the others plan their trip. From their limited GPS data and their collective memory of the terrain and landmarks, they were pretty confident they knew the approximate location of the door, and which glacier it was hidden beneath. The others had planned to backtrack along their route as closely as possible, to avoid missing the right crevasse, but what if another route were possible? Alex scanned the map. The ridge skirting the south of the glacier extended much further than where he and the others had accessed it before. If he followed the ridge, could he get beyond the crevasse-riddled terrain and access the furthest crevasse directly? It would be worth a try, if it came down to that.

Even though he was hoping for a message from Zoe at any minute, he decided it wouldn't hurt to start preparing. He looked at the gear scattered around his room. What would he need? A rope? The others brought two half ropes and were planning to leave one hanging down into the crevasse for when they were ready to leave. He should be able to use that to get down to them. If that was even where they were. Who knew what could have happened in the two days since they left on Friday afternoon.

Ice climbing gear? Probably a good idea. And his own tent, sleeping bag, and sleeping mat. Lots of first aid supplies, just in case.

Food. He would need to bring lots of food. Of course, the others had brought an emergency meal or two, anyone who spends much time in the wilderness knows to do that, but he would be surprised if their rations would last them longer than Monday evening. If it took him longer than that to get them out of there, they would only have whatever supplies Alex could manage to bring with him.

Unfortunately, there wasn't much to bring. He looked over the results of his foraging with disappointment. Of course, the others had brought most everything of use with them, and Alex had no time to go to a store. He glanced out the window. That car with the tinted windows was still there. Wait—someone was getting into the car. Alex ducked out of sight and peered through the curtains. The car didn't leave, or even turn on. Alex watched it for another ten minutes, but nothing happened. No, he wasn't going to go out shopping anywhere.

Alex went through the kitchen cupboards again. Tinned beans. Not ideal, but better than nothing. Mac n' cheese, dried fruit, instant soup packets. He pulled out his own stash of trip food. There were a few things left from last week's trip. Next he raided Tyler's room. He knew Tyler kept a box of granola bars under his bed and a bag of candy in his sock drawer. Tyler hadn't been nearly secretive enough.

Putting everything together, he figured he had about four meals for the five of them. Hopefully that would be enough.

What about light? Headlamps and flashlights would be no good if electronics wouldn't work. The others took a propane lantern, but Alex didn't have time to track down something like that, and most of the candles had probably been taken too. Alex went to check. The only candles left behind were tea lights.

Frustrated, Alex continued to search the house. There must be something he could use. Glancing at the table, he noticed the centrepiece that Jani had brought over ages ago—a small, dollar store lantern to put tea lights in. That would have to do. But he did have a clock. He'd found an old wind-up clock at the thrift store last semester and bought it because he thought it was cool. Now it would really come in handy.

By the time Alex had finished his planning and packing, it was midnight. He checked his phone for the five hundredth time. Still no message from Zoe, and they were supposed to be at base camp six hours ago. He didn't want to wait any longer.

How would he get there? The others took Tyler's car, and the only other person with a car in their group was Jae. Jae's car wasn't great for logging roads, and anyway Alex didn't trust the Agency to not be keeping an eye on it. He'd have to borrow a car. Who could he get a car from this time of night?

Mac. Of course. He always had extra cars lying around, and he'd been with SAR for years now. He'd be a good person to have his back if things went really bad. Quickly he dialed the number.

"Hey Mac," Alex said as his friend answered the call. "I hope it's not too late."

"Alex!" Mac's cheerful voice sounded loud on the phone after the quiet of the apartment. "No worries, I was just working on a project."

"That's good," Alex smiled. "Hey Mac, I have a favour to ask. Some friends of mine are in a tough spot and I need a car to go help them. Mind if I borrow one?"

"Sure thing! The Geo or the Sidekick?"

"The Sidekick would be great. Mind if I swing by in, say, half an hour or so?"

"Works for me. I'll be in the shop."

"Okay, thanks." Alex breathed a sigh of relief. Now just to get to Mac's farm without any trouble.

Quickly, Alex pulled on his coat and heaved his pack onto his back, groaning inwardly at its weight—much heavier than his pack normally would be for a weekend trip. After getting his bike and helmet from the gear room, Alex cautiously opened the door and slipped outside, locking it shut behind him. The black car was still in the visitor's spot, but if Alex went around the far side of the building, he might not be noticed. There was a spot he knew about where someone had cut the chain link fence, and the gap was large enough to get a bike through. From there he could bike on back roads and get to Mac's in thirty minutes. Maybe less. From there it was a four hour drive to the trailhead and an eight kilometer hike to the basecamp. He should be there by nine in the morning.

Chapter 5

Alex eased his pack to the ground and looked around the empty campsite—the last known location of his friends, 57 hours ago. Even though he didn't expect to find anything, he gave the area a thorough search. All the evidence pointed to the fact that the area had been used as a campsite. Very helpful.

Walking back over to his pack, Alex stumbled from weariness. He had been up all night, and the half hour nap he had at the trailhead had not been long enough. He needed to sleep. Two hours. That should be enough.

Alex woke to his alarm two hours later, feeling slightly less like death than he had two hours earlier. The morning sun was warm, the alpine flowers nodded in the breeze, and a chipmunk scampered away as Alex stirred and got to his feet. Surrounded by the peace of the mountains, it was hard to feel as anxious as he had during his escape from Monksford. He stretched and looked around. All signs pointed to it being a beautiful day. Then he saw them. Dark clouds on the southern horizon. Alex's stomach sank like a rock.

Quickly, he rolled up his sleeping mat and shoved it in his pack, then he grabbed a couple granola bars.

Breakfast on the trail today. He had to make it to the others before those clouds reached the mountain. As he started bushwhacking his way up to the ridge, he remembered what Jani had said about the weather report—clear skies for the weekend, and then the weather would turn unstable again.

Alex pushed himself hard, barely stopping to take a breath. The wind was not blowing as strong as the last time he was on the mountain. Maybe he would make it in time. Maybe.

An hour later he was on top of the ridge. The glacier stretched out below him to the north, silent and foreboding. No sign of any movement.

Alex continued cautiously along the ridge, watching for signs of his friends. Was that—yes, that was the spot where they had made it off the glacier. The others had planned to retrace their route. Did they come this way? Alex climbed down to the snowpack. He needed to know for sure. Yes, there were footprints in the snow. Four sets of footprints moving in single file onto the glacier.

Should he follow them? That would be the best way to know beyond a doubt which way they went. But two days had passed since they had come this way. Two days of sun and warm temperatures. Who knew what that could have done to the snow bridges and crevasses? He couldn't risk it. Even though he might lose their trail, he had to go around the long way.

Back on the ridge, a biting southern wind had sprung up, chilling him through his jacket. The clouds were looming larger than ever. Alex turned and started to jog along the ridge. Soon he was forced to slow to a walk as the ridge became rougher and rockier. As he scrambled along, he kept glancing down at the glacier. The view from the ridge afforded him a good view of the crevasses far below. He even thought he could see his friends' tracks winding back and forth between the crevasses.

Almost an hour later, a rumble of thunder made him glance to the south. The storm was much too close for comfort. If it hit him up here it would be difficult to keep his footing. Looking back down at the glacier, he saw that he was abreast of what appeared to be the final and largest crevasse. Time to climb down. He scrambled to the edge of the ridge and looked down. 50 metres, at least. Not a cliff, but certainly a class four scramble. It would not be an easy downclimb, especially with his overweight pack.

Alex hesitated. This was not a good idea. By rights it should be SAR out on the mountain right now, not him. If it hadn't been for that creep at the wedding. All of his training and courses screamed in his mind: Safety first. Always.

He shook his head. Too late to turn back now. Zoe was out there somewhere. And Tyler and the others. He needed to find them and make sure they were safe. He turned around and slowly began climbing down, placing each hand and foot carefully. Three points of contact at all times. A rock shifted beneath his foot and tumbled down to the glacier below. "Rock!" Alex called, then snorted. Not that there was anyone below him to warn. No one even knew he was there, except Mac. "If you don't hear from me in two days," he'd told Mac, "then call out SAR and tell them where our base camp was. And if any creeps come nosing, you don't know anything." Mac had laughed. Two days would be a long time to wait if he had a fall.

Just focus. One step at a time.

Finally Alex stood with both feet solidly on the surface of the glacier. Deep breath. Okay, now to cross over to the crevasse. Glaciers are extremely dangerous terrain; he would have to be cautious.

As he stepped away from the shelter of the ridge, a shadow fell over the sun. Dark clouds billowed across the sky and snowflakes whirled through the air, stinging his eyes. Crap. Alex ran toward the crevasse as fast as his feet could carry him.

He approached the lip of the crevasse just as the visibility started to close in. Where was Zoe's anchor? Quickly, he searched along the perimeter. After an eternally long two minutes, he found it. A quick inspection showed it to still be secure. Good enough. Alex set up a quick rappel and stepped backwards out of the howling wind into the icy silence below.

Chapter 6

As soon as his feet touched the rock below, Alex unclipped and ran along the crevasse, rounded the corner, and there was the door. He paused. The door stood still and solemn, glimmering in the ethereal ice-blue light. It took a moment for him to notice the two small tents tucked away to one side.

Quickly, Alex checked inside the tents. No one was there. What had they left behind? Two sleeping bags and mats in Tyler and Jae's tent. One sleeping bag and mat in the other tent. Four sets of crampons, tucked under the fly of a tent. That was it.

With their sleeping gear left behind, they weren't expecting to spend a night away from their tents. They had one sleeping bag and mat with them in case of an emergency. Their crampons were there, so they couldn't have gone back up on the glacier. That meant they had either travelled the other way along the crevasse for some strange, unknown reason, or they went through the door. But if they went through the door, why was the door closed now? Surely Zoe would have thought to wedge it open. Alex tried pushing on the door—just in case—but it didn't budge.

Stepping back, Alex ran his eyes up and down the door. If the others were in there, they must have figured out how to open it. He'd have to figure it out too.

The door was tall—easily twenty feet. Along the top, sides, and bottom of the door was a wide geometric pattern, or border, eleven squares wide and twelve squares high. Each square contained a geometric design. Some of the designs looked similar to each other, others were unique. Within the border, the design of the door was much simpler: A symmetrical pattern of larger squares, triangles, and other angular shapes. All of the patterns were raised out of the door, clean and sharp. Whatever kind of metal this door was made of, it may have been a bit tarnished, but it certainly didn't seem worn down by the elements. Down the center of the door was a hairline crack. It must be a double door.

He looked at the border pattern again. Was that some kind of code or language? If it was, that could be the key to opening the door. Were there any other options? There were no signs of excessive force being used against the door, so the others probably didn't force their way in. The only unusual thing he found was two small rough patches on the door, at about his head height, one on each side of the center crack.

Looking high up on the door, he thought he could see two more similar rough patches, though it was hard to tell. The sky was getting uncomfortably dark for it only being mid-afternoon. The thickly falling snowflakes were already coating the ground.

If the door wasn't giving him the clues he needed, maybe something else would. Alex put his pack down by the tents and set out to do a thorough search of the surrounding area. The rock wall on each side of the door was smooth, without any markings. Translucent icicles hung down from the glacier above, meeting the ground to form pillars of ice. Everything was eerily quiet. He followed the walls of rock and ice along one side of the open space and back down the other, but nothing unusual caught his eye.

As he went back to search the tents again, he noticed something catching the light, tucked in between the tents and the icy wall. Kneeling down to investigate, he found two metal rings, each about the size of his fist. Carefully he picked them up and brought them to the center of the open space, where the fading light was still somewhat helpful. The rings were made of the same metal as the door—that much was obvious. They were thick and smooth all around, except for on one side where a large protrusion ended in an abrupt, jagged way. Here the metal was shinier, as if it hadn't experienced the same weathering that the rest of the metal had. Strange.

Carrying them over to the door, Alex held one of the rings up against one of the rough patches. It was the same size as the jagged protrusion on the ring. Maybe it used to be attached, and something broke it off. But the rough patches on the door seemed just as weathered as the rest of the door, while the break on the rings was shiny and new. He tried fitting the two rings together. Although the broken patches were the same size, they didn't fit together the way Alex thought they might.

Alex looked at the door. There were those two rough patches up near the top. Could the rings have broken off from there? The only way to know for sure would be to climb up and have a closer look. Alex moved closer to the door. The raised design was deep enough to make easy handholds and footholds, but he didn't like the idea of free climbing up twenty feet, especially when there was no one around to help if he fell. He had to do something, though, and the rings were the only lead he had.

Alex shoved the rings in his pocket along with his gloves and started to climb. It was harder than it looked. His thick mountaineering boots kept sliding off the ledges, and the metal of the door was bitterly cold. Probably shouldn't lick it.

There. The rough patches were just in reach. Alex balanced himself carefully with one hand, and gingerly pulled out one of the rings with the other. It fit into the right hand rough spot perfectly. And the upper rough spots were shiny and new-looking as well. So these rings used to be attached near the top of the doors, and they broke off quite recently. Jae, what did you do? Alex shook his head and chuckled. No. This high off the ground, it was definitely Tyler.

So what were these rings for? Alex felt his legs getting tired. He needed to downclimb before he slipped, but he also didn't want to have to climb up again if he didn't need to. Hold on just a minute more. These rings—they were kind of high for handles. He tried pushing on the rough patches. Then he tried wiggling them. They moved. The rings had been attached to separate pieces of metal protruding from the door. Now that was something! And they moved more up and down than they did side to side. That would have to be enough to work with. Carefully, Alex made his way back down to the ground.

With aching legs, he sat down to think. These metal rings were meant to be moved in some way when they were attached to the door. Maybe they even opened the door. The others must have guessed that too, tied their rope to them, and pulled. But instead of opening the door, they broke the rings off.

So that didn't get him any closer to actually opening the door—unless he could find some way of attaching them back on again. Or could he pull on the mechanism somehow without the rings there? There had been a small crack all around the metal rods the rings used to be attached to. Maybe wide enough for the point of his crampons? But he'd need to be secured. No more clinging by his fingernails to ice-cold metal this time. He looked at the ice hanging down above the door. That should work.

Going through his gear, Alex got out everything that he would need to build an ice anchor and clipped it to his harness. He stepped back into his crampons and made sure they were properly secured.

No point wasting any time. Alex put his hands back on the piercingly cold metal of the door and started to climb again. This time, he placed the front points of his crampons on each small ledge as he stepped upward. Climbing with his crampons felt more secure than just his boots.

Knowing how cold his hands would get, Alex climbed quickly. Soon he was at the top of the door. Balancing himself carefully, Alex reached up to the ice hanging over the door. He could just reach high enough. Working as quickly and carefully as his numbing hands allowed, Alex built an ice anchor and clipped in.

With a sigh of relief, Alex sat back, resting in his harness. He blew warm air on his hands as he eyed the crack above one of the broken patches. Moving his foot, he slid the point of his crampon into the crack and pushed down. It moved. Shifting his weight, he slid the point of his other crampon into the crack above the other broken patch.

With a click, the door opened, swinging inwards on silent hinges. Yes! Wait ... the door pulled Alex with it. His chest hit the upper door frame, his crampons slid out of the cracks, and he was dangling in midair. Thanking his anchor for holding, Alex surveyed his situation. He got the door open, but now he was stuck up in the air with no way to get down. The smooth rock face offered nothing to hold onto. He didn't have any rope, just short pieces of cordelette, like the one he used to clip into the ice screws. Warm air flowed past his legs, out of the open door. A drip of water landed on his face. Was the ice melting? Alex looked up. He needed to find a way down. Fast.

Another gust of warm air made Alex look down. The door was closing. Slowly, slowly it approached until Alex could rest his feet against it again. The door closed, and with a soft click, it was still. Well, he had a way to get down now. Alex got his balance on the door and stood up. Unclipping himself from the anchor, he carefully climbed back down to the ground.

Alex stepped back and surveyed the door. He knew how to get it open, but how would he get down after opening it? This time he would have to be prepared. He sat down by his pack to go through his climbing gear. He didn't have any rope. Well, there was a rope hanging down the side of the crevasse, not too far away. Should he go get that? But that was their way out. If he took down the rope, they would have to ice climb to get back to the surface of the glacier. Not ideal, especially if they needed to get out in a hurry.

Alex collected all of his cordelette. If he tied it all together, would it be long enough? It should be. Not strong enough to take a fall, but he wasn't planning on falling. He just needed a way to lower himself to the ground before the door closed again. He'd have to get past a knot or two, which would make the rappel more difficult than normal, but not impossible.

With the cordelette all tied together, Alex laid it out on the ground. Pretending that he was hanging up above the door, Alex tied himself in and walked through the entire process of lowering himself to the ground. When he was sure it would work and that he hadn't forgotten anything, he walked back to look at the door. How was his anchor doing? It was hard to tell in the dim light and falling snow. All around the foot of the door the snow had melted. Had the warm air from the door weakened his ice? That could be really bad news for his anchor. Maybe he should give the ice a little longer to cool down again, just to be safe.

The door swam in Alex's vision. He blinked and shook his head. Maybe he should nap for a couple minutes. Alex crawled into one of the tents to get away from the falling snow, and flopped down onto Tyler's mat. Oh that felt good. A short nap—just five minutes. He'd set his alarm ... and ...

Alex forced his eyes open. Shadows filled the tent. What time was it? He pulled out his alarm clock. Five thirty? He'd slept for over an hour! Heaping insults on himself, Alex crawled out of the tent. Snow had continued to fall while he was asleep, covering the ground by the door where the earlier snow had been melted. Well, the ice should be solid again at least. Alex brushed the snow off his gear and got ready for his climb. He was stiff all over, and a dull throb at the back of his eyes threatened a headache. Impatient as he was to start climbing, he forced himself to drink some water and eat a couple of bites first.

Finally, he was ready to climb. His crampons clicked against the hard metal of the door. As he climbed Alex noticed that there were no marks on the door from his previous climb. Had his crampons not scratched it at all? What kind of metal was this?

His hands were numb and he was shivering by the time he made it to his anchor at the top of the door. Carefully, he reached up and clipped himself in. His anchor looked okay. How solid was it? Carefully, he sat down into his harness until his full weight was hanging off the anchor. As long as there weren't any sudden movements, it should be fine. He made sure everything was ready for his rappel, then shoved his crampons into the cracks. The door started to open.

As warm air rushed by him, Alex quickly lowered himself. It took a little while to bypass the knot, and he heard the *tic* of water on his helmet, but his anchor held and soon his feet were back on solid ground.

Quickly, Alex unclipped, grabbed his pack, and shoved it up against the door. Would that keep it from closing? He looked around. What else could he use to prop open the door? A block of ice would just melt … but it would buy him some time. He lifted a fallen chunk of ice and laid it against the other side of the door. He watched. The door didn't move.

A dark passageway stretched out before Alex, straight and smooth. From what he could see, it was the exact size of the door which now stood open, flush with each side of the passageway. He could not see far into the darkness, but it seemed that the passage sloped downward slightly. Warm air flowed from it, but apart from that all was silent and still.

"Hello!" Alex called. His voice sounded strange and loud. It echoed down the corridor. Silence. Well, it was worth a try. He turned his attention to the door. Could there be some way of securing it open? He slid the ice over to let one side close halfway. It was very dark behind the door. He pulled out the small lantern and a tea light, lighting it with a match. The small candle didn't give off much light, but it was something. He looked all over the back of the door and the wall behind it, but they were completely smooth. Nothing to secure the door, and no sign of a latch. He shoved that door back all the way open and tried the other side. Nothing there either.

He'd just have to prop the door open really well and pray that it stayed open. With no latch on the inside, it would be bad news if it shut somehow. Was that what had happened to the others? Did they get shut in and go searching for another way out? Alex shivered.

What could he use to secure the doors? He couldn't leave his pack behind, and the others hadn't left enough gear behind to make a heavy doorstop. The warm air meant that ice wouldn't be a good idea, there was already a thin trail of water trickling away from the block of ice that he was using. Would he have to go hunting for rocks? That could take a really long time. He leaned up against the door and his climbing gear clattered. What about a piton? He could use one like a wedge. Alex sorted through his gear and unclipped his thinnest piton. Kneeling down, he tried sliding it under the door. It didn't fit, but it would if the point was a bit thinner. His Leatherman had a file on it.

Pulling out his Leatherman, Alex sat down, leaning his back against the door—the side that the melting ice was holding open. He flicked out the file and started sliding it along the edge of the piton. Several minutes later, Alex tried sliding the piton under the door again. This time the pointed end slid in the crack under the door, while the thick end held the door firmly in place. Perfect. He left the piton under the door and moved the ice away to see how it would hold. While he waited, he unclipped another piton and filed it down for the other door. In the time that took, the wedged door didn't move at all. That was promising, but he wouldn't trust it until he'd given it a good long test. Wedging the other door, Alex shifted his pack so that the door was being held by the piton, but the pack would be there to catch the door if it did slip.

With that done, Alex set about packing up the gear the others had left behind. He rolled up the sleeping mats and stuffed the sleeping bags into their stuff sacks. Then he took down the tents and piled everything up against the doors. He looked around the area for rocks, but he didn't find any. Would it be worth piling ice against the doors, even if it did just melt? Alex decided against it—that would get the gear all wet.

Wanting to give the doors a longer test, Alex pulled out his camping stove and one of the heavier meals he had scavenged—a can of chili. As the chili warmed in his small pot, Alex realized just how hungry he was. It was his first real meal all day. He didn't even let it come to a boil—as soon as it was warm enough, he wolfed it down.

When he was finished, he washed his pot and spoon with some snow and re-packed everything in his pack, including his crampons and cordelette. He filled the empty can with ice and set it against the door, just because. He sighed and looked around. There was nothing else to do. The doors had been held in place all that time. He would just have to trust them.

He lifted his small tea light lantern and stepped forward into the darkness.

Chapter 7

The passage led on and on. The walls, floor, and ceiling were all the same smooth stone, leading straight ahead and sloping gently down. Even after Alex's eyes adjusted to the darkness, the small tea light candle did not shed much light on the subject. Alex had to keep moving it from side to side to make sure he didn't miss anything.

After what seemed like a long time, Alex checked his clock. Just over an hour since he set out down the passage. How long would it go on for? He kept moving forward at a moderate pace. He could have walked faster, but he didn't want to miss anything.

Something large and white loomed in front of him. Alex stopped, then moved the light forward to investigate. He had reached the end of the passage. A wall of stone stretched before him, of the same stone as the passage, but this wall was not smooth; it was adorned from ceiling to floor with elaborate carvings. Alex moved the light of the candle across its surface. He could see similarities to the carving on the door, though this one was much more complex. He could see images of winged figures, grotesque creatures, and a small orb with beams of light shining from it. As a whole, the image was stately and symmetrical.

Was that a glimmer of light? Alex turned and lifted his lantern. A passageway opened to the right. Small lights flickered in the deeper darkness of the passageway, drawing his gaze. He stepped towards it. The lights moved. He stepped forward again. The lights moved, flickering in the light of the candle. It was another mural. The sharply cut angles and images reflected his light, refracting it and multiplying it. It was a picture of some kind of flying creature.

Alex stepped again and the creature moved. Freezing, he looked at it sharply. It stopped moving. He stepped back, and the image returned to its original position. He stepped forward, and once again the image shifted—a fluid, natural movement, as if it was a living creature, not a mural. Holding his light close to the wall, he inspected the image. It appeared to be carved into the stone wall, crafted with incredible detail and precision, in such a way that the image changed depending on the way you looked at it.

Alex moved forward and watched as the creature dove from a great height, plummeting toward a small village far below. There were people in the village, looking up with awe and wonder. They had never seen a creature like that before.

Alex stopped. How did he know that? It wasn't like an image could show that kind of information. But something about its incredibly vivid nature led his mind to fill in the gaps that the image could not possibly have explained.

As long as he stood still, the image remained still, but as soon as he moved the image moved, almost as if he was watching a movie. He lifted a foot to move forward, but instead forced himself to take a step backward. The image reversed, very reluctantly, step after step, until he was back at the original mural. He looked around. There was a second passage to the left of the mural.

Alex frowned. Two passages, one on each side of the corridor like a T intersection. No sign of which way the others might have gone. To the right was the moving image. What was to the left? Alex stepped into the left-hand passage and a wave of exhaustion swept over him. Every step took a concerted effort. There were more images, but they were fuzzy and unclear. Or was his mind refusing to bring them into focus? He stopped and shook his head. It didn't help. Maybe he should take a nap at the crossroads before deciding which way to go.

As soon as Alex turned to go back, the image came into focus: A barren wilderness littered with crumbling ruins. A bird took flight and flew away into the darkening sky. And once again Alex found himself at the crossroads.

He sat down with his back resting against the wall, waiting for the exhaustion to pass. Should he sleep? It was already early evening, and three or four hours of sleep wasn't much to go on. But he had really been hoping to find some sign of Zoe and the others. The small globe of light from his lantern didn't reach far, just enough to outline the two passage openings, pools of deeper black in the darkness.

Which way did Zoe go? Both passages had images along the wall. The right-hand passage had images that moved easily when moving down it, but that made it difficult to move backward. The left-hand passage was exhausting to move down, but returning had been easy. It was as if the passages wanted him to go to the right, not the left. But did that mean Zoe went to the right? She hated anyone telling her what to do. But she would also see the logic in following the passages in the way they were made to be followed.

Alex sighed. Ultimately, he would just have to guess, or his fatigue would make the decision for him. Going down the right-hand passage would be easy. If he wanted to go left, he would have to sleep first.

Alex stood up and adjusted his pack. He could go on for a bit longer. Holding up his lantern, Alex stepped into the right-hand passage.

Moving slowly, Alex watched the mural in fascination. The skill it would take to create such detailed images and make them appear to move in such a life-like way! Alex watched as a small village met a strange flying creature and received a small gem that shone like the sun. The people were clever and used the gem to invent many wonderful things and solve many mysteries.

The images rushed forward. Again and again Alex forced himself to stop and cast his light around to make sure he wasn't missing anything, but the passageway continued on, straight as a ruler. The incredible moving pictures on the left, and a blank, smooth wall on the right. The stone floor did not yield any clues of who may have gone this way before. Alex didn't feel as tired now. He wanted to know what happened next in the story.

The village grew into a city and became prosperous. Their vast knowledge became known throughout the land, and people came from all around to ask them difficult questions. One sage was known for solving clever riddles, and was always able to give an answer. One day a delegation came to him from a distant nation, and—

The story stopped abruptly. Alex blinked. The passageway turned sharply to the left, but that was not what had jarred him. There was a door, an open door in the wall of murals, right where the passage turned. And there, propping the door open, was a mountaineering axe.

Alex knelt down and ran his hand along its cold, smooth surface. Zoe's mountaineering axe. He'd know it anywhere. Relief surged through Alex's body. He was on the right track. Zoe had been this way and had gone through this door—and this time she'd left it propped open!

Alex looked at the door. It was covered with designs and more of the strange patterns that had been on the larger front door. It seemed to be some kind of puzzle or riddle, as if it continued the mural's story, showing one of the riddles of the great sage. There weren't any kinds of handles or latches on the door. Good thing Zoe had wedged her axe in to keep it open. Inside the door was a large, dark room that his small candle did not illuminate.

"Hello!" Alex called into the darkness. "Zoe? Tyler? Anybody? Are you in there?" He waited, but there was no reply. From the echo, Alex judged that it was a large room, but not massive. Time to check it out.

He stepped through the door. The air was warmer inside. Almost stuffy. His small pool of light didn't make much of a difference in the massive darkness. Not having any other landmarks to navigate by, he started to follow the wall. It was covered with the same strange script Alex had seen on both of the doors—and *covered* was not an exaggeration. From the floor to as high as the light of his candle could reach, Alex could see patterns of geometrical shapes. It was clearly some sort of language. How Zoe must have loved this! It would be like a goldmine to her. Of course, she would have attempted to decipher it. If anyone could, Zoe could. And she wouldn't give up easily. A fond smile lingered on Alex's face as he passed row after row of text, interspersed with images of plants and animals and strange, unidentifiable things.

He reached the end of the room. Forty paces. He turned and followed the next wall. Twenty-seven paces. He turned again.

One, two, three, Alex counted his steps. He was walking faster now. He could do another circuit later and examine the carvings for clues. Right now he wanted to know if there was anything unusual about this room. Twenty-seven, twenty-eight, twenty-nine, a door!

Alex stopped short. An open door—he moved his light closer—a sliding door that was now tucked away in some recess in the wall. And there, at its base, it was held open by a long-shafted mountaineering axe. The one he had lent to Jae.

"Hey Jae!" Alex called through the door. "I want my axe back!" No reply came from the darkness, but his voice did not echo the same way it had in the first room. This room sounded smaller.

First things first—finish examining one room before moving on to the next. Pulling his head back, he turned and finished following the wall. Nine more paces. That made it about the same length as the first wall. He turned and followed the fourth wall. Just as he was reaching twenty-seven paces, his candle illuminated the propped-open door that he had entered through. Okay. Large rectangle room. One door in, one door out. But was there anything in the middle? Or had the others left anything behind?

Alex frowned. Well, the room may be big, but it didn't seem like it would be possible to get lost in it. Time to comb the middle for anything interesting that may be found.

After half an hour of zigzagging across the room, Alex reluctantly conceded that there was nothing to be found. The floor in the room was bare and smooth, and there were no further signs of his friends. But did the walls hold any clues? He had to find out before moving on. Alex set out to do another circuit of the room. This time he examined the carvings more closely.

Row upon row of strange symbols lined the walls. If only he had the time to try to figure out what they meant! There was a pattern to the symbols, and certain symbols were used so frequently that it must be possible to decipher them. If he wasn't so tired. And if time wasn't so pressing. Alex sighed. A second circuit of the room hadn't offered him any more useful information. If he could sit for a while and rest—even for half an hour—he might be able to figure something out. But what if the next room had an easier clue? Or even a sign of the others! He could always come back later.

Stepping over the axe, Alex moved into the next room. His small candle illuminated just as little as it had in the previous room, but the echoes of his movements sounded smaller, and the room felt warmer. Holding up his candle, Alex examined the wall. More carvings. The same geometric patterns as before, but these seemed more complex and detailed. He followed them.

Something crinkled beneath his feet. Startled, Alex lowered his candle. A plastic wrapper! Some kind of health food energy bar. Gosh, guys, didn't anyone teach you not to litter? Alex chuckled. They must have stopped to eat here.

A quick circuit of the room showed it to be a triangular shape, roughly half the size of the previous room, with another door on the opposite side of the room, once again propped open with a mountaineering axe—this one was Jani's.

"Hello!" Alex called into the darkness beyond the door. "Jani! Zoe! Can you hear me?" His voice echoed through a large space. His eyes widened. This room sounded much larger. He shook his head. Finish checking this room first before moving on.

Being a smaller room, it didn't take long. The walls were just as covered with carvings as the previous room, or even more so if that were possible. Where the wrapper had been, Alex found some crumbs strewn around, and it may have been his imagination, but he was almost certain he could smell beef jerky.

That was all. Time to check the next room.

Stepping through the door, Alex was enveloped with the senses of a larger, warmer, stuffier room that was just as dark. If only he had a bigger light, this would be so much faster. Well, start with another circuit of the room.

The walls were once again covered with the same carvings, and lowering the light to the ground showed that the floor was also covered with markings—the same geometrical symbols, but larger and more complex.

Alex was following along the second wall when he found a door. This door wasn't propped open. It was broken open.

Alex blinked. What happened here? Pieces of the stone door remained stuck to the sides of the door frame, and the rest of the door lay in shattered pieces on the floor. A closer examination showed that this had been a very thin stone door. Much thinner than any of the doors he had seen so far. He held his flickering light up to the door frame. The door appeared to be attached to the frame on both sides. Strange. Was this a door that wasn't made to be opened? But then, why was it so thin? And why was it *broken*?

The pieces of the door were all directly under the door frame or on the far side, so someone on this side must have pushed it in. He leaned through the opening, trying not to disturb any of the rubble. There, in the crushed rock dust—that looked like a shoeprint.

Wait. Finish checking this room first. Alex reluctantly moved away from the broken door and continued along the wall. A few steps later he found another door. This door was closed. Curious, Alex gave it a shove. It didn't break. Okay. He continued on.

A few steps later he found another door. This one was also closed. Three doors on one wall. He followed along the next wall. It didn't have any doors. And the final wall didn't have any doors either.

Back at the door he had entered through, Alex stopped to think. This room seemed to be a kind of trapezoidal shape, with a set of three doors in the longer wall. One door was broken and the other two were closed. So did the others go through the broken door? The footprint seemed to indicate so. But he couldn't move on until he had checked the middle of the room too, and with such a big room that was going to take longer. Might as well get to it.

Alex began his regular routine of crisscrossing the floor. It was a lot more interesting this time, because of the carvings on the floor.

He was crossing the floor for the fifth time when something reflected the light from his candle. Alex stepped toward it. A backpack. Jani's backpack! There was no Jani attached to it.

"Jani!" Alex shouted to the darkness around him. "Jani, are you here?"

Silence.

Quickly, Alex opened the pack and started pulling out Jani's things. Snacks. Jacket. Stove. Water bladder. All of Jani's things were there. Why was Jani's pack left there? Where did she go?

Throwing everything back in the pack, Alex grabbed it in one hand and his lantern in the other. What else had been left behind? He lifted his light as high as he could and looked around. Another reflector caught the light. Alex rushed over. Tyler's pack!

Quickly, Alex rummaged through Tyler's pack. Everything was there. Alex's heart was pounding. Why would Tyler leave his pack behind? What happened to him?

Scooping up Tyler's pack along with Jani's, Alex continued searching. He crossed and recrossed the room, but did not find any more packs. Was that a good thing? He supposed it must be. But why were any packs left behind at all? Had the others not stayed together? He had been assuming that he was searching for one group of missing people, but what if they had split up and gone different directions? If that was the case, he couldn't assume that they all went through the broken door. What if some of the group had gone through a different door and it had closed behind them? His head pounded. He needed to sit and rest, but he couldn't stop now. He needed to figure out what happened.

He set out to examine the broken door again, walking in roughly the correct direction. Instead, he found one of the closed doors. Turning sharply to correct his course, he felt something under his foot. He stopped and lowered his light. It was a logbook. And on the front page, in a messy scribble he knew well, was written "Zoe Wieland".

Chapter 8

Zoe's logbook. Alex snatched it up, a feeling of dread in his stomach. Zoe would never leave her logbook behind. Ever. But maybe it would have answers. He shoved it in a pocket, picked his lantern back up, and carried everything over to the broken door. Sitting against the wall, Alex opened up the logbook and flipped to the last page of writing.

> 1600 - Second riddle room completed. Propped the door open with an axe. Debate over whether to postpone our return to base camp. Curiosity prevailed. Attempting the third riddle.

Alex smiled. He could almost hear Zoe's voice. That entry was written at four in the afternoon. On Sunday? He flipped back a couple of pages to check. Yes, that was Sunday. No wonder they were discussing what to do. Even if they left right away they would have been late getting back to base camp. That was the last entry in the logbook. Whatever happened after that, Zoe didn't have a chance to write it down. So that didn't really help him figure out what to do next.

Alex checked his clock. Eight forty-five. He leaned his head back and closed his eyes, exhaustion dragging at his limbs. Should he just call it a night? He'd be able to think better if he had a proper sleep. Maybe there was something really obvious and he was just missing it.

No. He wanted to read the rest of Zoe's logbook first, but he might as well get comfortable. He took off his backpack and his boots and settled back against the wall. His feet ached. How many hours had he been going for now? He decided it wasn't worth counting it up. Positioning his little lantern to get as much light as possible, Alex flipped back to the first page of the logbook.

Day 1
1600 - Parked at trailhead. Weather: sunny, clear skies, gentle westerly wind. Jae didn't shut up all drive.

2027 - Arrived at basecamp. Sunny and warm. Will set up tents and make supper.

2130 - All going to sleep. Tomorrow up at 0430.

Day 2
0430 - Quick breakfast, sent SPOT OK message to Alex as agreed. Weather: clear. Starry sky, no wind.

0500 - Leaving camp.

0630 - At top of ridge. Stopped for break. Sun is up but not shining on glacier yet. A few clouds to the east. Moderate wind.

0715 - Found glacier access. Roped up.

0937 - Found the location of our previous anchor. Set up new anchor. Glacier traverse was difficult with many detours necessary.

1000 - Setting up camp by the door. Attempted to send SPOT OK message to Alex, but SPOT does not operate. As suspected, no electronics are functioning.

1245 - Efforts to open door unsuccessful so far. Jani insisted on lunch break.

1330 - Tyler climbed doors and found that the two rings high on the door are movable. While shifting them, Tyler fell and landed poorly on his ankle. Jani is tending to it.

1415 - Tyler climbed the door again to feed the rope through the rings. Pulling the ropes resulted in an audible clicking sound, but the doors did not move. We are certain the rings control some sort of latching mechanism, but it seems stiff or jammed.

1430 - After several tries, the successful approach was pulling the ropes as hard as we could. The door opened, but the rings snapped off in the process. Maybe we were pulling them at the wrong angle. Inside the door we can see a dark passage that slopes gradually down. The air inside is cold but does not smell unpleasant.

1510 - Long debate over whether to bring overnight gear or leave it by the door. Decided to bring one set in case of emergency and leave the rest behind, since inclement weather in an underground passage seems unlikely. We wedged the doors open with blocks of ice. Once Jae has finished taking photographs we will explore down the passageway.

1630 - We have reached the first feature of the passage: a large mural with a passage opening on either side. We are taking a break to eat before examining it. Never mind, Tyler is already.

1700 - Decided to go down the right-hand passage.

2000 - Assuming our mechanical watch has not malfunctioned, we followed the passage of carvings for nearly three hours. The carvings appear to be formed in a way that tricks your mind into perceiving them as moving images, and also seems to affect one's perception of time (or interferes with your watches) since we were all surprised by how much time had passed. I would be interested in examining the carvings more closely to see how they are made. I documented the entire sequence of images in my notebook. After all that walking, the passage led us back to our starting place at the large mural. We did not notice any other doors or passageways. There was some interest in exploring further, but instead we have decided to return to the crevasse for the night, since it is not far away, and we can refill our water.

2115 - Arrived back at our tents. Making supper.

2230 - Going to sleep. Tomorrow up at 0700.

Day 3
0645 - Woke up, making breakfast. Weather: another fair day.

0730 - All are now awake and eating breakfast.

0800 - Going back through the door to explore again. We will be looking specifically for any doors missed in yesterday's exploration.

0930 - Found a door hidden in the moving mural at the first left-hand turn. It appears to be some kind of puzzle.

1015 - Figured out how to open the door. Propped it open with a mountaineering axe to ensure it didn't close again. The room beyond has walls lined with script with a similar appearance to the script on the door.

1100 - To be able to open the next door it appears that I will need to decode the language first.

1330 - Jani insisted that I stop and eat something.

1430 - The riddle is solved and the door opened. Tyler propped it open with another axe. We will move into the next room.

1600 - Second riddle room completed. Propped the door open with an axe. Debate over whether to postpone our return to base camp. Curiosity prevailed. Attempting the third riddle.

Alex flipped back through the entries. So they wedged the door with blocks of ice. That would explain why the door was shut; the ice must have melted in the hot air. But Zoe mentioned that the air in the passage was cold. Where did all this hot air come from? Zoe would have recorded something like that. It would have been a shock, if they went back and found that the doors had closed behind them. The thought made Alex feel sick.

It was disappointing that the logbook didn't contain any of Zoe's deciphering, but of course she had a separate notebook for that. Alex closed the logbook. Somehow reading about his friends made the darkness seem so much emptier.

What happened here that made Zoe and the others leave so quickly? It must have been something serious. Would he have to try to figure out what Zoe had learned in her study of the language? Under normal circumstances he would enjoy the challenge, but these were far from normal circumstances. What mattered now was finding the others as quickly as possible, and he had a lead that was much more promising than hours of studying—a smashed in door. At least one of his friends had gone that way, and they'd clearly been in a hurry.

Alex willed his aching feet back into his boots. He'd push on a little longer.

What to bring? He couldn't carry three packs. Well, he could, but not as a long-term thing. His goal, however, was to come back this way, with his friends, so he decided to leave Jani and Tyler's packs by the busted door. He carefully slid Zoe's logbook into a pocket and hoisted up his pack. Staggering a little, he steadied himself against the wall and lifted his small lantern. The hot, stuffy air seemed to be worse near the broken door. He was sweating, and he'd only been sitting still. Careful not to disturb any of the rubble lying around the door, Alex stepped through.

Immediately, he checked for footprints. There were several, but they were all over each other, and seemed to be facing every direction. He could see at least two different tread patterns, but the door's blast zone didn't go far enough to be much more help.

What was that? Alex picked up a long, thin cylinder that was lying on the ground. It was wooden, with a smooth, dark surface, except for one end that appeared to be broken.

Lifting his lantern, Alex looked around. There—something on the wall! A closer examination showed it to be a small metal grate covering a hole in the wall. Beside the grate was a lever with a broken handle. A broken wooden handle. Alex held up the wooden cylinder to match, even though he didn't need to. What was with those guys and breaking things? He tried moving the lever, but without the handle it proved impossible. With his lantern in one hand and his newly acquired stick in the other, Alex continued to explore the room. It was small—the smallest room he'd found so far. Maybe that was why it was so hot. Or was it possible that this room was the source of the heat?

Opposite the broken door, there was one other entrance to the room: an open doorway that had no door. Satisfied that there was nothing else to discover, Alex moved forward. He had only gone a couple of steps down the passage when two new passageways appeared. Alex frowned. Which way should he go? The bare rock floor didn't show any signs of his friends' passing. With a grin, Alex tossed his stick onto the ground. It pointed straight ahead. Alex picked up the stick and continued on straight ahead. The passage made a sharp turn to the right, then came to an abrupt stop. A dead end. Alex turned back and tried the right-hand passage. It divided into two. He paused. There was something uncomfortably familiar about this. It was almost like a maze or ... a labyrinth. That's what it was, he was certain. But his goal wasn't to find his way through, it was to find his friends. He'd have to check every passageway, systematically, or he'd risk missing them. A trail of breadcrumbs would have been nice. Alex went back to the start of the labyrinth and tightened his pack.

Almost an hour later, Alex was satisfied that he had checked every passageway in the labyrinth. He'd seen the way that led into another room, presumably the exit of the labyrinth, but he hadn't stopped to investigate it, leaving that for after he had finished exploring the entire labyrinth. He had noticed several more metal grates, though none of them had levers attached like the first one.

Now that he could say with certainty that his friends were not in the labyrinth, it was time to look beyond it. Having built a model of the labyrinth in his mind, he quickly made his way to the exit.

Emerging into the room beyond, Alex started coughing. The floor was covered in dust, but the dust didn't show any footprints. Strange. He was sure that he hadn't missed any other ways out of the labyrinth. Had his friends not come this way after all?

Stubbornly, Alex pushed on. He needed a more concrete sign than just a lack of footprints. Was there anything else in this room? There, on the wall, a vent with a lever. And just like the first one, the lever was broken.

So they had been here. Clearly. But why weren't there any footprints when the dust was so thick? And why was there so much dust in this room? Alex kept exploring. Instead of finding a wooden handle on the ground, he found a rock. And then another. Then a large boulder, and Alex stood before a door. A doorway filled with massive rocks.

Alex blinked. What were all these rocks doing here? He tried pushing one out of the way, but it was very heavy. It almost looked like there had been a rockslide on the other side of the door, but that didn't make sense. This was inside a mountain, not outside.

A quick survey of the room showed no other ways out. A dead end.

His own thought stopped him short. A *dead* end? Had the others been caught in a cave-in?

"Zoe!" Alex yelled, "Zoe, can you hear me?" The rumbling of settling rock filled the silence. Alex ground his teeth in frustration. "Zoe! Are you in there?"

He began to pace. This rockfall was new. It had to be new, or why would it be settling like that? It would explain why there were no footprints, if the others came through before the rockfall filled the room with dust. So where were they? Did they enter the next room, only to find that the ceiling above their heads was unstable? He looked up. The light from his small lantern didn't shine far enough to allow for a close inspection of the ceiling. He hadn't been worrying about a cave in. He should be more careful about yelling like that.

What should he do? If the others were trapped but still alive, somewhere in there, he had to go get help. There was no other way. He couldn't move all this rock by himself, and Search and Rescue would be able to think of something.

He was striding back toward the labyrinth when the light around him dimmed, flickered, and went out. Darkness engulfed Alex completely. He held up his lantern. The final stub of wick glowed faintly red, then disappeared into the blackness. The smell of the smouldering candle lingered in the air.

Hands shaking, Alex unzipped the pocket where he kept his extra candles. He fumbled as he exchanged the old candle for a new one. Now where were his matches?

A muffled sound caught Alex's attention. What was that? He stopped and listened. Silence. Then a rumbling and sliding of rock. Holding out his arms, Alex hurried through the blackness until he felt the heap of boulders. Standing very still, he listened intently. There it was again. A muffled sound. Could it be someone yelling?

"Hello?" Alex called through a gap in the boulders.

The muffled sound again.

"I can't hear you!" Alex called as loud as he dared.

A rumble of settling rock.

Silence.

What was that? A faint flicker of light, reflecting between the boulders.

"Is someone there?" he called, but there was no reply.

Alex started pacing again, back and forth in the blackness. He couldn't just leave, but what could he do?

Another rumble of moving stone. Alex went back to the rubble-filled door. There was another flicker of light, trickling down through the boulders. "Hello?" he called.

Then he heard it—clearly a voice this time. Muffled and distant, a voice called, "Alex?"

It was Zoe.

Chapter 9

"Zoe!" Relief crashed over Alex, followed closely by a wave of concern. "Are you okay?"

"I'm okay." Zoe's voice echoed strangely.

"And the others? Are they with you?"

"Yes. We're all here and we're all okay. Tyler twisted his ankle again, and Jani is bruised and sore, but that's it."

"You're trapped?"

"The rockfall blocked our way out."

"How big is the rockfall?"

"It filled this whole room."

"Wait—then where are you?"

"We're on top of the rocks. We got as close to the door as we can, but we're still far above you."

"Above me? How tall is that room?"

"No idea. Our light doesn't shine far enough."

"Your light is okay? How are the rest of your supplies?"

"We lost Jani's and Tyler's packs. He had our extra propane, and our rope, and Jani had the stove. We've been rationing our water and food, so we haven't run out yet, and we're being careful with the light too."

"I found the packs you left behind. And your logbook, Zoe. Tyler, are you close enough to hear me?"

"Yeah," Tyler's voice sounded even more muffled. "Man, you have no idea how good it is to hear your voice."

"It's good to hear yours too. Hey, can you see any way of moving some of these rocks? If we can make a hole, I could pass your supplies up."

"I don't know ... these rocks are huge. I think we're pretty high above you."

"Alex," Zoe interjected, "you could send the bags down through the trap door."

"Trap door?" Alex blinked. "Okay, tell me what happened."

"Jani fell through a trap door in the third riddle room."

"It shut behind her," Tyler added, "we couldn't hear her or talk to her. She was just gone! It was awful!"

Alex could only imagine. Tyler must have been panicking.

"We heard her voice through one of the doors," Zoe continued, "so we went into the next room, which was the labyrinth."

"Tyler broke the door down." Jae contributed.

"After the labyrinth we went into this room," Zoe continued. "At the far end there was a grate in the wall where we found Jani. The trap door had dropped her into a tunnel, which she followed to the grate. Tyler pried the grate open, and—"

"Hey!" Jae protested, "you missed the bit where Tyler broke the lever in the labyrinth and hot air started pouring out of the vents."

"That part wasn't necessary," Zoe replied curtly. "Alex passed through there, and he would have seen enough evidence of what happened to figure it out for himself."

"And what about this room? You didn't tell him about it at all! It was big and long, and the floor was all uneven, and we had to climb from block to block. It was—"

"Jae," Alex interrupted, "you can tell me about it later. Let Zoe finish."

There was a moment of silence, then Zoe continued. "We got the grate open, but the ceiling started to collapse. We all got through the grate into the tunnel where Jani was, so we didn't get hurt, except for Tyler's foot. We explored the tunnel, but it doesn't seem to lead anywhere. There are two more grates along it, like the one we climbed through. We were considering trying to open one of them when we discovered that we could climb out on top of the rockfall and heard you shouting. Now that you know where we are, that simplifies things."

"Yes," Alex agreed. He'd been thinking very quickly. "If I can drop supplies to you, you would be safe to stay in place for another two or three days. I'll go get SAR, and with their help we can get you out of there, without having to explore any unknown passageways that just might collapse on you."

"Forget it, Jae, we are not going exploring," Zoe retorted in response to something Alex could not hear. "There's no reason for us to go kill ourselves while we're waiting for help to arrive."

"Where was the trap door in the room?" Alex inter-jected before the conversation could be derailed. "Did you do something to set it off?"

"It was in the exact centre of the room," Zoe explained. "There must have been some sort of trig-ger, because we'd been in that room for over an hour, and I'm sure someone must have stepped in that exact spot already. There was a series of gongs that Tyler was messing with, so it might have been that."

"But I'd been doing that for a long time," Tyler added. "It almost had all the right tones to play the Halo theme music!"

"What were you playing when the trap door opened?"

"I don't know, I was just messing around."

"Okay, I guess I'll pile your stuff on the trapdoor and 'mess around' with the gongs until the trapdoor drops it down to you. You can get to the drop point?"

"Yes we can," Zoe confirmed. "When are you going to drop it? It would take us about an hour to get over there."

A wave of fatigue made Alex sit down quite abruptly. "Um ... I might sleep now, and drop your gear in the morning. Will you be fine till then?"

"Yeah, we have enough to last till then. What time in the morning?"

Alex thought for a moment. "Let's say around eight or nine, so I have time beforehand to sort out the gear and pack it for dropping."

"We'll have someone in place ready to receive it by eight, and we'll send someone here in case you need to talk to us."

"Thanks, Zoe. I'm glad you're all doing okay. Talk to you in the morning!"

"Goodnight, Alex," called a chorus of voices. The small glimmer of light flickered and disappeared from his sight. Alex pulled out his matches and lit his candle. The light flickered up immediately, a welcome relief from the deep darkness. Well, the others had gotten themselves into a bit of a situation, but not as bad as it could be. And now they had a plan.

Wearily, Alex got to his feet and stumbled toward the labyrinth. He wasn't about to spend the night somewhere where the ceiling just might cave in. He stopped by the broken door just long enough to pick up the packs from where he had left them, then trudged wearily through the riddle rooms, never lifting his eyes from the ground. He didn't stop until he reached the start of the murals. It felt safer there, and fresh, cool air was seeping along the ground. He rested the three packs along the wall and pulled out his sleeping bag and mat. Right—wind the clock. He looked at the time. Eleven thirty. Pulling off his boots and socks, he slid into the soft folds of his sleeping bag. Oh that felt good.

Chapter 10

Alex woke with a start. What time was it? Did he remember to set his alarm? The complete darkness in these tunnels did not change with the sunrise. Where was his lantern? He waved his arm around and knocked the lantern over. Oops. He righted it. Where were the matches? In his pack, of course. Alex sat up and reached for his pack. There it was. After fumbling around for a few moments, he managed to procure a match. He lit it, and used the flare of light to check the time. Seven thirty? He'd planned to set his alarm for seven! The match sputtered out, and Alex struck another match to light the candle. The candle wouldn't light. Had it burned out? Alex shook his head. He must have forgotten to blow it out before he fell asleep. He fished out another candle, put it in the lantern, and lit it. No time for a cooked breakfast, he'd have to make do with a granola bar.

As Alex munched, he pulled everything out of all three packs. He put all the heavy food into Jani and Tyler's packs, and gave them most of the water. What about the rope? Alex frowned. If everything went according to plan, he wouldn't need it, but as long as Zoe and the others were staying put, they wouldn't need it either. Might as well keep it. He quickly sorted through the rest of the gear. There was enough to get the others through another day or two. Longer if they were careful about it. He swung his pack up onto his back. It was a lot lighter now. That was nice. He heaved the other two packs over his shoulder and lifted his lantern.

Back in the third riddle room, Alex set down the extra packs and went to examine the centre of the room. He quickly realized his mistake. With his lantern only illuminating a small area, it was impossible to tell if he was actually in the centre of the room. He checked the time. Eight-thirty. Not too bad. He walked briskly back to the door where he entered and began counting his paces along the wall. Then he counted his paces along the adjacent wall. Retracing his steps, he counted his paces until he was halfway along the wall. Thankfully, the floor was tiled. He could follow the tiles and know that he wasn't veering off course. He counted his paces until he guessed that he was in the centre of the room, or close to it. He looked at the tiles below his feet. The last thing he wanted was to fall down the trap door himself and get stuck with the others, without the extra gear. Every tile was decorated with one of the designs that also covered the walls, but one design looked particularly familiar. Maybe it was a design that he had also seen on the door. Whether it was or not, it seemed to be as close to the center of the room as he could guess. He knelt down and examined it closely. Was that a hairline crack all around the tile?

His confidence growing, Alex straightened. Now to grab the packs and—

He stopped, and carefully set his lantern down beside the trap door. Now he would be able to find it again.

After collecting the packs, Alex balanced them carefully on the trap door and stepped back. Now where were the gongs that Tyler had told him about? What did they look like? He certainly hadn't seen any gongs in his exploration of the room yesterday. He frowned. Well, the others had been messing around and the trap door randomly let go, so now he would mess around, and hopefully it would happen again.

He trotted expectantly toward the wall where the set of three doors was. He tried pushing on each of the doors—the ones that weren't already broken. He pushed the designs on the door frames. Nothing seemed to happen. He began walking around the room, pushing and poking anything on the wall that looked interesting.

He was about halfway along the second wall when he pushed a small knob on the wall and a bell chimed, low and clear. Alex stopped and pushed it again. The bell tolled again. Interesting. Alex kept moving along the wall, poking and prodding. A few paces later, he pushed a smooth, hand-sized space on the wall, and the sound of a gong echoed through the silence. Alex felt around and found several more spots that struck unseen gongs within the wall. Each gong had a different tone.

Feeling a little bit silly, Alex played bits and snatches of songs, as best as he could. He carried on for a couple of minutes, just for good measure, then went to check on the backpacks. They were still there. Alex went back to the gongs. He attempted playing the theme music from Halo, even though he didn't know it very well. He tried playing the music from every video game he could think of that Tyler ever played. He checked on the backpacks, but they hadn't moved. Carefully, Alex leaned over the trap door and gave it a shove downwards, but it didn't budge.

Alex continued his circuit of the room, poking at anything that might have caught Tyler's eye. He made it all the way around the room and back to the gongs again. He'd found a couple more bells, and a few points along the wall that moved without making any sounds. Still nothing happened. Now what? He could keep "messing around" forever, but still not do exactly what the others had done to trigger the trap door. Maybe he should talk with them again and see if they had any other suggestions.

Leaving Tyler and Jani's packs on the trapdoor, Alex made his way through the labyrinth and back to the cave-in.

"Hello!" he called through the boulders. "Can someone hear me?"

"Hello!" It was Jani's voice. "I can hear you. What is it?"

"I can't seem to get the trap door to work. Do you have any other ideas of what might have triggered it?"

"Um, I don't know. I was sitting by the door we came through. Zoe was standing by the centre door, trying to figure out what the writing said above it, and Tyler was playing music on the gongs. Zoe was trying to say something to us, but Tyler wasn't being quiet, so I walked across the room to ask him to stop, but the floor dropped out from beneath me and I fell down. I'm not sure what Jae was doing." Jani's voice sounded tight and worried.

"Jani, are you doing alright?"

"I'm fine," she replied quickly. "I'm a bit sore from the fall, but Tyler says I didn't break anything."

"I'm glad. Could you call the others together? I want to see if anyone has any ideas of other things I should try."

"Okay, I'll get them."

Alex listened as Jani shouted to someone who was beyond his hearing.

"Okay," she reported, "they will come, but it will take a while for them to all get here."

Alex settled down to wait.

"You there, Alex?"

Startled, Alex opened his eyes. "Yeah, I'm here!"

"Jani said you were having a problem with the trap door?" Zoe's voice filtered down through the rock pile.

"I couldn't get it to work. Any other ideas of things I should try?"

"I've been thinking about it, but I can't come up with anything else. Tyler?"

"I already told you what I was doing." Tyler replied. Alex could almost hear his shrug.

"Jae," Alex called, "can you think of anything I should try?"

Jae mumbled something.

"What was that?"

"Never mind," Jae called.

"What were you doing when Jani fell?"

"I don't know ... I guess there was one circle that I pressed, exactly opposite the center door. That was just before Jani fell."

"Why didn't you tell us that before?" Zoe demanded.

"No one asked me," Jae muttered defensively.

"Okay, I'll try that," Alex called. "Anything *else* I should try?"

Jae was silent.

"Anything?"

"I guess that's all we can think of," Jani called. "Hopefully it works."

Alex returned to the riddle room. Counting his paces along the wall opposite the doors, he found what should be about the center of the wall. Where was this circle Jae was talking about? There it was, a shallow half-sphere protruding from the wall, down close to the ground. He hadn't noticed it before. As soon as he pressed it, there was a soft click behind him, and a scraping of buckles and canvas against stone. He didn't need to check, even though he did. The packs were gone.

Relieved, Alex hurried back to the cave-in. "Are you still there, Jani?"

"Yes," Jani called back. "Did it work?"

"Yes, it dropped the packs down. Did you get them alright?"

"I don't think Zoe has made it there yet. It takes a long time to cross all the boulders and then follow the tunnel down. But when she gets there she'll call up to Jae, and he'll call to Tyler, and then Tyler will tell me, so we shouldn't have to wait too long."

"Okay. I'll wait to hear before I go. I want to know for sure that you've got them alright."

About half an hour later, Alex heard a distant voice shouting.

"They got them!" Jani relayed the news to him. "Both packs landed safely."

"Good. Those packs have enough food and water for two days, plus the stove and extra propane for your light. I'll be down off the mountain and in touch with SAR by this evening, and all going well I'll be back here with help by suppertime tomorrow."

"Okay." Jani's voice sounded small.

"Hang in there, Jani. I'll get help, and we'll get you out of there."

"Thanks."

"Say hi to Zoe and the rest for me. I'm going to get going now and not waste any more time."

"Okay. Goodbye, Alex."

"See you soon!" Alex straightened his pack and set off through the labyrinth at a brisk pace. The sooner he could contact Search and Rescue, the better.

An hour and a half later, Alex saw daylight in the tunnel ahead of him, and a sharp gust of icy wind blew out his candle. Hurrying forward, Alex saw the doors, still open, and white sky beyond. Snow drifted down the passageway to meet him and crunched underfoot. As he approached the doors, the snow became deeper, and deeper. Three feet of snow, at least, and the sky was obscured with whirling flakes. The storm hadn't stopped. It was a blizzard. Getting down the mountain would be impossible. Even getting off the glacier would be impossible. There was no way that he could contact SAR and no way that anyone could get up the mountain to help them. They were alone.

Chapter 11

Alex stared at the whirling snow. There was no way to know how long the storm would last, and until it stopped he couldn't signal for help. He pulled out his SPOT device, just to check, but it didn't work. What a mess. No one even knew where they were or when they were supposed to be back. Except Mac. He'd told Mac to call out Search and Rescue if they didn't return in two days. That would be tonight at midnight. But that didn't mean that help would be right on its way. SAR wouldn't be able to search for them until the storm let up, and even then SAR would only know the location of their base camp. He would need to be up on the glacier surface to signal them, or SAR might miss them completely, unless ... he could set up some wickets by their anchor. SAR would be able to see the reflectors from the air, as soon as the storm let up. Perfect! Then he could spend his time trying to get the others out, without worrying about getting back to the surface in time to signal SAR. He could even leave a note for them.

Shrugging off his pack, Alex rummaged through it, looking for his logbook. There it was. Alex pulled it out and glanced at the cover. "Zoe Wieland".

Wait, what? Alex stared at it. He had sent Zoe's logbook back to her in the supply drop. He was sure he had. Dropping Zoe's logbook, he started rummaging through his pack again, but his own logbook was not there. How did that happen? Mentally, Alex kicked himself. He couldn't be making mistakes like that, that was how you got yourself killed out in the mountains.

Sighing, he reached down to pick up Zoe's logbook, and stopped. It had fallen open to the last page, and there was writing on it that Alex hadn't noticed before. Zoe had drawn a detailed copy of the design on the door, and along each side of the picture were scribbled some words:

> *One for you was strong mind and quick for thought.*
> *Two for you is strong body and quick for body movement.*
> *Three for you will be strong soul and bright for god(s?).*
> *Four for you not (?) and never for (?) (?).*

Alex snatched it up. Small lines connected the different words to the different symbols in the door's elaborate border. A translation! Each side of the door contained one phrase, and each corner had an elaborate image that appeared to be several symbols combined into one. What luck that he kept Zoe's logbook after all! It wasn't a full translation of the language, and it seemed that there were at least a couple symbols that

Zoe couldn't decipher, but it was something he could start with.

One for you was strong mind and quick for thought.

What did that mean? Strong of mind and quick of thought. That sounded like someone who was smart or clever.

Two for you is strong body and quick for body movement.

That seemed straightforward enough. It was talking about someone who was physically strong.

Three for you will be strong soul and bright for god(s?).

Bright for gods? Maybe a religious or a holy person?

Four for you not (?) and never for (?) (?).

Clearly that line had stumped Zoe, but at least it seemed to be talking about somebody who was not something. Okay.

One for the clever.
Two for the strong.
Three for the holy.
Four for the ... not something.

But one or two or three or four of what? The inscription didn't seem to say. Alex glanced from the sketch in his hand to the massive door that stretched above him. He knew—more or less—what it said now, but he still didn't know what it meant.

Alex stared at the drawing for a while longer. Something was strangely familiar about it. Of course it was familiar, he'd spent ages staring at the door yesterday, but it wasn't that. It was ... Alex looked up at the real life door beside him, then down at the drawing. It made him think of the rooms that he had been in. A square, and then a triangle, and then a trapezoid, and then three doors that would have led to three different rooms ... it was a map. Alex stared at it. It couldn't be. That was just too easy! But it was too strange to be a coincidence. The pattern exactly matched the rooms he had been in so far. The inscription said "One for the clever", and the first door they found led to a series of rooms covered in riddles. Did that mean there were three more doors—a door for the strong, a door for the holy, and a door for those who were not something? If it did, maybe there was another way to reach his friends!

Using the map he could pinpoint pretty precisely where his friends must be. Zoe had spoken about a large, long room, and said that the grate was at the far end. That wasn't far from where the second door should be. Even if the doors between the rooms followed the same pattern, that was just four rooms he'd have to make it through. If only he had more of Zoe's notes on the language. He flipped through the logbook, but there wasn't anything else he hadn't seen before. Satisfied that he wasn't missing anything, he slipped the logbook into his pocket. His first task was to set up the wickets.

Tramping through the accumulated snow, Alex reached the rope that was still hanging down the side of the crevasse. He could hear the wind howling across the glacier far above him.

Clipping into the rope, he made the ascent quickly. Even though he was prepared for the wind, it ripped the breath right out of his lungs. Bowing his head into the blinding snow, he crawled away from the edge and staggered to his feet. Unclipping the long bamboo rods from the side of his pack, he jammed one as deep as he could into the snow. Taking three steps forward, he planted the next one. That would have to do. He only had three.

Creeping back to the crevasse edge, Alex made sure his belay device was ready for the rappel. He glanced around. The wind whipped the stinging snow into his face and chilled his bones. He could barely see the wickets, just steps away from him, their orange reflectors swaying wildly in the wind. Hopefully they would bring help soon. Leaning back, he began his descent.

Returning to the door, Alex cleared a patch of snow and set up his campstove. As eager as he was to get going, he knew he shouldn't pass up the opportunity to refill his water and eat a proper meal. With snow melting in the pot, Alex leaned back against the rock wall and pulled out the logbook. He flipped to a blank page and began to write:

Four climbers are trapped by a cave-in deep inside this cave. Take the first right, then the next left, and follow the open doorways until you reach the cave-in. I am trying another route (first right, second left) to see if I can find another way to them. Tyler has a twisted ankle, but the other three trapped climbers are in good health and they have enough food and water to last until Thursday. Alex

Ripping the page out of the logbook, Alex rolled the note around the final wicket and tied it firmly in place with some reflective ribbon. Where to leave it? He could stick it in the snow right in front of the door, but it might fall over and be missed. Instead, he leaned the wicket against the rock wall nearby. That should be obvious enough.

With his water bladder full and his stomach full, Alex lit his candle and checked his clock. Three in the afternoon. Time to go.

Walking down the corridor at a brisk rate, Alex pondered his next move. He could try to tell Zoe and the others of the change of plans, but that could easily take an hour. And what if they didn't hear him? They weren't expecting him to return for another day at least. They might be completely out of earshot, and that time would be wasted. He might as well do his best to get to them first, and if he found a dead end he could always return to update them later. Even so, he paused as he passed the door, propped open with Zoe's ice axe. It felt a lot like leaving them behind.

Steeling himself, he continued. The murals along the wall immediately demanded his attention. He had passed the first set of murals enough times that he barely even watched them anymore, but these murals were new to him. Picking up the story, he followed the tale of the empire's rise to power. Responding to the surrounding threats, the empire increased its military might until all opposition was cowed before them. With peace established, the warriors engaged in many great competitions, vying for positions of fame and honour.

Alex stopped as the corridor turned sharply. This was the second corner, so there should be another door, if his suspicions were correct. He didn't see a door, but where the door might have been was a great mural of two warriors fighting in an arena. With no weapons or armour, it looked like they were engaged in some kind of wrestling match or test of strength. Well, the second way was apparently for the "strong", so that made sense.

He examined the mural closely. Sure enough, there was a hairline crack that betrayed that it may be a door after all. But how to open it? The first door—the door of the clever—was opened by a puzzle. Would the second door be opened by strength? He felt a little uneasy. He was strong enough, but he definitely wasn't ripped. His thin, wiry build was more suited to an endurance runner than a wrestler.

He tried pushing on the door. Nothing happened. He pushed again, harder. Still nothing. Frowning, he stepped back and examined the mural again. What if there was a particular trigger point? He tried hitting the figures at different places. On the head. On the stomach. On the arms. Still nothing, except a stinging hand. Backing up as far as the turn in the corridor allowed, he ran toward the door and kicked it as hard as he could. With a click, it swung open.

Alex blinked and peered through the opening. It was impossible to see anything in the blackness. Which way to go? If the map was correct, going around the left side of the room would get him closer to his friends' approximate location, but if the doors followed the same pattern as the riddle rooms, going around the right side would be faster.

Holding up his lantern, he examined the wall to the right, running his hand along the smooth stone. No elaborate inscriptions here. Cautiously, he followed along the wall.

After several steps there was a soft click and swish. Something hard slammed into Alex's back and he staggered forward. Spinning around, the light of the candle just caught something white moving beyond his sight. Another swish—felt, rather than heard. Alex ducked and felt something pass centimetres above his head.

Pressing himself against the wall, Alex tried to get his bearings. If only he had a bigger light. But he didn't, so he'd have to make do with what he had. As a child on his parents' farm in Southern Ontario, he would often go walking through the forest at night. He'd gotten to the point where he'd know where the trees and stumps were before he felt them. Carefully, he blew out his candle so that his other senses wouldn't be distracted.

Clipping the lantern to his belt, he pressed one hand firmly on the wall and walked resolutely forward. Immediately, he felt something swinging at him from his left. He ducked and heard it crash against the wall above his head. He lunged forward and then rolled to the side as something whizzed above. Standing, he felt the floor give way beneath him. He jumped, and slammed chest-first into the edge of the floor. Scrambling, he made it up. The wall no longer within his reach, his gut said keep moving forward. Something slammed into the ground behind him. A whizz, and again Alex ducked and rolled. Jump. Dodge. Dive. Heart pounding. Muscles burning. Whizz. Crash. Slam. His hand met the wall, firm and secure. Alex hugged against it, breathing hard.

Making a rough mental estimate of how far he'd gone, Alex forced himself to keep moving. A rush of air, and he threw himself to the ground. Something large whizzed above his head. Thump. The noise echoed strangely, somewhere beyond him. Interested, Alex tried to move toward the echo. Dodging and rolling, it was hard to move one certain direction. Finally, the echo sounded loud, just ahead of him. Muscles tensed for action, Alex stood and listened. No clicks or rushes of air.

Letting himself breathe, Alex carefully pulled out a match and lit it. The flare of light showed an open doorway, just two paces in front of him. He lifted the lantern to light it, and saw that one of the glass panels was shattered. Another one was cracked. Carefully, he lit the candle.

His arm ached. Pulling up his sleeve, Alex found a large bruise, already turning purple.

Cautiously, he moved closer to the doorway. Holding the light through the opening didn't reveal anything about the new room. He lowered the light to inspect the floor. There was no floor.

Instinctively, Alex stepped back. Where the floor of the next room should have been, there was black nothingness. Frowning, Alex pulled out a second candle and lit it. Carefully, he pulled the old candle out of the lantern, still burning, and gave it a gentle toss, out into the blackness. It fell, flickered, and went out. No sound returned. After waiting over a minute, Alex decided that the depth of the pit didn't matter after that. A dead end? He put the new candle into the lantern. Leaning carefully through the door, he examined the walls. They were brick, each brick staggered at a different depth. It would be pretty easy climbing. Easy climbing, with high consequence ... if he fell, it would be game over.

Alex sat down to think, but not many thoughts came. He could carry on, or he could go back. Go back and try another way? He didn't relish the thought of going back through the room he had just made it through. That was not going to be fun. But he didn't relish the idea of death by falling down an infinite abyss either. Could he build an anchor somehow?

Getting up, Alex examined the door frame. He couldn't see any way of securing a rope, but the room behind him had lots of moving parts. Could he loop a rope around one of them? Lifting his lantern, he moved cautiously along the wall.

Click.

Alex ducked instinctively and felt something swing above his head. He looked up, and it was gone. Moving back to his starting position, Alex tried again. This time he jumped backward, instead of ducking, and caught a glimpse of a panel swinging out from the wall, ready to smack an unsuspecting passerby in the back of the head. It returned to its position on the wall as quickly as it had emerged. If he could wedge it open somehow, maybe he could loop a rope around it.

Returning to his perch by the door, Alex rummaged through his pack, looking for something he could spare. Unzipping a side pocket, he pulled out the two metal rings that he had found broken off in the crevasse. Probably shouldn't use those. Sorting through his climbing gear, he chose his thickest piton. It wasn't as thick of a wedge as he would have liked, but if he jammed it in sideways it should work pretty well.

Setting his lantern down so he'd have both hands free, Alex walked carefully toward the trap. As soon as it triggered he ducked, then jumped up and shoved the piton in the joint by the wall. The returning panel smacked into his face, and Alex ricocheted back into the wall. The panel, caught by the piton, stopped centimetres from his face.

Rubbing his nose, Alex inspected the panel. It appeared to be securely wedged. He tried to shift the piton, but it wouldn't budge. That was good; the rope shouldn't dislodge it.

Getting out his rope, Alex looped it around the panel and clipped it into his harness. He swung his pack up onto his back and clipped the lantern to a gear loop. The candle flickered wildly, but he couldn't spare a hand for it, and some light was better than none.

Double checking that everything was in order, Alex leaned around the edge of the door and got a grip on the wall. He climbed quickly but carefully, checking each handhold and foothold before trusting his weight to it. It was easy climbing, but a long way to go in the dark when you couldn't see the end of the route. When he reached the first corner he stopped for a short rest, wedged between the two walls. He didn't like to think about what would happen if he fell. The rope might keep him from an untimely death, but he was so strung out that there would be quite a nasty swing with lots of scrapes and bruises. Well, he just wouldn't fall. Resolutely, he started traversing the second wall.

Finally, his flickering light showed a dark opening in the wall just ahead of him. With aching arms and calves, he pulled himself into the open doorway. With a sigh, he sat down and leaned back against the door frame. So far everything seemed on track for being the same route as the riddle rooms, but with physical tests instead of mental ones. If the pattern held, the next room would be very large. What kind of challenge would it hold? He wasn't in a hurry to find out.

Carefully, he unclipped one end of the rope and pulled the other end until it came free from his makeshift anchor. When the rope was properly coiled and put away, Alex stretched and stood up. Thinking better of it, he sat back down again and got out a granola bar. It wasn't quite supper time yet, but something to eat would do him good.

Five minutes later, Alex felt ready to continue. He checked his lantern. It didn't seem any worse for being rattled around during the climb. He stepped cautiously into the new room and examined the wall. It was plain and smooth like the first room. He took a couple careful steps, but nothing happened. Encouraged, Alex continued to follow the wall.

He walked until he guessed he should be meeting the next wall, but no wall appeared. Puzzled, Alex continued forward. The room was larger than he expected. Much larger.

"Hello!" Alex shouted. The echo indicated a large room, but not unreasonably large.

Bright light filled the room, as sudden as if someone had flicked a switch. Alex's mouth gaped open. "What the—" he gasped, spinning around. It was a bright, white light, so bright he could hardly see. He squinted. The room was only about as large as he expected, and—he shook his head—he was only standing steps from the door he had entered by. The floor was moving, moving him slowly but steadily back toward the door. He started walking again, briskly, but the floor matched his pace, only allowing him to make slow progress forward.

Where was the light coming from? Now that his eyes were adjusting, he craned his neck in every direction but couldn't see a light source. Maybe he'd get a better view from the center of the room. Changing his course, he noticed that the floor changed too, continually trying to push him back the way that he had come. There was only one other door in the room, so he set his course straight for it and increased his pace. The floor also increased its pace, but he was able to make slow progress.

Sudden darkness engulfed him. Alarmed, Alex took a quick step and stumbled. The ground jerked beneath him and he fell to his knees with a crash. Scrambling back to his feet, he began to run. His lantern! He turned, and saw the small, flickering light sweep away from him, illuminate the empty doorway for one brief moment, and fall into the black chasm beyond.

In complete darkness, Alex ran. Was he gaining ground, or was he being swept back toward the brink just like his lantern? He fumbled in his pocket, trying to pull out another candle. It was stuck, he couldn't get it, not while keeping this pace.

"Hello!" he called again to the darkness. "Some light would be nice!"

To his astonishment, the light reappeared. A quick glance showed that he was closer to the chasm than he wanted to be. He readjusted his course for the far door and slowed his pace to a sustainable lope. To his dismay, the ground moved him backward. He picked up his pace again. Finally he started to make head-way.

Without slowing, he craned his neck around, trying to see the source of the light.

"Hey!" he ventured in a loud voice. "Where's the light coming from?"

The light went out.

"Hey!" Alex protested. "I *want* the light!"

The light reappeared. Then went out again.

"Oh come on!" Alex groaned. "Light on, and *stay* on!"

Light flooded the room again.

"Thank—" The light flickered, and Alex glared at the ceiling. The light stayed. "Thank you," Alex fin-ished.

The pace was a hard one to keep up. Soon Alex was breathing heavily. It almost seemed like he wasn't getting anywhere, except for the distant door that drew imperceptibly nearer.

Finally Alex looked over his shoulder and saw that he was halfway. He resisted the urge to run faster; the floor would only speed up to match him. He focused on the pace of his strides and let everything else fade from his mind. Keep running. Keep running. His legs ached. His lungs ached, and his pack felt heavier and heavier. The continual jostling hurt his back.

There—the door! It was almost within reach. He ran faster; he couldn't help it. He ran, with his hand stretched out. He reached, grabbed the handle, and black darkness engulfed him. The ground whipped his feet out from under him and his face slammed into the door. Hanging onto the handle with all his strength, he struggled to his feet, opened the door, and threw himself through it. He hit the ground and grabbed onto what felt like the door frame.

"Um ... light?" he called. There was no response. But the world was no longer moving underneath him. He felt around. It was the door frame. He planted himself firmly on the space within the door frame where, in theory, no further traps or challenges would be triggered. Leaning against the door frame, Alex breathed a sigh of relief.

Chapter 12

After a long drink of water, Alex fished a candle out of his pack and lit it. Not a tea light—they wouldn't be too useful now that his lantern was gone—but he had taken some tall tapered candles from Tyler's pack. Those would be easier to carry. Maybe he could rig something up so the wax wouldn't drip on his hand.

He didn't feel too eager to move on to whatever challenge this next room may hold. His legs felt like jello, and his head was pounding. Maybe he should eat something. Alex pulled out a granola bar and noticed that he only had one more left. He'd need to start taking time for proper meals, or he'd run out of quick food.

As he munched, Alex checked the time. Six thirty? He had been running for over an hour. No wonder he felt awful. Alex leaned his head back and closed his eyes.

Finally his breathing returned to normal. Without getting up, Alex examined what he could of this new room from his place of relative safety in the doorway. From what he could see, it appeared to be more of a corridor than a room, but his candle did not shed any light on what kind of obstacle it might contain.

"Anyone want to give me some light in here?" he shouted. Maybe the mysterious light would appear in this room too. "Hello?" No light appeared.

Beyond his sight, his voice echoed strangely, then magnified and took on a voice of its own. "Hello? Hello?" a voice called; a shaft of light pierced the darkness far down the corridor, coming through a grate high in the wall.

Alex sat up. "Zoe!" he called, "Zoe, I'm here!"

"Alex?"

The voice was clearer now, and the light solidified into a grid-shaped pattern.

"Zoe! I'm down here! Through the grate!"

A shadow blocked some of the light. "Alex, what are you doing down there?"

"Short version: I can't get off the mountain because of weather, so I thought I'd see if I could get you out a different way."

"Did you find a way out?" Jae's voice butted in eagerly.

"What's happening?" Jani's voice echoed from further away.

"Alex found another way out," Tyler called back to her.

"More or less," Alex corrected. "First we've got to get all of you down through that grate. How does it look on your end?"

"Looks like most of the grates we've seen so far," Tyler offered. "With enough force it should come open."

"How far down are you?" Zoe asked.

"Could you give me a little more light? Thanks. You're a good fifteen feet up off the ground, and halfway along what appears to be a long, empty corridor."

"Appears to be?" Zoe questioned.

"I have yet to go through a room that has been that simple."

"I see. You have my rope?"

"By your rope you mean my rope that I lent to you? Yeah, I have it."

"Smart ass."

"I missed you too, Zoe," Alex grinned and got slowly to his feet. He didn't feel quite as shaky now. He noted with interest that there was a door at the far end of the corridor. Not that he wanted to find out what was beyond it. His friends were his objective.

"If we let down some cordelette through the grate, could you tie the rope to it?" Zoe called down.

"Probably. I should see what's up with this room first so we know what we're up against."

"Okay. Anything I can do?"

"Just hang tight for a couple minutes and I'll let you know."

Cautiously, Alex stepped out into the corridor. With a rattle, the floor gave way beneath him.

"Crap!" Alex flung himself back toward the door and just managed to grab the threshold.

"Alex? What—" Zoe called.

"Are you okay?" Jani called.

"Just a sec," Alex muttered through clenched teeth as he pulled himself back onto the solid space immediately in front of the door.

With firm ground beneath him once again, he leaned against the door frame and breathed a heavy sigh. He knew this wasn't going to be easy.

A small click at his feet made Alex look down. The floor was back in its place, looking just the same as it had before. Alex leaned forward and gave the floor a firm shove. It tipped down a little, then returned. He shoved harder. The floor by his feet fell, but the floor at the far end of the corridor rose, blocking his view of the far door. Silently, the floor slid back into place and stopped with a click.

"Alex?" Zoe's voice echoed down the corridor.

"I'm okay," he called. "The floor collapsed under me, but I managed to pull myself back up. It looks like the floor isn't stable at all. It's like a giant seesaw with the fulcrum right about where your grate is. That's going to make it hard to get to you."

An absence caught Alex's attention. Where did his candle go? After a brief glance around, Alex gave the floor another shove and peered down as well as he could. As the floor sank, a black gap opened at its end. His candle must have fallen down. That was concerning—what would happen if a person fell down? He'd rather not find out.

"—Any ideas?" Alex only caught the end of Zoe's question.

"Um, how much cordelette do you have between all of you?"

"At least forty metres."

"That should be enough. Can you tie it all together and drop it through the grate? And maybe tie a climbing nut or something to the end. I'm going to see if tilting this floor will make the end of the cordelette slide down to me."

"Roger."

Alex waited. A few minutes later, Zoe called again. "We have the cordelette ready. Should we send it through?"

"Yes, I'm ready for it. Make sure you have a good hold on your end."

Alex watched as the thin line of cordelette inched its way down from the grate and formed a small heap on the ground. There was only a small climbing nut tied to the end. The grate must not have permitted a larger one. Once the pile of cordelette was a decent size, Alex gave the floor a firm shove. The pile didn't budge. Alex pushed the floor down as hard as he could. The cordelette shifted, but not much.

"It's not working," Alex called up to Zoe. "Give me a minute to rig up a way to make the ramp tilt further."

"Okay."

Alex got out his rope and clipped several climbing nuts to the end. Then he stuck the head of his mountaineering axe over the edge and sat on the handle. He draped the rope over the axe head so that the climbing nuts could be lowered onto the ramp a foot or so from the edge. Hopefully that would stop them from slipping off.

"Alex?" Zoe's voice echoed down the corridor. "We're going to pull the cord up a little and try swinging it. Maybe we can get it partway to you."

"Sure, go ahead. Give a countdown and I'll drop the ramp right when you're letting go."

Alex watched as someone's fingers reached through the grate and started to swing the cordelette back and forth. "Three. Two. One. Go!" Zoe called.

Alex dropped his weight. The cordelette swung towards him and dropped. It hit the angled floor, tumbled lower and lower, then stopped.

Carefully, Alex lifted his weight and the ramp rose. When it clicked into place, Alex reached out with his axe and just managed to hook the end of the cordelette. "I've got it!" Alex called. "Good idea, Zoe!"

"That was all Jani, actually," Zoe called back.

"Nice one, Jani! Hang tight and I'll tie the rope on for you to pull back up." Alex unclipped his weights and firmly fastened the end of the rope to the cordelette. "Pull away!"

Alex watched the rope snake down the corridor and up to the grate. "Let me know when it's secure!"

"Secure!" came the call a few moments later.

"Great. I'll secure it on my end too, then we'll have a lifeline between us. Can you get the grate open, or did you want some help from the outside?"

"Help would be good, if you can manage it. It's hard to get decent leverage in here," Zoe explained.

"Sure, I'll see what I can do." Alex wasn't too worried about falling, as long as he could be clipped into the rope. Leaning into the darkness of the room behind him, Alex pulled the door almost shut, stuck his axe through the gap, and turned it sideways. He looped the end of the rope around the shaft, and tied it securely. Letting go of the door, Alex gave the rope a good sharp tug. The anchor held well. Leaving his pack on the threshold, Alex grabbed his other axe and clipped it to his harness.

"Here I come!" he called. Grabbing the rope with one hand, he started to run. The ground gave way beneath him, then stopped with a thud at a 45 degree angle. Alex held onto the rope with both hands and walked slowly up the incline. Glancing over his shoulder, he saw a dark hole at the bottom of the ramp. It was definitely big enough for a person to fall in.

As Alex reached the middle of the corridor, the ramp flattened beneath his feet, teetering from side to side. Putting his feet against the wall, Alex climbed up to the grate and clipped into it with a tether from his harness.

"Hey," he said, peering through the metal grate, "how's it going in there?"

"Good to see you, Alex." Zoe gave a half grin. Beyond her, Tyler was sitting on the floor with Jani standing beside him. She smiled up at Alex, but her eyes looked large and haunted. Jae was leaning against the cold stone wall, holding his camera tightly. They were all covered with smears of dirt, and their features stood out sharply in the stark light of the propane lantern. They looked like prisoners. Alex couldn't shake the hollow feeling that landed in his gut. But he would get them out. That's why he was there.

"Any advice on how to tackle this grate?" Alex asked with forced cheerfulness.

Zoe shrugged. "We just pried the last one off with our axes."

"And then the ceiling caved in," Jani added in a whisper.

"You're worried the ceiling might cave in again?" Alex looked up. The ceiling looked solid enough. "Well, I guess we'll have to risk it. I'm going to do whatever I can to get you out of there."

Leaning back, Alex jammed his axe behind the edge of the grate and started to lever it away from the wall. It wasn't easy. The grate was firmly attached, and his axe kept almost slipping out of his grasp.

Finally he had the top edge bent out enough that he could get the whole point of his axe into the gap. He pried it as hard as he could. With a crack, one of the corner pins fell out. Alex leaned back to rest his arm and survey the situation. It was rather humorous—working to remove the very grate he was clipped into. Rather like sawing off the branch that you were sitting on.

"So, Zoe," Alex mused, "what's the rope tied off to?"

"We tied it off to Tyler's butt, because that is definitely too big to fit through the grate."

Alex laughed, more than he had laughed in days. The sound seemed loud and out of place in the echoing corridor, but it felt good. Alex shook his head. "Gosh I've missed you guys."

"It's tied to the next grate, down that way," Jani said, pointing down their narrow tunnel.

"That's good," Alex smiled. "I don't want to count on this grate too much. But I am thinking about trying to bend it down without removing it completely. It would give us more to hold onto."

Zoe nodded. "The grate's open enough now, we could probably help you with it from this side. But we'd have to go get our stuff."

"Sure," Alex agreed. "We'll need your stuff over here anyway."

Zoe nodded. "Jani, Jae, let's grab the packs. Tyler, you hold down the fort. Mind if we take the light?"

"Go for it," Alex nodded. "I could use a breather anyway."

Zoe, Jani, and Jae shuffled off down the narrow passage, leaving Alex and Tyler in darkness.

"It's not very far," Tyler offered. "They'll be back soon."

"Oh I'm not worried." Alex grinned to the darkness. "You guys have been along this passage quite a bit, haven't you?"

"Not really. We explored it a lot at first, trying to find a way out, but lately we've just been sitting on our asses in the dark. Hey, if you're rescuing us, does that mean we get to eat more now? Zoe has us on strict rations."

Alex laughed. "Sorry Tyler, but even once I get you out of there, we won't be able to get off the mountain until the storm lets up. Rationing may still be necessary."

"Dang it," Tyler groaned. "How bad is the weather?"

"A visibility of about three metres, when I was up there."

"Shoot. That's not good."

Light filtered down the passage, announcing Zoe's return. "What's not good?" she demanded.

"The storm up above," Alex explained. "It's pretty severe, but hopefully it will be past by the time we make our way out."

Zoe nodded and set her pack against the wall. Jani carried two packs—hers and Tyler's. Jae didn't set his down.

Alex lifted his axe. "Well, I guess it's time to bust you guys out of there."

It didn't take long to get the second pin to snap, but bending the grate proved to be a challenge. Alex adjusted his anchor to hang off the top of the grate, and he used his body weight to try to bend it down. Zoe helped as she could from behind the grate, but it was too tight of a space for anyone else to join in.

Finally the grate was bent parallel to the floor. Alex eyed the remaining pins with suspicion. "I'm going to climb up and see how this grate holds with someone sitting on it."

Making sure he was securely fastened to the rope, Alex grabbed the edge of the grate and pulled himself up. The grate held.

Alex peered through the opening. "It looks like we're good to go!"

Zoe stared at him in consternation. "Alex, what did you do to your face?"

"I was getting better acquainted with a hard surface or two. Is it that bad?" Alex felt his nose and winced. "Yeah, I guess it's that bad."

Zoe shook her head. "Okay, what's the plan?"

"Do you still have that cordelette handy? Good. I'll clip into that and stand below the grate to help steady the ramp while each of you traverse across to the doorway."

"Packs first?"

"Oh yeah, the packs. Maybe each person can take their pack with them, but we'll attach them to the rope with a separate sling."

"Sure. Jani, you're up first."

"Me?" Jani's eyes widened. "Oh … okay."

Tyler squeezed her hand. "You can do it, Jani."

"Should I wear my pack?" Jani asked, turning to Alex.

Alex shook his head. "I don't think you'll fit through the hole with your pack on, but Zoe can lower it down after you." He turned to Zoe. "You got some cordelette for me?"

Zoe nodded. Carefully, Alex lowered himself down and found his balance. He clipped into the chain of cordelette that Zoe lowered and unclipped from the rope. "I'm ready when you are, Jani!"

Cautiously, Jani poked her head through the opening. She wiggled through until her head hung over the edge of the grate. "It's a long way down," she said in a quivering voice.

"It's not too bad," Alex urged her. "Maybe try coming through feet first. Then you won't have to turn around."

Jani withdrew back through the hole, and a few moments later her feet emerged. Carefully, she lowered herself over the side of the grate.

"Good job, Jani," Alex nodded. "You're almost down."

Jani grabbed the rope with both hands and lowered herself to the floor. Alex shifted his weight to stop the floor from tipping.

"Incoming!" called Zoe from above, and Jani's pack descended on a second chain of cordelette.

"Okay, Jani," Alex said, "You're heading for that door there where you can see my pack. I'll do my best to stop the floor from tipping under you. Just whatever you do, don't step through the door into the next room."

Jani nodded and slowly moved toward the door, one careful step at a time.

Alex opened his mouth to urge her faster, then thought better of it. The slow pace gave him plenty of time to counterbalance.

"Alex," she called as she reached the end of the ramp, "if I step off, that will make you fall."

"I'll be fine," Alex called. "That's why I'm clipped in."

"But if I hold this end of the ramp down, you won't fall, and the floor will be steadier for everyone else."

"That's true," Alex nodded. "Good thought, Jani."

Jae was sent down next, then Tyler. They crowded onto the small landing in front of the door. With Jani holding down the far end and Alex being the counter-weight, the floor stayed fairly steady.

Alex was glad this wasn't proving too hard for the group, but his heart sank as he thought about the route they would have to take to get out. Moving floors, high-consequence climbing, and a homicidal obstacle course. Zoe and Tyler would probably make it okay, but Jani was very cautious and Jae wasn't much of a climber.

Zoe stuck her head into the corridor. "Everyone make sure you're secure. I'm untying the rope." A few moments later, Zoe reappeared in the window and looped the rope through the grate. "You solid, Alex?"

"Yup, as long as Jani's good to keep holding me up."

"I'm fine," Jani called.

Zoe unclipped the cordelette from the grate and fastened it to the rope. She lowered her pack and the lantern, then slid down the rope herself.

"Everything's down?" Alex asked.

Zoe nodded.

"Great. Head over to the door and make sure that no one goes through it, no matter what!"

Zoe crossed lightly to the threshold where the others waited. "There isn't much room over here," she commented in a dry voice.

"Yeah ... sorry about that," Alex winced. "I'll get there as soon as I can." He crossed back to the center of the room. Zoe had everything ready for him, and the loose end of the rope was tied off securely to the anchor to make a taut double thickness of rope. He clipped himself to the rope with a carabiner on a short leash, then untied the cordelette. Backing up as far as the leash allowed him, Alex grabbed the carabiner, then ran toward the door as fast as he could. The floor fell, and he jumped. With a jerk, the rope caught him, his eyes level with Zoe's boots about three metres in front of him.

"You alright?" Jani asked.

"Yeah." Alex looked up at his friends crowded on the landing. Tyler and Jae were sitting on their packs, with Jani squeezed between them, holding the lantern up high. Zoe had attached herself to the rope with a prusik and was leaning back off the edge, trying to maintain her personal bubble as much as possible.

Something bumped the bottom of Alex's boot. It was the floor. Pulling his knees up, Alex let the floor rise as much as he could, then he launched himself forward with a sharp jump, pushing the carabiner in front of him. He moved a few centimetres. The floor came back up and Alex tried again. A few more centimetres. Alex frowned. The slack in the rope made it harder than he expected, but some progress was better than none. He continued to worm his way forward.

After a few minutes he paused to catch his breath. "Hey Zoe, how far can you reach?"

Keeping one hand on the rope, Zoe leaned out toward Alex.

Alex reached for her hand, but he wasn't quite close enough. One more jump would do it. He drew his legs up and leapt as far as he could.

A sharp crack split the silence and the rope shook. Alex grabbed the rope, glancing over his shoulder. One of the pins holding the grate had snapped; the grate swung at a precarious angle, held by one final pin.

"Grab my hand!" yelled Zoe.

Alex reached up and grabbed it.

With a crack and a clang, the grate fell to the ground. Alex's carabiner dropped, held only by the leash attached to his harness. With one hand in Zoe's and the other clinging to the rope, he watched as the grate tumbled down the ramp and disappeared into the darkness beneath his feet.

"Give me your other hand!" It was Tyler.

"Just a sec," Alex grunted, looping the rope around his foot so he could put his weight on it. "There." He reached up, grabbed Tyler's hand, and held on as Tyler and Zoe pulled him up onto the landing.

"Thanks." Alex smiled at Zoe and Tyler, then slowly lowered himself to sit on the edge of the landing. He didn't like how shaky he was feeling. It had been a really long day.

Zoe started reeling in the rest of the rope. "Do we want to keep the grate?"

Alex shrugged. "See if it will come up. Might come in handy, but if it's too much work just leave it."

Alex watched Zoe tug at the rope, and tried to steel himself for the return journey. His whole body felt like lead. How on earth would he get everyone back the way he had come?

Zoe gave up on the rope and handed it over to Tyler. Alex looked at her tight, strained expression. Whether he was ready to move on or not, he couldn't make Zoe stay in this cramped space anymore. "Well, Tyler?" Alex looked up at his friend. "Any luck with the grate?"

"It's really stuck on something."

"Then we'll leave it. Just pull the rope out."

Tyler untied the rope and pulled it through, coiling it neatly. Alex squeezed through to the door and took apart his anchor. He took a deep breath. "Okay, here's the deal. The room on the other side of this door has a moving floor. We will need to be careful and make sure to walk very slowly, because the faster we move, the faster the floor will move. There's a door to the right, which is where we are going, but the room beyond that door doesn't have any floor, so whatever you do, don't let the floor push you through it."

Carefully he opened the door. The yellow light of the propane lantern illuminated a small circle of floor. Alex leaned through the door. "Hey!" he yelled into the blackness, "could we have some light in here?"

Brilliant light filled the room.

"What?!" Tyler, Jani, Zoe, and Jae exclaimed together.

"Wait, there's light? That you can just turn on?" Tyler gaped.

"No way!" Jae laughed.

"Where did it come from?" Jani demanded.

Alex stopped short in surprise. The room was different. Four pillars of coloured light shone down in the center of the room, and where the door should have been there was nothing but a blank wall. Not blank—all the walls were covered with ornate designs, and now the door was on the left. A closed door. What happened? How did the room change? Or was it ... a completely different room?

"Are you telling me," Tyler hadn't stopped talking, "that all this time we could have had light if we'd just asked for it?!"

"Where is it coming from?" Jani still wanted to know.

"How is it—"

"IT KNOWS ENGLISH?!"

Everyone turned to stare at Zoe. Alex blinked. "I guess so?"

"How is that possible?" Zoe demanded. "Everywhere we have looked in this place there has only been one language, one very unusual language that does not, as far as I can tell, have any connection to any modern languages, but you speak a command, in English, and not only is there a response, but a response that was clearly able to hear, and understand, and comply with your command? What the heck!"

Alex shrugged. "Honestly, I hadn't even thought of that. There does seem to be something that responds to my call for light, but only in this room, for some reason. Speaking of this room ..." he grimaced, "it appears to be completely different than it was when I passed through it earlier."

"What?!" everyone demanded again.

"The light is different, the door is on the wrong side, and the walls are decorated rather than plain." He stepped out through the door. "And the floor isn't moving."

"Alex—" Jani bit her lip.

"What?"

"Are you sure you should go in there? What if there's a trap?"

Alex looked around. "Well, there might be. But we've got to get out of here, and that's not going to happen by sitting and waiting. Come on, let's explore the room."

Cautiously, the others stepped through the door. Nothing seemed to happen.

First, Alex went to examine the spot where the door should have been. There was no sign of it, no cracks or outline or any kind of indication that there had once been a door in that wall. He turned to Zoe. "This design on the wall, is it connected to the language at all?"

Zoe shook her head. "Not as far as I can tell."

Jae was approaching the pillars of light in the centre of the room.

"Jae, leave those alone," Alex advised. "We don't want to trigger something just yet."

Jae joined them by the wall. "So if we can't go back the way you came, how do you know that we can get out at all?"

"I don't know," Alex admitted. "But I have some ideas. I just want to make sure we're not in any immediate danger first."

"And then what?"

"I want to sleep."

"What?"

"I've been going since seven thirty this morning, and it is currently ..." he checked his clock, "almost nine in the evening. If I don't sleep soon, I am going to fall over."

"Yeah, I guess," Jae conceded.

Alex walked back to Tyler and Jani who were sitting down, not far from the door they had entered through. "Have you eaten?"

"Well, we've eaten what Zoe says was our ration for today," Tyler admitted with a wry face, "but I wouldn't mind some more if you're offering."

Alex laughed and opened his pack. "Well, I haven't had supper yet, so I'm going to eat. Maybe I'll share a little."

Zoe joined them as Alex set up his stove and got some water on to boil. "You think it will be safe enough to spend the night here?"

Alex shrugged. "I think so. Nothing dramatic has happened in here yet, so that's a good sign."

Tyler gave a dry laugh. "Have things been rather dramatic for you?"

Alex gave them a brief rendition of his experiences since he entered the second door.

"That's crazy," Jani said with wide eyes. "The rooms we went through weren't anything like that.

They were mostly just riddles and writing all over the walls."

"That's just it," Alex nodded. "That's because you went through the first door. Look at this." He pulled out Zoe's logbook and flipped to the last page.

"Hey! That's my logbook!" Zoe cried, snatching it from him.

"Yeah. Funny story about that. I was so certain I sent you yours and kept mine, but it was because I ended up with your logbook that I was able to come find you. Look at this." He took the logbook back from Zoe and showed everyone the last page. "That's the design on the door, but it's also a map of these rooms and passages. See? That's the first door you went through, and all the riddle rooms." He traced the map with his finger. "I went through this door, through this way, and this corridor is where we met. Now we're in this room."

"So with this as a map, we can find our way out!" Tyler grinned. "Gosh, that's a relief."

"And there's more," Alex continued. "Zoe has the translation written around the edges here: *One for you was strong mind and quick for thought.* So that's like people who are clever, right? Two is for the strong, three for the holy, and four for the ... something."

"Three hapax legomena in one sentence," Zoe interjected with a frown. "I looked everywhere but I couldn't find those ideograms in any other place. But the symbol for *not* here seems to be characterizing this by its dissimilarity to something particular. It's just not clear what. Those three symbols do seem to be related, though."

"Thanks, Zoe." Alex gave her a wink, then turned to Jani. "So you see, the first set of rooms were full of riddles and translations because that was the way of the clever. The second door was the way of the strong, so it was full of traps and challenges. The door to go back that way has disappeared, so we will have to try to get out through the third door."

Jani looked down at the map. "The way of the holy?"

Alex nodded.

"What does that mean?"

"I have no idea. Hopefully it will be easier getting out than getting in."

"And if it isn't?"

"Then we'll figure that out when we get to it."

Jani didn't look convinced.

"What is Jae doing?" Zoe interrupted in an unimpressed voice.

The rest of the group turned to look. Jae, who had returned to the centre of the room, was trying to get close to one of the lights, but whenever he stepped toward it, it moved away from him. It gave Alex the distinct impression of a cat chasing an oversized laser pointer.

"Should I stop him?" Jani wondered.

"It doesn't seem to be doing any harm," Alex admitted. "I say we leave him to it."

When his supper was finished, Alex spread out his sleeping bag and mat, leaving the others to decide how they wanted to arrange themselves. He didn't feel too uneasy about this room. Maybe it was his exhaustion, or maybe it was the thought that they weren't in the way of the strong anymore. Whatever the way of the holy might contain, it couldn't be as difficult as what he'd had to navigate that day.

As soon as his head touched the floor, he was asleep.

Chapter 13

Alex woke up in complete darkness. Where was he? Not in his bed in the apartment—the absence of the obnoxious fluorescent streetlight outside his window confirmed that. Besides, he was in his sleeping bag. Of course—he and his friends were spending the night in the room that no longer appeared to be trying to kill him. But where was the light? As Alex sat up, his back spasmed and his head pounded. Thinking better of it, he lay back down. "Anyone awake?" he asked into the darkness.

"I'm awake," Zoe replied, not far from his elbow.

"Do you know what time it is?"

"I haven't checked recently."

Alex reached for his pack and pulled out his clock. Striking a match, he checked the time. Ten o'clock? He'd slept for over twelve hours! He should have set an alarm.

Alex made himself sit up again. "Hey! Could we have some light in here?"

Blinding light filled the room and a chorus of groans assailed his ears.

"Too bright!" Tyler protested.

Zoe covered her eyes with her arm. "At least you could have warned us!"

"Sorry."

"Is it gone yet?" Jae's muffled voice called from under his pillow.

While Jani and Tyler made breakfast for everyone, Alex repackaged his sleeping gear. All going well, they'd be out in a couple hours, and then they'd be able to start their descent, or at the very worst have to wait in the crevasse for the storm to pass. He didn't expect getting out to be that simple, but as long as they made it out today, they should be fine. Filling up his bowl with oatmeal, he went to sit by Zoe, who was staring at the sketch of the door in her logbook.

"I can't believe it's a map," she said without looking up. "I should have seen that."

"You didn't have any reason to suspect it," Alex reassured her, "and you've had other things on your mind."

"Like being trapped and quite possibly dying down here?"

"And figuring out the language."

"It was too easy." Zoe shook her head. "I mean, it *was* hard, for sure, but decoding a completely unfamiliar language, in an unfamiliar context ... it should have been impossible. I should have needed a Rosetta Stone, or some other kind of bridge in translation, but there was nothing. It should have been impossible."

"Maybe you're better at this than you thought," Alex grinned.

"I think it was written to be translated."

"What?"

"Whoever invented this language intentionally made it simple and accessible. The inscriptions are repetitive and only become complex very gradually, with next to no culturally dependent information. It was only in the third room that I was running into things that I had no context to understand."

"Strange."

"And now there's a light that responds to English?"

"Yeah, go figure."

"This place doesn't make sense. I don't like things that don't make sense."

Alex gave Zoe an understanding smile. "Maybe it will make more sense as we go. Speaking of which ..." he pushed himself up onto his feet. "Let's get going."

Once everything was cleaned up and packed up, Alex looked around the group. Everyone seemed to be in good spirits, at least better than when he first saw them yesterday. Zoe eyed the room with suspicion. Jani continued to hover close to Tyler who was limping slightly. Alex made a mental note to check on Tyler's ankle the next time the group needed a break. Now it was time to get moving.

"Will we need this?" Tyler asked, indicating the lantern.

"Probably," Alex nodded. Sure enough, as soon as Alex touched the door, the light disappeared.

"What happened?" Jani gasped.

"It appears we lost the light again." Alex sighed. "Can someone light the lantern?"

With a hiss, the propane lantern flared up into a globe of light, casting stark shadows over the group huddled around it.

Alex looked up at the ornate door. "Okay, we're about to go into the way of the 'holy'. I have no idea what we'll find there, but please stay together and try not to touch anything. We're going to try to get through this with as little complication as possible." He exchanged a glance with Zoe, then looked back at the door. There didn't appear to be any kind of handle on it, but as he looked the design on the door began to move and morph. Coloured lights flickered along the curving designs, leading inward, always inward, toward the centre of the door where a nebulous glow was forming. Alex reached out his hand and touched it.

An explosion of force erupted from the door, knocking everyone backwards. Alex landed on his back, crushing his pack beneath him. Darkness closed in around him. "Damn," he muttered, struggling back to his feet.

"Ow," Jae groaned from somewhere to his left. "What the hell was that?"

"Apparently the door saying 'you shall not pass'," Zoe commented dryly. "You don't need to be a linguistics major to figure that one out."

The darkness split apart with a whoosh from the propane lantern. Somehow Jani had managed to keep it from being broken.

Tyler was still lying over his pack. "I fold," he groaned. "Can I go home now?"

"We're working on that." Alex reached out a hand. "Come on, Tyler. Back on your feet."

"I don't wanna," Tyler protested, but he allowed himself to be helped into a sitting position. "What happened to 'as little complication as possible'?"

Why had he touched the door? Alex shrugged. For some reason he had been so sure that was what would open it. He glanced over at the door—where the door should have been. Now there was a dark opening into the next room. "Hey! It worked!"

"Worked?" Zoe asked incredulously. "More like 'tried to kill us'."

"But at least it's open now. Let's get going before it changes its mind."

Making sure everyone was on their feet, Alex led the way into the next room. Zoe followed close behind, her blazing eyes daring the absent door to show its face again.

Jani followed next, carrying the lantern, with Tyler leaning on her other arm. His limp was worse now.

"Next time, Alex," Jae commented as he followed last, "could you at least let me take a picture first before you blow things up?"

"I'll keep that in mind," Alex responded dryly as he turned to survey the new room they had entered. The lantern gave just enough light to show that it was a triangular room, just as he expected. The walls were ornately decorated, and to his relief the doorway on the opposite wall did not appear to contain a door.

"What's that?" Tyler gestured. In the narrow corner of the room was a small pillar or pedestal, about a metre tall.

"I'll go look," Jae said eagerly.

"Wait!" Alex gestured to Jae who was already halfway to the pillar. "We don't need to nose around, the door is already open."

"Can't I at least take a picture?" Jae protested.

Zoe sent him a withering glare.

"Jae," Alex spoke as gently as he could. "We don't need more pictures. We need to get out of here."

"But I need pictures. For my articles."

"You are not posting or sharing anything about this place!"

"What?" Jae looked shocked. "You can't say that. My career needs this. *I* need this!"

"You do *not* need this, and you do *not* need to become rich, or famous, or whatever else you are hoping to get out of it." Alex glared at Jae. "Do you want to know why I came out here to find you by myself, when it would have been much safer and smarter to call SAR in the first place? There are people out there. People who saw your article and were so *interested* that within hours they had found out all of our names, where we lived, what we were doing, and even cornered me at my own cousin's wedding to question me about your whereabouts. There is a whole society of creeps out there that is bound and determined to track us down, and I am as sure as hell not going to let you publish anything else that is going to draw their attention again!"

Silence rang in Alex's ears as he realized that he had been yelling. Everyone stared at him. Because he'd been yelling, probably. He sighed. "Getting out of here alive is our first problem. Our second problem will be avoiding the 'Historical Acquisitions Agency'."

He gestured toward the door. They could discuss this more once they were out. Just one more room to go.

The others followed him silently through the door. Alex looked around as the lantern illuminated ... another triangular room. Alex frowned. That wasn't right. According to the map this room should be rectangular.

"Okay ... that's interesting." Zoe was eyeing the room with a suspicious glare. She had also noticed the discrepancy.

"What's wrong?" Jani glanced from Zoe to Alex.

Alex reached for the lantern. "Could I borrow that?" Pushing past Jae, Alex leaned back through the door, scrutinizing everything the light touched. He turned back to the others. "It's the same. Exactly the same. The designs on the walls, everything."

"And ..." Tyler prompted.

"That doesn't match the map." Zoe explained.

"But there's still a door to go through, so do we need to worry about it?" Tyler grinned hopefully.

Alex wanted to argue, but maybe Tyler was right. Maybe. He could tell the room that it was the wrong shape till he was blue in the face, but that wouldn't do anything for them. He handed the lantern to Tyler. "Okay, let's try the door."

As they walked through the door into the next room, Alex's heart sank. This room was exactly the same. Again.

"I'm guessing that's not good?" Tyler asked.

Zoe was poring over the map in her logbook. "It doesn't make sense. Everything else matched. Why doesn't this match?"

Alex frowned. Either the map was wrong, or this was somehow part of the challenge of the way of the holy. He gestured to the others. "I want to try something." He unclipped a climbing nut from his harness—one that he could make do without—and set it on the floor. "Let's see if these are really different rooms or if they might just be the same room over and over."

Zoe frowned. "But that doesn't—"

"Nothing here makes sense, Zoe. Come on, the experiment will only take a minute or two."

Leaving the climbing nut on the floor, they all returned to the previous room. It was unchanged. They returned to the room before that, which was also just the way they left it, with nothing on the floor. Satisfied that his question was answered, Alex led everyone back to where he had set down the nut. He stared at it for a while, then noticed that everyone was waiting for him to say something.

"There's something going on," he admitted, "but I haven't figured out what."

"Should we try the *next* room?" Tyler suggested.

Alex laughed. "Sure, why not?"

Alex was hardly surprised when the next room was another identical room to the one they just left, but without the climbing nut on the floor.

"And the next room!" Tyler cried with an exaggerated gesture, and set out with his half-limping gait.

As the others followed, Zoe moved to Alex's side. "Why are we doing this? We're just getting farther and farther from the map that we can follow."

"But do we have any other choice? It's not like we've passed another door that we can try instead." But what if there was another door? "Hey Tyler!" Alex hurried to catch up. When everyone was gathered together again, he continued, "What if there is a hidden door that we are missing? I think we should go back and look."

"But we haven't seen any hidden doors," Jae protested.

"Maybe because they were hidden," Zoe retorted under her breath.

"It won't hurt to look," Alex urged them. "Besides, we've already gone through five identical rooms. Who knows how many more there are?"

"Not that many more," Zoe interjected.

"How do you know?"

"Because these rooms are slowly moving us in a circle. Eventually we will circle around to where the other rooms are that we have been in and the pattern will have to stop."

"I guess that's true," Alex admitted. "How many degrees of a circle would you say each room is?"

"I can go look—"

"No." Alex cut Jae off. "We're leaving the corner with the pillar alone. We can see it from here well enough. Probably a bit smaller than a 45 degree angle? So we should really only have another couple rooms before we reach an area that we've already explored. I guess we could keep going then, and see what we find."

They walked through the next room, and the next room. Then five more rooms. Tyler's limp was getting worse, and Zoe was scowling darkly.

"Okay, we should have reached something by now," Alex admitted. But it was so easy to try just one more room. Easier than going all the way back to the start. He led the group into the next room and stopped short. There was a climbing nut on the floor. How was that possible?

"Damn," Tyler muttered under his breath as he stopped beside Alex. "How—"

"That's impossible!" Zoe exclaimed. She grabbed the lantern and stormed out of the room, back the way they had come.

"Zoe—" Alex called, but she didn't stop. Everyone hurried after her, through room after room, until Alex almost lost track of how many rooms. There was the climbing nut again, but Zoe did not stop until she was in the third room beyond it. Then she turned to wait for the others. Jae was breathing heavily. Tyler was limping severely, leaning on Jani's arm. Zoe just stared at them with blazing eyes.

Alex broke the silence. "It's gone, isn't it?"

Zoe nodded.

Jani frowned. "Gone?"

"The room we slept in. We appear to be in an endless circle of rooms that isn't letting us out."

"That's pretty cool," Tyler commented, glancing around at the room.

Alex shook his head. "It would be a lot 'cooler' if we weren't trapped in it."

"So how are we going to get out?" Jae wanted to know.

"I guess we look for hidden doors?" Alex had a feeling that it wasn't going to be that simple, but it was all he could think of at the moment.

Everyone lit candles and scattered around the room to look for anything that might indicate another way out, but Alex called Tyler back. "How's that ankle of yours?"

"Oh, it's alright."

Alex raised an eyebrow.

"Okay, it hurts," Tyler admitted, "but it's going to be fine."

"You have it wrapped up?"

Tyler nodded.

Alex sighed. "Just try to stay off it as much as you can, okay?"

A sudden bright light flooded the room.

"What—" Alex looked around. The pillar in the corner of the room was alight, with a large, white flame burning in the air just above it. Jae was sidling away from it as quickly as possible.

"Jae!" Alex exclaimed, "What did you—"

"I didn't—" Jae protested.

"I told you not to touch that!"

"I was just taking a—"

"I said no more pictures!"

"Leave him alone!" Jani jumped between Jae and Alex with eyes blazing. "You all keep picking on him and saying that what he wants doesn't matter. Well, I think that it does matter, and I demand that you start treating him like a person instead of a nuisance!"

Alex opened his mouth, but couldn't find any words to say. He needed some space. Turning, he walked out of the room.

The tread of his feet sounded loud in the silence that followed him. The room that he entered was as bright as the room he left. Alex frowned. Was there a flame burning in this room too? No. The light from the other room was shining into it as if there was no wall between them. He walked over to the wall. It was still there—he could touch it—but it was almost entirely transparent.

"Hey," he called to the others, "you've got to come see this."

They came.

"Wait, you can see through the wall?" Tyler grinned. "Cool! When did that happen?"

"I don't know. Maybe ..."

"When the fire appeared?" Jani asked pointedly.

"Maybe."

"Let's see if the next wall is see-through too!" Tyler suggested, already limping toward the door.

"Tyler ..." Jani rushed after him and offered him her arm.

As soon as Alex went through the door, he could see that this wall was not transparent. "That's interesting," he commented to Tyler.

"What's interesting?" Zoe asked as she came through the door.

"This wall isn't—"

Jae came through the door, and the light streaming from behind him instantly went out.

"What—" Alex bit his tongue and started again. "That's interesting. As soon as we all went through the door, the flame went out."

"Why would it do that?" Tyler wondered.

"Maybe it needs someone to be close to it," Jani mused thoughtfully.

"What, it has a motion sensor or something?" Zoe didn't sound convinced.

"The light lets you see through things that you couldn't before," Jani said quietly, almost to herself, then she turned to Alex. "Could I try something?"

"Sure." If Jani had an idea, he wasn't going to stop her.

"Stay here," Jani gestured, then went back through the door.

Tyler looked anxious. "Are you sure that we—"

The light reappeared.

"Hey!" Tyler cried, "We can see through this wall now!"

Jani nodded. "That's because I lit the flame in this room instead of the one beyond it."

It was strange to be able to see Jani directly, but only hear her voice coming through the doorway. Alex and the others went to join her.

"So it seems that the light of the flame only has an effect on the adjacent rooms," Alex summarized. "I wonder what it does."

"I wonder what happens if we light them all," Jani added thoughtfully.

"Let's try," Alex agreed. "How do you turn the flame on?"

"Just by walking close to it."

"I told you I didn't touch it," Jae muttered.

"Yeah, sorry for jumping on you like that. Come on, let's give this a try."

They went into the next room, and Jani walked down to the pillar to trigger the flame's appearance. Alex had a vague feeling that he was forgetting something, and it hit him as soon as they walked through the second door. Would the furthest flame continue burning? He looked back and could only see one flame. "Did the first flame go out again?"

Everyone else turned to look.

"I'll go check," Jae offered. In a few moments he returned. "It went out. Only the flame in the closer room is still burning."

Alex frowned. "I guess we can't light them all then."

"Yes we can," Jani offered, "we just have to spread out."

"But—" Alex thought for a moment. He didn't want to let the group split up, but what if they were onto something? "I guess we could try."

Tyler shook his head. "Alex, we're all together now. I don't want to risk losing someone again."

"Well, does anyone have any other ideas?"

No one responded.

"Then I guess we need to try it. Either that or keep searching for a hidden door."

"I think we should try it," Jani asserted.

Alex realized that everyone was waiting for him to make the final call. "Okay. We'll do it. Everyone keep a lit candle in case the lights go out again and we need to be able to find each other."

At Jani's suggestion, Tyler conceded to staying in their current room so that he wouldn't walk on his ankle more than necessary. It also happened to be the room with the climbing nut. Somehow that seemed appropriate.

Leaving Tyler behind, Alex, Jani, Zoe, and Jae lit the flame in the next room and then moved into the room beyond it.

"Hey, it's working," Jae commented, "I can still see both flames."

Three flames, Alex noted silently. The room beyond Tyler was still alight. How many more rooms were there to go?

"And we can see Tyler," Jani added.

"That's good," Alex nodded. "Jae, you stay and man this room."

Jae agreed, and Alex, Zoe, and Jani moved on, lighting the next two flames. Zoe offered to stay in the second room. It felt wrong to leave her behind, but Alex didn't protest. He moved on with Jani.

As Alex lit the next flame, he looked around. He could count seven flames now, lighting seven rooms that spread in a wide semicircle. They were over halfway. Looking back he could see Zoe and Jae in their rooms, and right across the circle he could see Tyler, sitting on the floor massaging his ankle. They seemed very close, but also very far away. Alex shook his head. Time to finish this and see what would happen.

After lighting the flame in the next room, Alex suggested that Jani stay there.

Jani shook her head. "No. I'd rather go on. If you don't mind," she added quickly.

Alex did mind, but he didn't have a good reason to object, so he let Jani go on. He listened as her footsteps faded into silence. There was a small whoosh, then Alex could see Jani through the wall, calmly walking away from the flame into the next room, the last dark gap in a circle of light.

A whoosh, and the circle of light was complete.

Alex looked around. Now what? He looked around the circle, wondering if the others would be able to hear him if he spoke to them.

The roaring of the flame in front of him grew louder, demanding his attention. Alex watched as the flame grew larger until it filled the entire end of the room, consuming the pillar beneath it, merging with the other flames into one massive ball of white fire.

He watched it swirl and morph and take the shape of a glowing, fiery door, beautiful and terrifying.

Alex couldn't tear his eyes away from it. "Uh, guys?" he called, "there's a door here!"

There's a door here! There's a door here! His voice echoed in his ears, or was everyone else calling the same thing? A roaring like a furnace crowded out any other sounds. What should they do? They hadn't made a plan. Going through a magical fire door sounded like a pretty bad idea, but what else were they supposed to do? Wandering in circles and never being able to find a way out sounded like a pretty bad option too.

He reached out his hand. The air in front of him was hot, but not dangerously so. He took a small step forward. The fire flashed and swirled, obscuring the image of the door. He froze. Slowly the image of the door reappeared.

"Turn around!" A voice echoed in Alex's ears. "Turn around! Walk in backwards!"

"What?" Alex shouted.

Turn around! Turn around! The voice echoed as if everyone was shouting it.

Why? Why backwards? It didn't make sense!

Turn around!

Tearing his eyes away from the mesmerizing sight, Alex turned his back toward the heat of the fire. The rest of the room seemed pitch black in comparison to the brightness. Dark splotches swirled in his vision. Clenching his fists, he forced himself to take a step backwards toward the fiery door. Then another step.

And another step. The roaring of the flame filled his ears. It was all around him.

And suddenly, silence. Alex stepped back sharply and bumped into something.

"Don't move," hissed Jani beside him.

"Why?" Tyler whispered from close behind Alex.

"Shhh."

A door materialized in front of Alex, shadowy and translucent. Wait ... it looked familiar! It reminded him of the door that Zoe had opened into the riddle rooms. He was about to ask Zoe about it, when the door whisked away and was replaced by a different shadowy door. Alex recognized it instantly.

"Hey!" he hissed as quietly as he could, "That's the door to the way of the strong! I went through that door!"

"Which door?" Tyler asked.

"Can't you see a door?"

"Yes, but are we all seeing the same door?"

Alex glanced over his shoulder. He couldn't see any other doors, or see any of his friends, even though he could hear them so close. That was disconcerting.

"My door shows a couple big blokes fighting," Tyler offered.

"That's it!"

"So should we go through it?" Jani asked softly.

"I don't—"

The door whisked away and was replaced by a new door. It was ornately decorated and reminded Alex of some of the designs they had seen on the walls recently. "Is that door for the way of the holy?" he asked aloud.

"How should we know?" Zoe demanded. "We haven't been through it yet!"

"But the first door was the door to the riddle rooms, right?"

"Yes," Zoe confirmed.

"And the second was the way of the strong. So this must be the right one!"

"The right one?" Jani queried.

"Yes, that's the way we're trying to get out."

"So we choose this door?"

"I think so. Which other one would we choose?"

"Are you sure?" Jani's voice was growing louder. "It's going to disappear any moment!"

"Choose it!"

"How?" Jae demanded.

"Just do something!" Alex shouted, and stepped into the door.

There was a blinding explosion. Alex tumbled across the room, slamming into something very hard. Lights swirled in his vision as he tried to get to his feet. His legs gave out and he sank to the floor again.

"Hello?" he called, "Anyone there?"

Silence rang in his ears. Cursing internally, Alex fumbled in his pocket for a candle and some matches. It took him three tries to light a match, because his hands were shaking, but finally he succeeded in lighting the candle. The small flame flickered, giving a dull, sickly light. Had he really done so much before with only a candle to light his way? The darkness seemed oppressive and overwhelming after the blazing brightness of the fiery door. He lifted up the candle, but that didn't help much. Wait—there was a door, right in front of him. It was ornately designed and reminded him somewhat of the shadowy door he had assumed to be the door to the way of the holy. But even if it was the right door, where were his friends?

Alex struggled to his feet. He really didn't want to have to search for his friends again, in the dark, with no idea of where to go, and nothing for light but a small candle. It just felt like too much.

"Hello?" he called into the darkness. "Light?"

Nothing happened. What was it that Zoe had said? That there must be some kind of presence that could hear and understand. But that was only in that one room ... or was it?

"Could we have some light in here?"

Nothing.

"Could I *please* have some light in here?"

Nothing.

Alex's temper rose. "So you think you're so great, huh? Just 'poof' making light out of nowhere. Well, I don't think you are so great. You only made light in one room! I bet you can't make light in here, even if you wanted to!"

Light sprang up all around him.

"Ha! I knew it!"

The light disappeared again.

"Okay, sorry, I won't gloat. I need the light to find my friends."

Slowly, the light returned. Alex looked around. Although the light was dim, he could see the extent of the room well enough. It was large, filled with all sorts of altars and basins and statues and strange things that Alex didn't understand. He was beside a large door, the door out of the way of the holy, he was quite certain. But where were his friends? There—a dark figure sitting against the wall. Alex hurried over. It was Tyler.

"Are you okay?" Alex asked, kneeling beside him.

Tyler looked at Alex with a confused expression. He opened his mouth like he was talking, but Alex couldn't hear anything.

"What?" Alex leaned closer.

Tyler spoke again, but Alex still couldn't hear him.

"I can't hear you!" He watched Tyler closely. Tyler mouthed, "I can't hear you either."

Alex frowned. Had their hearing been damaged by the explosion? That might be why he couldn't hear anyone respond to his calls. He mouthed to Tyler, "I'm going to go look for the others."

Tyler nodded and stood up, wincing as he put weight on his foot. Alex gestured for him to stay where he was. There was no point in Tyler injuring himself further.

Alex began to search the room. He found Zoe lying on the ground beside what looked like a dry fountain. She didn't respond to his touch, but a quick check of her vitals indicated that she was okay. Knowing that she hated being shaken awake, Alex made a mental note of where she was and went on to find the others.

He rounded a large altar and found Jani walking towards him. She greeted him gladly, though once again they couldn't hear each other speaking. Jani showed him that the glass on the lantern was cracked. As best as he could with pantomime, Alex encouraged her not to worry about it, and gestured for her to follow him.

A little further, they found Jae sitting against a pillar, blinking up at the unexpected light. He had a lot to say, even though Alex and Jani couldn't hear him, but Alex gathered that he had been worried when no one responded to his calling. He sent Jani and Jae towards Tyler and went back to Zoe. He stepped heavily as he walked, which had its intended effect. Zoe opened her eyes as he approached.

He could tell that she wanted to be left alone, but at his request she let him check for injuries. She seemed to be alright, but he made a mental note to watch for signs of concussion.

When the entire party was back together again, Alex led them over to the door.

"How do we open it?" Tyler mouthed at Alex.

Alex shrugged. "Any ideas?" he mouthed, turning to the rest of the group.

Everyone stood looking at each other.

Finally Alex walked up to the door and gave it a big shove. It didn't move, but his gesture seemed to have the desired effect as he watched the others laugh and step forward to help. They tried all pushing it together. They tried pushing and twisting different parts of the design on the door. Then Jani gestured to a small handle on one side of the door and pointed out that there was a matching one on the other side. Jani and Tyler grabbed the handles, and the large double doors swung silently open.

Alex cheered, even though no one could hear him, and they all hurried through the doors into the corridor beyond. It was the corridor of moving pictures—Alex recognized it easily. He sighed with relief. They made it! Just a couple of hours of easy walking and they would be out.

"Hey! I can hear again!" Tyler exclaimed.

It was true, Alex realized. He could hear their footsteps, Jani's breathless laugh, the rustle and creak of their packs, the large stone doors gently swinging shut, a small, unexpected click from behind him.

Alex turned around. A gun was pointed at his face.

Chapter 14

A gun. Alex stepped back involuntarily and held up his hands. There was a gun. His heart raced. It must be the Agency—who else could it be? But how had they found them so quickly? What were they doing here? Why did they have a gun? Bright lights flooded the corridor, almost blinding him.

Jani gasped.

"What the—" Tyler stammered.

Alex could feel Zoe's intake of breath. He resisted the urge to shield his eyes from the light. He could only just make out a group of uniformly dressed individuals, the foremost of which was pointing a handgun at him.

A middle-aged man in a well-cut suit stepped forward into the light. "Well, well. Alex Wieland. I thought we might just find you here."

Red anger flashed through Alex as he recognized the intruder from the wedding.

Tyler stepped beside Alex. "What's going on?"

"Oh, Alex and I are old friends," the man replied with a patronizing smile. "We were just getting reacquainted."

Alex glared. "I don't—"

"And none of your smart talk this time, Alex," the man purred. "You see, this time I have a gun." He gestured to a holster at his side as his eyes took in the rest of the group. "I see that you found your friends. How heartwarming."

Alex struggled to control his anger and speak with an even voice. "Yes, I found my friends, and now we want to go home. Let us go. We won't be in your way."

The man made a little scolding sound and shook his head. "Oh trust me, you won't be in the way. In fact, my supervisor is very interested in meeting you. I trust that you won't object."

"Do I have the option of objecting?"

"No. Just the option of making this more difficult than it has to be." He gestured his companions forward. "Of course we can't have any of you doing something rash. Don't mind the handcuffs; they're just a formality."

Five of the uniformed figures approached and handcuffed Alex and his friends. The strongly built woman with the handgun lowered it slightly, but didn't put it away.

"Alex ..." Jani said in a small voice, "what's happening?"

Before Alex could reply, their captors started marching them down the corridor. They were spread out, each accompanied by an escort, with the wedding crasher leading the way and the woman with the handgun coming behind.

As he walked, Alex listened to the tramp of their footsteps. Where were they taking them? The end of the mural passage? All the way out to the glacier? Either way they were in for a long walk.

He tried to pay attention to the murals as they passed, but his mind kept returning to the Historical Acquisitions Agency. How had they found them? Did that mean the storm had let up? Was Search and Rescue on its way?

Images on the wall flashed by him. Kings. Soldiers. Priests of some sort. People dying.

Alex was *certain* he had slipped out of the apartment unnoticed. How had the Agency managed to follow him? Or had they found the crevasse on their own?

An unexpected halt brought Alex's attention back to their current situation. Three of their captors were having a hurried conversation further down the passage, gesturing at Tyler who was leaning against the passage wall. His hunched shoulders showed how much pain he was in. Alex's heart sank. He'd forgotten about Tyler's ankle.

He turned to his escort. "My friend is hurt. Can I go to him?"

His escort gestured for him to wait. Just then, one of the larger captors approached Tyler, removing his handcuffs and his pack. Easing Tyler's arm over his shoulder, he helped him stand upright again. Jani appeared at Tyler's other side, and together they supported him as he limped gingerly forward.

The pace was slower after that. Alex grumbled inwardly at their captors for forcing Tyler to keep moving, but at least they were moving in the right direction. Even if they hadn't been captured he would've had to get Tyler out somehow.

Alex's escort was a man Alex guessed to be in his thirties, and a bit larger than he was. Alex watched him out of the corner of his eye for a while and decided he seemed approachable enough.

"What's your name? I'm Alex."

"Agent Mendoza."

"Nice to meet you, Mister Mendoza. Have you been with the Agency for long?"

"Four years." He squared his shoulders. "This is my first field mission."

"Good for you. Say, do you ever call it the HAA for short?"

A strange look crossed the man's face. "I ... I don't think I should be talking with you."

Alex shrugged, doing his best to hide a smile. Agent Mendoza would be alright. He couldn't say the same about the agent in charge, though. As soon as they got to the supervisor there was going to be trouble.

He turned his attention back to the murals. It appeared that the priests were killing the kings now, at the order of that shining orb he kept seeing images of. Beams of light shot out of it, destroying towers and palaces, reducing everything to a wasteland. Now the people were building something inside a mountain. Some kind of tomb or something? No, they didn't put the dead kings in it, they put the orb in it, and sealed it off.

The corridor turned at a sharp angle. Alex looked at the corner with interest. He couldn't see a door, but then the other entrances had been hard to spot too. He looked down the corridor ahead of him. Tyler and Jani appeared to be doing alright, thankfully, but it was hard to see Zoe or Jae in the shadows beyond them. Hopefully they were okay.

The remainder of the murals were pretty depressing, showing ruined cities and other crumbling landmarks that didn't mean much to Alex. He was more interested by the sounds echoing down the corridor towards them. There were people up ahead.

Finally the passage of murals ended and they stepped out into the wide, sloping corridor that led down from the glacier. Bright lights stung their eyes, and the smell of many people in a confined area assailed their senses. People were bustling back and forth, some appeared to be in uniform, some wore mountaineering gear. There were two people taking a rubbing of the large mural at the end of the corridor.

Their guards bustled them along. In a pile on one side of the corridor, Alex noticed his friends' climbing axes that had been wedged in the riddle room doors, along with their bundled up tents and sleeping bags that Alex had left up by the glacier. The bright lights they passed were gas lights of some sort, but fitted with large mirrors to amplify and direct their light.

Alex and his friends were deposited by a bare bit of wall partway along the corridor. Their handcuffs were removed, and they were directed to drop their packs and sit several paces away from them. Alex watched the wedding crasher and several of their other captors disappear into the crowd, leaving only a couple of guards. Not that that really mattered. With the sheer number of people in the corridor, not to mention the bright lights, there was no chance of them sneaking away.

Tyler leaned back against the stone wall and groaned.

Zoe leaned over to Alex. "This wouldn't happen to have something to do with that society of creepy creeps you mentioned?"

"Yep," Alex grimaced. "The very ones."

"What do they want from us?" Jani queried.

Alex glanced at the guards, but they didn't seem to be paying much attention. He shrugged. "Honestly, I don't know. I think they were looking for this place, but they've found it now. Maybe they want to find out what we know about it."

"Are we safe?"

Alex looked at Jani. He wanted to reassure her, but when he closed his eyes he could still see the gun that had been pointed at his face. He sighed. "I don't know."

Jani shivered.

"But at least none of us are trapped anymore," Alex continued. "We're together, and we're within an hour's walk of the door. And SAR should be out looking for us soon."

Zoe cocked an eyebrow. "Search and Rescue knows where to find us?"

"I gave Mac our base camp coordinates and left a couple of wickets up on the glacier by our anchor. It shouldn't take them long to find us, once they're on the mountain."

"But ..." Jani glanced around at their captors, busy with their work. There were twenty of them, at least.

"Let's take things as they come." Alex gave Jani a reassuring smile and turned to Tyler. "First of all, how's that ankle?"

Tyler moaned without opening his eyes, but moved his arm to give a thumbs up.

"Uh huh. Let's have a look at it."

He eased Tyler's boot off and unwrapped his ankle. It started to swell almost immediately. "Here, Tyler, let's get your foot up. Jani, could you give me a hand?" Together they got Tyler lying down. Alex took off his softshell jacket and bundled it up into a makeshift pillow. Jani lifted Tyler's foot up onto her knees.

"Hey," Alex gestured to the closest guard. "Excuse me, agent person. My friend has an injured ankle. We need ice for it. Can you get us something?"

The guard looked at Alex with a blank expression.

"We need ice. For Tyler's ankle."

The guard blinked. "I'll speak to Agent Batts." He turned and walked away.

"Do you suppose they have a medic of some sort?" Jani asked Alex as they watched the guard disappear from view. "This is a pretty large group."

"Good thought, Jani. I'll ask when he gets back." Alex knelt by Tyler and checked his breathing. It was a bit faster than it should be, but not enough to be alarming. His face was very pale and tight. Alex looked over at their pile of packs. What would happen if he went to get his water and first aid kit? He didn't want to make their situation any worse than it was already.

Ten minutes later the guard returned with a small blue ice pack, which Alex immediately passed over to Jani.

"Thanks." Alex nodded at the guard. "Do you have a medic or a first aid attendant here? Someone should really have a look at Tyler's ankle."

"I'll speak to Agent Batts."

"Okay. And while you're here, can we get our water out of our packs? We were marching for over an hour and you didn't even give us a chance to get a drink."

"I'll speak to Agent Batts."

"Seriously?"

The guard turned and left without responding.

"Alex?"

Alex turned to Jae. "What?"

"Maybe you should let me do the talking next time. I think that would go better for all of us."

A commotion far down the corridor drew Alex's attention. Several people were talking in excited voices, and the sound was drawing nearer. Alex glanced over at Zoe to see if she had noticed it, but she was sitting hunched against the wall with her eyes closed. Zoe could go through the smallest caves without feeling claustrophobic at all, but being surrounded by too many people was her worst nightmare. He had to get her out of here.

As the commotion grew louder, a woman in a casual khaki uniform strode up the corridor. She was tall, with a narrow face, her dark hair pulled back in a severe bun. The creases at the corners of her eyes betrayed an age that otherwise was impossible to pin down. She stopped directly in front of Alex and his friends, her piercing gaze quickly taking in the situation. With a gesture, she commanded silence from the clamouring agents that had followed her up the corridor.

"Parker, bring Doctor Nakano here at once. Sadik, bring food and water for our guests. First Detachment is on standby. The rest of you, return to your work. That is quite enough gawking."

As the crowd dispersed, the woman turned back to Alex and his friends and her stern expression relaxed. "Sorry to keep you waiting. I'm Karen Morani, Director of the North American Field Department of the Historical Acquisitions Agency."

"*Field* Department?" Alex muttered to himself. "Somebody's lost."

The woman's expression didn't change, but she turned her smile towards Alex. "Alex Wieland, I believe? I've heard so much about you." She held out her hand.

"All good things, I presume," Alex commented dryly, refusing the outstretched hand. A glint of cold steel flashed behind Morani's smiling eyes.

"Jae Kim," Jae interjected, stepping between them. "Pleased to meet you." He shook her proffered hand warmly. "I believe you read my article?"

His article? Is that really all he cares about? Alex rolled his eyes, but the conversation had moved on without him.

"You're a journalist, aren't you?" Morani was smiling at Jae. "I think your writing has great potential."

Oh no.

Jae smiled and gestured humbly. "They say a picture is worth a thousand words, but I think that pictures and words can work together to tell even more. Wouldn't you agree?"

"Oh, absolutely." Morani's eyebrows arched and she shifted her gaze to the rest of the group.

Jae turned to the others. "Let me introduce my friends. You've already met Alex," Jae shot him a death glare and moved on. "This is Janilee Misra, a good friend."

Morani nodded politely.

"This is Zoe Wieland, Alex's sister. And this is Tyler Harrison. You may have noticed his injury."

"Yes, I'm sorry to hear about your ankle, Tyler. Doctor Nakano will be here shortly to examine it."

"Thank you," Jae smiled. "This is a fortunate meeting. I imagine you've had some time to look around. What do you think of the place so far?"

"It's very interesting."

"Isn't it? The hall of moving pictures, for example. That is remarkable craftsmanship. Have you explored any of the inner rooms yet?"

"Yes, several. Our language experts are there now, working on a translation."

"Oh yes, it's an interesting language, isn't it? Zoe would have a lot to say about it, I'm sure. She's the one who translated it for us."

Morani raised her eyebrows. "By herself? Well done. I'm sure our team would love to hear her insights."

Zoe's glare said she'd be damned if she said a word to them.

"Have they not been able to translate it yet?" Jae asked innocently.

"They have made significant headway. Of course, we are also taking the additional time to ensure everything is well documented."

"Of course." Jae nodded. "You haven't had any trouble with the trap doors yet?"

"Trap doors?"

"We almost lost Jani down one. It was a pretty close call, but we were able to get her out, through Tyler's quick action. There's hardly been a room in this place that hasn't tried to kill us in some way or another."

"Excuse me for a moment." Morani turned away, calling an agent who was loitering nearby. There were some whispered orders, and the agent hurried off down the corridor. Morani turned back to Jae. "You were saying?"

Jae frowned for a moment. "Oh right. Tyler saving Jani. And then there was a cave in, which I'm sure you saw evidence of. You seem well prepared, so I imagine you've been reinforcing the ceilings wherever your agents are stationed for long. If Alex hadn't managed to find another way to get to us we'd probably still be trapped down there."

Morani gave Alex a sidelong glance. "That was lucky."

"Lucky for all of us, I'd say," Jae continued shamelessly. "This place really starts messing with your brain after a while. Doors appear and disappear, and you can go back through one to find a completely different room than the one you were in before, or find yourself crossing the same room over and over with no way to get out! It was beyond me, but Jani seemed to understand what we needed to do and we managed to get out, and only had to dodge two explosions!"

"Explosions?"

"This place doesn't like it when you do the wrong thing—it's almost like it has a personality of its own!"

A personality of its own. Alex glanced back down the corridor. He hadn't told anyone about his experience in the room of altars, but now that he thought about it, it didn't make sense at all. It was strange enough that he could ask for light—in English—and get it, but whatever it was that responded to him in the room of altars had acted more like an intelligent being than a voice command centre. It had pride, and a sense of humour that was almost playful. And it wasn't limited to only one room. Was there ... *something* living in these corridors, watching them? His spine tingled.

"—And since we couldn't go out the way Alex had made it in, we knew we had no choice but to try making it through the third door, which was where your people met us." Jae was still talking. "Of course, getting in is difficult, but getting out is no easy task either. You have to make sure you never turn your back at the wrong time."

"You seem to have learned a lot about this place," Morani stroked her chin thoughtfully, "and you have some very qualified people on your team."

"Oh yes," Jae agreed. "Alex, Jani, and Tyler are in outdoor leadership studies, and Zoe is studying linguistics. They all have weeks of experience in the backcountry. With a team like this, I'd say we could get in anywhere."

Alex shot Jae a sidelong glance. What was he doing?

Morani smiled. "It just so happens we could use a team of useful guides." She leaned in confidentially. "My agents are well trained, but I don't know if many of them could keep the kind of level head that you have shown. We are trying to find something which we believe may be in the center of this vault. Would you help us find it?"

Jae's eyes glittered. "That is an interesting proposition," he mused thoughtfully, "but our exploration has taken us four days so far, and our food supplies are getting low."

"Of course, as long as you are working for us, we will provide food and water for all of you."

"That would be helpful, as long as each person's rations can be carried on their person. Traps or obstacles could separate us, and we wouldn't want someone to go hungry."

"We could easily give each person their rations at the start of each day."

"With two days of extra rations in each person's pack, in case of another cave-in."

"Agreed."

"And we will need our own packs and other gear returned to us," Jae continued, "exactly as we left them, with nothing missing."

"Of course."

"And our pay?"

"Pay?" Morani smiled. "You're a bold one. Let's consider room and board your pay."

"But there is more we can offer, you know."

"Oh really?"

"As a photojournalist I would gladly document the entire expedition for you, for just two hundred dollars per day, provided my name is included with any photos you publish."

"One hundred dollars."

"One fifty. Meet you halfway and it's yours."

"Very well. One fifty."

"Wait, what?" Alex stammered. "You can't just—we're not helping these people! They're—they're criminals! Stalking us, invading our privacy, breaking into our apartment, threatening us at gunpoint! We're not having anything to do with them!"

"Alex—" Jae hissed, "we can't just—"

Morani gestured for Jae to be silent. "Let me address this. Agent Batts!"

The agent Alex met at the wedding approached briskly. "Commander?"

"Is it true that you and your division threatened our guests at gunpoint?"

"Yes, Commander."

"And I imagine you handcuffed them."

"Yes, Commander."

"You also authorized agents to enter their residence without permission?"

A look of surprise flicked across Agent Batts' face and his eyes went cold. "I never needed permission before."

"You never reported accessing a civilian's residence before." Morani stared pointedly at Agent Batts. He met her gaze without flinching.

After a long silence, Morani arched her eyebrows. "Interesting. When we return to headquarters I will be launching a formal investigation into your ... behaviour. Is that understood?"

"Yes, Commander." Agent Batts turned to leave.

"Batts?"

Agent Batts froze.

"You're getting sloppy."

Anger smouldered in Agent Batts' eyes. His gaze lingered on Alex's face for a brief moment, then he turned and strode up the corridor. Silence fell in his wake.

Morani watched Alex closely. "I know you don't trust us. Given the circumstances, however, I don't know if we have much choice. The vault has been opened and there is no turning back."

Alex gave her a skeptical glance. "Says who?"

Morani leaned forward confidentially. "This is a once in a lifetime opportunity, Alex. I'm sure you want to learn more about this place."

"Actually I want a nap. In my own bed."

"There is something about places like this. They get inside your mind, and you need to know, you need to go deeper."

"Or get away as quickly as possible?"

"It's a fascination. An obsession. You can't just walk away and never know. Can you?"

Her eyes flicked across the group and settled on Tyler's eager face.

"If I went with you," Alex interjected, "Would you let the others go free?"

"What?!" Tyler, Jani, and Zoe stared at Alex.

"You can't leave us behind!" Tyler protested.

"Tyler, you of all people aren't fit for going anywhere. You can't even walk! If anyone has to do something dangerous, it's going to be me, and I'm not leaving you here alone."

"Damn right you're not leaving me alone, because I'm coming too!"

"Jani, tell him that he can't walk on that ankle."

Jani looked sheepish. "It's true, Tyler, we can't let you walk on it. But Alex, we shouldn't split up again. What if we lose someone?"

"I think I might have a solution that would be satisfactory," Morani interjected. "There is no need to set out right away. You can rest until tomorrow. Doctor Nakano will tend to Tyler's ankle, and you can all have a good meal—oh, here's Agent Sadik with refreshments now."

A young man approached, offering everyone protein bars and bottled water.

Morani smiled as she watched Tyler tear into his food ravenously. "I'm sorry that this is the best we can offer at the moment, but supper is served at six, and I'll be sure that the cook is told about the extra numbers." Her nod to Agent Sadik told him to do just that.

Alex looked at the wrapping of his protein bar suspiciously. It didn't appear to be tampered with, and the plastic water bottle was still sealed. Was he that hungry? He supposed he was, and partook reluctantly.

Doctor Nakano arrived soon afterwards, and began to examine Tyler's ankle. She clearly knew what she was doing, but even so, Alex couldn't help hovering a little.

"Could I speak with you for a moment, Alex?"

Alex jumped. He didn't realize Morani was so close behind him. Ensuring his features remained composed, he gave a noncommittal shrug.

Morani gestured him away from the others to a spot where two chairs were set up. Alex followed, but refused to sit in the proffered chair.

Morani made herself comfortable in the other seat, looking up at him through steepled fingers. "Well, Alex, I believe that it is time for us to come to a decision. I know you want to leave, but unfortunately that is impossible. I am under strict orders that no one is to leave these premises until we have reached our objective."

"Orders?"

"The Historical Acquisitions Agency is a high ranking para-government organization. Going against orders is a serious offence."

"What even *is* the Historical Acquisitions Agency?"

"That is classified information."

Alex settled his face into an unimpressed glare. "Let us go."

"That is impossible. Not only is it forbidden, the weather has made the mountain completely impassable. Until the storm lifts, no one is going anywhere."

"How did you get here?"

"A small break in the storm was all that was necessary. The Agency is willing to take greater risks than Search and Rescue does."

Alex gave Morani a sharp glance. "Search and Rescue?"

Morani sat back in her chair. "Search and Rescue was alerted early Tuesday morning that a group of mountaineers was in danger on this mountain. As you can imagine, the Agency followed the news with some interest."

Alex watched Morani in silence.

Morani studied him for a moment, then continued. "There will be no Search and Rescue until the storm is over, and even then no one will depart from this location until we have obtained its artifact. Since we are trapped here together, I would appreciate your assistance."

"Our assistance? Like it's somehow a good idea to help you when we get nothing out of it? You're basically holding us hostage."

Morani raised her eyebrows slightly.

"Your offer was highway robbery, and you know it," Alex continued. "If you've ever looked into hiring a guide, you know what that costs, and it's not cheap. But you want us to essentially be your guides in a place where our lives are very much on the line and expect to only pay us with the food we eat and the encouragement that we can go home sooner? If you want me to trust you, pay us fairly."

Morani sighed. "I know you are worth more than I am offering. There is just one problem. This is a mission that no one knows about, that no one can know about, besides a few key people. You are not one of those people. It can't be in the books that we paid you, or that you were here at all."

Alex frowned. "If you're *that* kind of agency, I'm sure that you must have ... *ways* of doing things, under the radar, that can't be linked back to you. There could be other ways of compensating us fairly. Like ... a bursary, say, to go towards our university tuition. You don't have to hand us a cheque to pay us for our time."

Morani stroked her chin thoughtfully. "I could look into that."

"Do you promise?"

"I don't have the position to be able to make such promises, but I will do what I can."

Was that the best he was going to be able to get? Alex sighed. "And there's one other thing. Regardless of what I do, I want Tyler and Jani to stay behind here. I know enough first aid to know that one day is *not* enough for his ankle. It's going to be weeks before he will be able to walk on it normally again, and Jani won't want to be separated from him."

Morani looked at Alex thoughtfully for a while. "Tell me, Alex, when you were in the circle of repeating rooms, would you have made it through the flaming door if it hadn't been for Jani's insight?"

"No."

"And do you think your team would have made it through the challenges as well as they did without Tyler's humour and energy?"

"No."

"You need them, Alex. You're their leader, and you are very competent, but you cannot make it through this place on your own merit. You need Jani's insight, and Tyler's spirit, and Zoe's clever mind." She paused, then gave a little smile. "Jae's charisma didn't do you any harm either. I always keep my word." She straightened her shoulders. "I will hire you as a group or not at all. And you can be sure that we will use all the resources at our disposal to help Tyler's injury. We have a brace that can offer his ankle complete support while still fitting inside his boot, and he will be supplied with medication to reduce the swelling and remove any pain."

"I'm not sure—"

"Think about it. I will give you two hours, because we will need time to make our plans for tomorrow." Her eyes roamed down the corridor at the bustling scene. "My agents are well trained, and I am confident that they can complete their mission, but they are here because this is their job. You and your friends have something unique to offer. You are here because—"

"We're idiots?" Alex offered.

Morani smiled. "Perhaps."

"I guess I'll talk to the others and see what they want to do."

"You're the leader, Alex. They may have their own opinions, but in the end they will submit to whatever you decide."

Alex shrugged and turned away. Maybe it was true, but he wasn't the kind of leader who would tell them to risk their lives. They had to decide that for themselves.

Chapter 15

Alex waited silently beside his friends. Tyler and Jae were having a lively debate over the merits of different protein bars. Jani chimed in occasionally. Alex smiled as he watched them. Making friends had always been hard for him, especially when he was younger. If it hadn't been for his sister, he would have been a very lonely child. People usually found him too intense, or socially awkward, but Tyler, Jani, and Jae didn't seem to mind. Well, sometimes he wasn't so sure about Jae. Jae was a latecomer to the group, and Alex had a hard time understanding him. He had different values and a different way of seeing the world. Today, even more than usual, Alex wasn't sure what Jae was trying to do. It had almost sounded like he was *trying* to convince Morani that she needed their help. If that was Jae's plan, it had worked, unless that was what Morani already had in mind. Jae kept talking about getting famous, but would he really try to force his friends into helping the Agency, just for that? Surely he knew just how dangerous and stupid that would be.

Wouldn't he?

Alex turned his gaze to Zoe. She was sitting hunched against the wall, ignoring the conversation going on around her. Alex didn't like the thought of helping the Agency, but he also didn't like the thought of Zoe being stuck in this crowded corridor for goodness knows how long. If they couldn't leave, it would almost be better for Zoe to go back into the vault, to be able to explore and solve puzzles, especially if the Agency would let them work alone as a team. That was unlikely, but even having to function with a couple of tagalongs would be better for her than sitting here with nothing to do, overstimulated and overwhelmed.

Alex shifted position to draw attention to himself.

"Alex!" Jani slid over so there was room for him in the circle.

Alex sat down. As the silence extended, he realized that they were all watching him intently.

"Are we going to help them?" Tyler asked at last.

Alex sighed. "We need to talk about that. Morani intends to keep us here until they finish their business in the area. Something about secrecy and following orders. She says we could be of use to them, but you know as well as I do how dangerous it is in there. We managed to get out alive—all of us—and I don't want to jeopardize that by going back in."

Tyler frowned thoughtfully. "I don't know, Alex. We know what to expect in there now, so it shouldn't be as dangerous."

"But that's just it, we know what we're up against, and it isn't good. We could go back to the way of the clever, but that would mostly just mean sitting around there instead of sitting around here, and I doubt that Zoe is keen to work with the Agency's translation team. I am definitely never going through the way of the strong again, no matter what anyone says. That was hell. And I don't relish the thought of being blown up for a third time in the way of the holy."

"But there is one way that we haven't tried yet." Jani spoke quietly. "We could go that way."

"Jani, I don't—"

"Hear me out, Alex. We don't know who the fourth way is for. All Zoe figured out was that it is for those who are not something. Well, I can think of a lot of things we are not. We're not members of the Agency, we're not willing to threaten or harm people to get what we want, and we're not even after whatever it is that the Agency is trying to find. We're not like them, so maybe we can find a way in."

"That's painting things a little strong," Tyler protested. "Didn't their boss say that the guy who threatened us wasn't following orders?"

"She did," Alex agreed, "but that doesn't mean it's true."

"Can't we give her the benefit of the doubt? I really want to see what's at the center of this place."

"Tyler, you're crazy. You of all people should realize how bad of an idea it is to walk on that ankle of yours."

"It's not that bad."

"It *is* that bad!"

"But Alex, I was talking with Doctor Nakano, and she was telling me about this air cast they have that would work really well for me. And she might even let me keep it after! Wouldn't that be great?"

"Not as great as not needing it in the first place."

"Oh come on, Alex. This is what we wanted, to explore this place and find out what it is. We'll never get another opportunity like this. I know we were ready to call it off, but now we've been given another chance to keep going, and the Agency will even help us out with food and water."

"They're not 'helping us out', they've taken us hostage!"

"Alex, can't we just take them on their word and enjoy the adventure?"

"Tyler, we can't trust them."

"Whether we trust them or not," Jani spoke up, "Morani says we have a chance of making it in, even more than her agents do, and I agree. They need our help. I think we should do it."

"Jani, seriously?"

"It's like we're meant to do this, Alex. It would feel wrong to stop now."

"Zoe," Alex turned to his sister, "back me up on this. You know it's a bad idea to go back in there."

"It is a bad idea," Zoe spoke in a strained voice, "but staying here is hell. If we go, at least we'll be doing something, something that we're good at, instead of just sitting here."

Alex's heart sank. Of course Zoe felt that way, but if she wasn't going to stand with him on it, then ...

Jae leaned forward. "Alex—"

Alex rolled his eyes. "This is the find of the century, I know."

Jae glared at him. "Maybe. But have you considered that as long as we are helping them, we have the power in this situation. As soon as we are just sitting here, being a burden, they get to call all the shots."

Alex eyed Jae suspiciously. Was that really his angle? Or was he just trying to play his suspicion of Morani to get what he wanted?

"Trust me on this, Alex. We need to go in there."

Alex stared at his friends, looking from face to face. They really did want to go back into the vault, every one of them. Even though it was dangerous, and stupid, and possibly deadly. But they were waiting ... waiting for what he was going to say. And if he said no, then they wouldn't go. It was that simple.

But it wasn't that simple. He wasn't that kind of leader that just told people what to do regardless of what they wanted. He said he wouldn't tell them to put themselves in danger, but what should he do when they *wanted* to put themselves in danger? He wouldn't stop them. But he wasn't going to let them go without him this time.

Alex sighed. "It looks like you get your way, Jae. I'll tell Morani that we will go with them, provided certain conditions are met."

Jae's eyes twinkled. "Are you sure you don't want *me* to do the talking?"

"No. There are certain things I want to make very clear to her."

Jae winced.

"Okay, okay." Alex sighed. "I'll do my best to be diplomatic."

Looking around, he spotted Morani talking with a couple of agents further down the corridor. Brushing past the guards, Alex marched right over to her.

Morani stopped mid-sentence and turned to him.

Alex crossed his arms. "My friends have decided they want to help you, but only if you meet our conditions." Alex held up a finger. "First, you must keep the agreement you made with Jae regarding food, water, and our belongings, and keep your word regarding medical care for Tyler. You must also recognize our authority as guides to say what is safe and what is not. If we deem a room or an obstacle to be too dangerous, we retain the right to say that we will not go that way, and no one can force us to do so. We may also, at any time, decide that the endeavour as a whole has become too dangerous, and we may return here, with no penalty or negative repercussions from you or any member of your agency. You will do everything within your power to reimburse us *fairly* for our time and expertise. And after we leave this place, we will be free of all obligations to you or the Historical Acquisitions Agency and we may go about our lives as we wish. Do you agree?"

A shuffling behind him made Alex glance over his shoulder. Zoe, Jani, Tyler, and Jae were all standing behind him. Jae gave a quick motion with his hands.

Alex turned back to Morani, "And I want the entire agreement in writing, and signed."

Morani's eyes twinkled. "Of course, Alex. A written contract is an excellent idea. We can go over the details and get it all written up over supper." She turned her attention to the papers that she was carrying.

Alex blinked. Was that it? He'd been expecting at least some sort of pushback.

Morani glanced back up at him, as if surprised that he was still standing there.

Alex stammered. "I don't—"

Jae pushed past him. "What Alex means to say is, if there is any way we can be of assistance for the next hour or two until supper, we would be glad to be of service. I'm sure you could always use an extra helping hand or two." He flashed a charming smile.

Morani matched him, smile for smile. "Thank you for your offer, that is very thoughtful. I believe, however, that you would do well to take this opportunity to rest. We want you to be in top form for tomorrow."

"Thank you for your consideration." Jae gave a half bow. "Then if it is no trouble we will retrieve our packs and other equipment and take care of any routine maintenance that may need to be done before tomorrow's expedition."

Morani nodded. "That would be time well spent. You will hear the bell when supper is ready." She turned her piercing gaze on Alex for a moment, then turned and walked away.

Alex glared at Jae. "What did you say that for?"

"Say what?"

"You *know* what I—ow!"

Tyler, his face beaming, pounded Alex enthusiastically on the back. "Thanks, man! I can't believe we get to do this!"

"Do what?"

"Explore this old vault, of course, like we're Indiana Jones or something. And working with a real secret agency and everything!"

"Tyler. We still haven't—"

"Come on, let's go get our gear!" Tyler set off at an eager hobble.

Alex shook his head. Maybe if he was lucky it would prove impossible to write the contract in a way that would satisfy everyone. Then they wouldn't be able to go after all, and it wouldn't be because he said no. Somehow he had a feeling that he wasn't going to get out of it that easily. He sighed. "Well, at least we have our gear back now."

Jae winked. "You're welcome."

Sprawled out along one side of the corridor, Alex and his friends sorted through their gear. The tents and sleeping bags they had left behind at the door were still wet from the snow, so Zoe and Jae did their best to spread them out to dry, propping them up with hiking poles and the shafts of their axes. Various agents continued to bustle up and down the corridor, but paid them little attention.

Alex managed to take Jani aside for a moment. "Are you sure you want to help these people, Jani? I know Tyler's gone crazy for it, but that doesn't mean that you need to agree with him."

Jani lowered her eyes. "I know. Tyler gets his obsessions, and then I have to play second fiddle. But I really did mean what I said earlier. It's been uncanny, how well we've been able to make our way through this place so far. It feels like this is something that we're supposed to do. And if we can't go home until it's done, we might as well do it sooner rather than later."

Alex sighed. "I guess that's one way of looking at it. But Jani, going back to what you said earlier, about how you always have to take a back seat to Tyler's obsessions ... are you okay with that? I mean, I live with him, and I know how challenging it can be. It's not that he isn't a great guy—he's the best friend I've ever had, besides Zoe—but you've been his girlfriend for ages now. No one should have to—" Alex checked himself and shrugged. "I just think you could do better than that."

"Maybe." Jani's face grew thoughtful. She stared across to where Tyler was trying to shape the tents and sleeping bags into a makeshift blanket fort, while somehow staying off his injured ankle. "There's been times when I've wondered that too. But when it comes down to it, I can't imagine life without him. He's so full of joy and fun. Everything is an adventure when he's around, even on the most ordinary day. Sometimes it is hard, but ... I love him, Alex. Even if he gets so excited sometimes that he forgets I exist." She gave a wry little smile.

Across the corridor, Tyler's blanket fort collapsed on top of him. Alex and Jani exchanged a glance.

"Should we rescue him?" Jani asked.

"Nah. Let him flail a bit longer."

Jani laughed, but soon went to free Tyler from the heap of bedding.

Alex watched them for a while, lost in thought. Did Tyler even realize how much Jani cared about him? He had a keeper, that was for sure. Now he needed to grow up and realize just how lucky he was.

A little while later, the dinner bell rang. To Alex's amusement, two long tables had been set up and surrounded with plastic chairs. He exchanged an incredulous glance with Zoe. Didn't the Agency have better things to carry up the mountain?

Further up the corridor, a third table held food, plastic water bottles, napkins, and a stack of paper plates. Something smelled good, but Alex hung back, not eager to join the noisy throng of agents that gathered around the tables. Zoe seemed to agree, and they waited together for the rush to die down. After a while, an agent who looked as if she could be Zoe's age approached them and ushered them to the food table, where their plates were filled with potatoes, bread, and a thick, unidentifiable stew. They found Tyler and Jani sitting at one of the tables.

Alex set his plate down. "Where's Jae?"

Jani glanced around. "I haven't seen him."

Alex shrugged and pulled out a chair. His eye caught Agent Batts watching him from across the corridor. He felt his face get hot.

"Excuse me."

Startled, Alex turned to see an agent standing behind him.

"You are requested to join Commander Morani for supper."

"Oh. Right." Alex looked down at his friends, then back to the agent. "Okay, I'll come."

He followed the agent down the corridor to a place where Morani sat at a small, private table. Jae sat in one of the two chairs across from her. They broke off their conversation as Alex approached, and Morani smiled.

"Thank you for coming, Alex. I thought this would be a more suitable place to discuss our contract." She gestured him toward the empty chair.

Alex complied. The chairs—including Morani's— were the same hard plastic as the ones the rest of the agents were using, and the plate in front of Morani held the same kind of food. Jae had his supper with him too. Alex realized he had left his plate on the table where Zoe and the others were. Well, he wasn't very hungry anyways.

"I see you haven't brought your supper. Parker will get it for you." Morani nodded to the agent who was standing nearby.

Alex shifted in his seat. "Thanks." He cast a side- ways glance at Jae. He should have guessed that Jae wouldn't let himself be left out of anything important.

Morani pushed her plate to the side. "I invited Jae to be part of our discussion. I thought he might bring a useful perspective."

Alex shrugged. "Alright. If Jae is ready we might as well start."

Jae saluted with a dinner roll.

Morani smiled and pushed a paper across the table to Alex. "I took the liberty of drafting up a contract based on our earlier conversation. I thought it could be a helpful starting point."

Alex glanced at Jae. It was true, that would be helpful, but he wished he'd thought of doing that himself.

He looked down at the document. "*Employer*?"

Morani raised an eyebrow. "If you are working for the Historical Acquisitions Agency and getting reimbursed for your time, I believe that would make us your employer. Would it not?"

"I'm not about to go from hating this Agency's guts to signing on as an employee just a few hours later."

"Alex—" Jae interposed quickly, "—it's more like a contractor situation, isn't it? So we aren't really employees. We're independent contractors that are being hired for a specific job."

"Right." Alex still didn't like it, but it was better than being an employee.

Morani handed Jae a red pen. "I agree. Go ahead and mark that in."

Alex read on. "Okay, it says here that remuneration is to be determined, but that's too vague. I want to know what value you place on the work that we are doing and exactly how much you will be attempting to pay us."

"What do you want to be paid?"

Alex did some quick calculations. "Two hundred dollars per guide per day." It wasn't industry standard, but technically they were still students.

Morani nodded at Jae. "Write that in. Of course I can't make any promises, but if your work impresses me, I might be able to increase the amount. Jae, we will accept your photography services at the same rate."

Alex caught an eager glint in Jae's eyes. He turned to Morani. "It is also industry standard to pay your guides a deposit beforehand."

"Alex..." Jae hissed under his breath, "you can hardly expect her to have—"

"You want a deposit?" Morani gave a slow smile.

"Yes, I think that would be fair."

"How much do you want?"

"Industry standard is twenty-five percent."

"That is a hefty sum to be carrying around a mountain." Morani's eyes twinkled. She knew what she was going to offer, Alex was sure of that, but she wanted to see what he would say. It was like a game of chess. If he played well, he could ensure every word on that contract was the way he wanted it. Morani had made her move. Time to see what he could do.

Late that night after everyone had gone to bed, Alex could still feel Morani's gaze burning in the back of his mind. It made him uncomfortable, like she knew what he was thinking. Morani wasn't being completely honest with them, he was sure, but what could he do about it? He had to admit that he was satisfied with the contract, but somehow he felt like Morani had gotten what she wanted too, and he didn't like that. His gut kept screaming that this was a bad idea, that they shouldn't be doing this at all. The problem was that all the alternatives he could come up with were even worse.

Alex shivered. The icy air creeping down the corridor from the glacier far above somehow managed to seep through his sleeping bag. Small lights had been left burning along the corridor to stave off the pitch darkness, an unavoidable reminder of the Agency that wouldn't let them go. Alex watched the light flicker on the ceiling and listened to Zoe's slow, even breathing close beside him.

It was a long time before he fell asleep.

Chapter 16

Early morning came far too early, although deep within the ancient stone it was impossible to tell noon from midnight. Alex dragged himself into the world of wakefulness with considerable difficulty. His head pounded. A vague memory of swirling lights and blinding flashes echoed in his mind. He hadn't slept well, and the thought of what he and his friends were about to do sat like a weight on his chest. But he was a guide—or training to be one. He would do whatever it would take to get his friends safely through the vault and out again.

With his own pack ready to go, Alex watched his friends make their preparations. The plan was for an early start. Agent Sadik had already dropped off water and rations—three days worth—and Doctor Nakano had come to help Tyler into the special brace. It wrapped tightly around his leg and ankle, supporting his weight and immobilizing the injury, while being remarkably lightweight and flexible at the same time. It wasn't a cure, but Alex couldn't help but be impressed. It was better than any brace he'd seen before.

With nothing else to do before departure, they waited for Morani and her agents to finish their preparations. Morani herself was going to be part of the expedition, along with three of her agents. Alex had grumbled about the large party size, but Jae had kicked him under the table and Alex let it stand. He couldn't help but feel a little smug that he and his friends were ready to go before anyone else was.

Tyler danced in a circle, testing out his new brace. "Hey Alex, check this out! My ankle isn't hurting at all!"

"Tyler, stop it," Jani laughed, chasing him down until he plopped to the ground beside Zoe, panting heavily.

"... Okay, maybe it still hurts a little." He winced.

Zoe punched him on the shoulder.

"Ouch! What was that for?"

"Now your ankle doesn't hurt."

Tyler bowed dramatically. "Thank you, Doctor Zoe. But I am sorry to report that my ankle still hurts."

Jani punched him on the other shoulder. "How's it now?"

"Hey! Alex, they're ganging up on me."

Alex laughed. "Sorry to say, I think you earned that, Tyler."

"Excuse me."

The agent that Morani had called Parker stood patiently beside Alex.

"Yes. Are we needed?"

"The expedition will be ready to leave soon. The Commander would like you to meet her by the great mural."

"Right. Okay gang! Sounds like we're off." Alex swung his pack onto his back and followed Parker down the corridor.

Morani waved a greeting as they approached. She had been speaking with a large, muscular woman whose aging face bore a stoic expression. Alex recognized her as the woman who had been holding the handgun when Agent Batts had captured them.

Morani gestured to her companion. "Alex, let me introduce Agent Ventura. She will be part of our expedition."

Alex gave her a skeptical look.

"Yes, she will be armed," Morani continued, correctly reading Alex's expression, "but that isn't for keeping you in line. She is a trained bodyguard, which may be very helpful in overcoming certain kinds of challenges. The next member of the team is Fredrik Lundqvist." She gestured to a tall, lanky young man who smiled nervously. "He is a student of archaeology who has been completing his internship with us. He will be keeping our records."

Alex nodded a greeting. Fredrik looked down and fidgeted with his notebook.

"And the final member of our team is Agent Batts, whom you have already met."

"Wait, you're bringing *him*?"

Morani looked sideways at Alex. "I know you don't have a good relationship with Agent Batts, but he is our head of research for this mission. His presence will be invaluable."

"I thought you were removing him because of his behaviour."

"I said I would investigate his conduct as soon as this mission is finished, but in the meantime his knowledge is critical to our success. He has been researching this lead for years."

"I'm not going to go with him."

Jae brushed past Alex and managed to elbow him in the back in the process.

Alex glared. "... At least I'm not very happy about it."

"I'm sorry for your discomfort, but rest assured that he is here to assist *me*. You won't need to have anything to do with him."

Alex caught a glimpse of Agent Batts across the corridor and gave him a cold stare. He hadn't thought to include any restrictions on who could be a part of the expedition when he'd signed the contract. It was too late now.

As it often does with a large travelling party, it took much longer to embark than planned, but finally they set off down the corridor of murals. Alex was instructed to lead the way, and he invited Zoe to walk beside him. They didn't talk much. Alex was more than aware of Morani's piercing gaze following close behind him.

It was ten thirty by Alex's clock when they arrived at the corner where the fourth door should be. The mural here showed the building of the great vault. Could this be that vault? And if so, was the mysterious gem still hidden somewhere inside? That seemed to be Morani's guess.

> *One for the clever.*
> *Two for the strong.*
> *Three for the holy.*
> *Four for the ...*

What kind of challenge would lead into the way for those who are "not"?

Alex looked around. Everyone was watching him.

Silently cursing Morani, Alex turned to his friends. "Any ideas?"

As they looked at each other awkwardly, Alex's heart sank. Was this what it was going to be like with Morani and her agents watching over their shoulders?

Well, time for delegation. Subtly. He wasn't about to invite Morani's knowing smile.

Alex examined the wall closely. "Tyler, would you say this is a single door or double?"

As Tyler started to trace the hairline crack, Alex turned to Zoe. "Any sign of text that could give us a clue on how to get in? And Jae, have you gotten a picture yet? I happen to know you give me heck when doors explode before you've had a chance to get a picture."

Alex's gaze briefly passed Morani's face. Her eyes had that infuriating twinkle. She knew what he was doing. Of course she did.

"It's a single door, as best as I can tell," Tyler reported. "No sign of latches or anything."

"And no text," Zoe added.

Alex frowned. "So we really have no clue about this door, other than it's something to do with 'not' ..."

"And that's *not* much help," Tyler concluded with a wink.

"Yeah. Something like that."

Alex was surprised that Morani hadn't stepped in and said anything yet. Was she just going to watch him squirm?

"I've got the picture," Jae announced. "You can push and poke it as much as you like now."

Alex sighed. Well, someone had to do it first. He gave the door a solid push. Nothing happened.

Tyler joined him in an instant, and together they pushed and prodded and tried whatever else came to mind.

Finally Alex stopped and leaned against a wall to catch his breath. He jerked a thumb at Morani. "Your turn."

"I wouldn't dream of it," Morani smiled, "you're doing so well."

Alex rolled his eyes. Well, physical force didn't seem to be working, and there was no text, so it couldn't be a riddle. What options did that leave?

"We don't know much about their religion," he said slowly, "except for what we saw in the way of the holy. Any ideas for what might open this door if it's a religious thing?"

"I dunno," Zoe frowned. "If it was something religious I think it would have blown us up by now for doing the wrong thing."

"True. Any other ideas then?"

"This is the door of the not," Jani said thoughtfully. "Maybe it's not a door at all."

"Not a door?" Tyler protested, "What do you mean?"

The door of the not. How do you get through a door that's not a door? Alex stared at it with narrowing eyes. *The door is not.*

Alex reached out his hand to touch it. His hand went right through the door.

There was an audible gasp from everyone behind him. Alex withdrew his hand and tried again. Once again his hand passed through the door as if there was nothing there.

He turned slowly. "It seems that we have found the way through the door, since apparently there is no door there at all."

Tyler's mouth was open. "But—but I touched the door! It was real!"

Alex shrugged. "Why don't you try it now?"

Tyler's hand smacked audibly against the door. "Ow!" He shook his stinging fingers. "Seems solid to me."

"What happens if you tell yourself that there is no door there?"

Tyler's face settled into a thoughtful frown and he reached his hand out again, more cautiously this time. His hand went right through the door. He burst into an incredulous grin. "No way!" Quickly, he pulled his hand out again. "What happens if you change your mind about the door while your hand is still in it?"

"No need to find out," Alex nodded decisively. "We're not going to be hanging out in the doorway." He turned to Morani. "Who would you like to enter first?"

Morani raised an eyebrow. "Perhaps we should share that honour?"

"I would prefer to be sweep and make sure nobody is left behind."

Morani nodded. "Very admirable of you. Tyler seems eager enough, and maybe Batts? Three at a time, each group with one of the lights."

"Um," Tyler frowned, "not to contradict you, Commander, but if there's any chance of the groups getting split up, I want to go with Jani."

"If you like. Jani with us, Batts and Lundqvist with our good photographer, and Ventura with the Wielands. Ventura is also good at making sure no one is left behind."

Alex felt his face get hot. He had *not* been considering a quiet getaway, unlike what Morani seemed to be implying. Thankfully, he didn't need to say anything, as Morani was already preparing to go through the door. She took Tyler's hand firmly, and Tyler reached his other hand out to Jani, who was carrying one of the lanterns.

Alex felt his stomach turn. What if Tyler and Jani went through that door that wasn't really there and never came back out again? He wanted to say something, but no words came.

Morani, Tyler, and Jani stepped through the door. They disappeared.

Alex felt more shaken than he wanted to admit, but he wasn't about to show that in front of Agent Batts.

Jae was fussing over his camera. "If only there was a way to catch that …"

Agent Batts strolled to his side. "Our turn, Mister Photographer."

Fredrik Lundqvist had been taking notes on his clipboard. He dropped his pencil two times as Agent Batts prepared to go through the door. Finally Batts managed to navigate Jae and the intern into an acceptable position and stepped through the door.

Alex felt his own anxiety lessen as they disappeared. He turned to Zoe. "Well, I guess it's our turn now."

Zoe was staring at the door.

Alex did a quick glance around to make sure nothing had been left behind. Agent Ventura stood beside him, as expressive and unmoving as a brick wall. Alex held out an awkward hand. "Shall we?"

Ventura nodded towards Zoe. "You should speak to your sister first."

"Zoe?" Alex noticed now that she was shaking. "What's wrong?"

"I can't do it, Alex."

"Can't do what?"

"I can't walk through that door."

"But everyone else has gone through alright. If there were any problems we would have heard about it by now." Not necessarily true, but it wasn't like they had much choice.

"No. I can't walk through a door. It isn't possible!"

"I know it's unusual, but Tyler has gone through, and Jani and Jae. It must be possible. Why don't you try just putting your hand through?"

Zoe reached out slowly. Her hand met the door and stopped. "See? I can't."

"Just pretend the door isn't there."

"I can't just pretend the door isn't there. I can clearly see that it is there!"

"What if it's like a hologram?"

Zoe rolled her eyes. "You can't touch a hologram!"

"Well, um, what were those things called ..." Alex tried to think quickly, "... you know, in quantum mechanics, how observation can change the way particles behave. We don't understand it, but we can still run experiments on it. Right? Let's try an experiment. Close your eyes and put your hand out."

Zoe shot him a skeptical glance, but did as he asked.

"Great. Now take two steps backwards."

"Backwards?"

"Yeah, backwards. Good. Now one step forward."

Zoe took a tentative step forward.

"Okay, you're still a long way from the door. Take another step. Keep your hand stretched out, you're not there yet. And another step."

As Zoe stepped forward her hand went right through the door.

"Good. Now turn around."

Zoe turned toward Alex.

"Perfect. You can open your eyes now."

Zoe blinked. "Did it work?"

Alex grinned. "Yup. Want to try it with your eyes open?"

"No."

"Well," Alex glanced over at Agent Ventura, "the others are waiting for us. Zoe, do you feel like you can step through the door if your eyes are closed? Or should I spin you around first?"

Zoe made a face. "Fine, I'll try. No spinning."

Alex gave her a reassuring smile, but her eyes were already closed. He took Zoe's hand and reached his other hand out to Agent Ventura who picked up the lantern. "Okay, two steps backwards. That puts us about six steps away from the door. One, two, three, four—"

They stepped through the door.

Chapter 17

It was dark. The lantern Agent Ventura held aloft was still shining, but did not penetrate as far into the darkness as it should have. Alex looked around. Two globes of light shone in the distance: the other lanterns, presumably, but they seemed very far away.

Alex glanced at Zoe. "You can open your eyes now."

"You didn't finish counting."

"Five six. You good now?"

Zoe made a face at him. "I won't be *good* until we get somewhere that makes sense. Where are we now?"

Alex shrugged. "The first room I guess, but it seems a lot bigger than it should be."

"I suppose at this point nothing should surprise me anymore."

"Shall we go find the others then?"

"Do we have to?"

Alex glanced at Agent Ventura. "Yeah, I'm pretty sure we have to."

Zoe sighed. "And let me guess, you're not going to let go of my hand."

"Sorry. Not till we figure out what is going on with this darkness. There's something wrong about it."

Zoe glanced around. "For one thing, it isn't reflecting off any of the walls."

It was true. Alex craned his neck in every direction but couldn't see any walls showing through the darkness. He frowned. "Agent Ventura, we'll be on our way to join the others shortly, but could we look around for a moment first? It's strange that we can't see the door we just came through."

"Not that it was actually a door," Zoe grumbled under her breath.

Agent Ventura turned and held the lantern aloft. "The door is not where it should be."

"Could we try taking, say, about six steps that way?" Alex pointed back the way they had come.

Agent Ventura frowned. "Are you suggesting we go back through the door?"

"Not really, I just want to see if the door is actually still there."

"Very well, but we will return through the door immediately."

"Yeah, of course."

"Wait, I don't—" Zoe started, but Alex was already walking forward, dragging the others with him.

"One, two, three, four, five, six."

The darkness around them was unchanged. There was no door.

"—Oh." Zoe frowned.

Alex sighed. "I was afraid of that. Well, let's go find the others."

As they walked toward the distant globes of light, Alex started to recognize the shadowy figures of his friends. There was Jae taking a picture. Jani and Tyler were talking with Morani. It almost looked like they were floating inside glowing spheres of light. Where was the ground?

Alex looked down, then wished he hadn't. There was nothing beneath his feet.

"Agent Ventura, could you lower the lantern down to the ground for a moment?"

Agent Ventura set the lantern on the ground, or rather where the ground should have been. It hung in the air with nothing beneath it.

Alex ran his hand along what should have been the ground. It felt solid enough. He shook his head. "No walls, no door, no floor. At least, no floor that we can see."

Zoe looked unimpressed. "Great. First a door that isn't a door. Now a room that isn't a room."

"Let's catch up with the others."

They didn't have to walk as far as Alex expected. The strange behaviour of the lights made it hard to judge distances properly.

"Find anything yet?" Alex asked as the globes of light converged.

"Hey Alex!" Tyler grinned. "Isn't this neat?"

"Maybe." Alex shrugged. "I think a nice obvious door would be even better, if you know what I mean."

"Where is your inquisitive mind, Alex?" Morani gave a bemused smile. "This isn't a race, you know."

Maybe not. Alex sighed. It was a job now, and the hundred dollar deposit in his pocket proved it. Each of them had received a hundred dollars from Morani as a deposit for the money that they would hopefully receive when this was done. Alex had held his ground on it, but having the money in his pocket felt worse than he thought it would. It called into question the fact that he was being forced to do this.

Tyler remained enthusiastic. "You'd have to be pretty smart to figure out how to make a room like this. At first I wondered if it was mirrors, but that doesn't fit quite right."

"Maybe it's just a mind game."

Tyler shrugged and grinned. "Maybe. I wonder if—hey, what's that?"

Alex and Tyler hurried over. It was a marble flagstone, set into what would have been the floor, if there was a floor. Morani was beside them in an instant.

The flagstone was decorated with engravings and held in the center a curious dial, with writing all around it.

Morani's eyes glittered in the lantern light. "We've found the key. This will show us what this room is really for."

"Or maybe how to get out of this room?" Alex added under his breath.

Morani stood up. "Zoe, I believe you have had some success with this language?"

Zoe gave Morani a look of deep suspicion, but slowly approached the flagstone. Kneeling beside it, she slid her notebook out of its pocket, opened to a blank page, then froze.

"Try to give her some space," Alex offered.

Morani took a step back and everyone else dispersed. Zoe meticulously copied down the inscription. Slowly, her expression of discomfort faded into a look of intense concentration.

Alex stood guard as the others milled about and waited. Out of the corner of his eye he watched Jae sneak closer for a photograph. Should he stop him? No. Zoe was in the zone now. Not even the apocalypse would distract her.

Morani waited nearby, unmoving as stone. She was probably too far away to read what Zoe was writing, but her eyes followed Zoe's hand intently. Alex breathed a sigh of relief as Zoe lifted her head and smiled. A smile like that meant she'd figured it out.

"May I read it?"

Alex looked at Morani in surprise. He hadn't heard her ask for something nicely before.

"Here. I made a copy for you." Zoe ripped a page out of her notebook and handed it to Morani.

Morani read it aloud. "Sky and fire. Death and darkness. Ice and water. Pain and stone. Your door here what finds you."

"It sounds awkward, but that is what it's saying, as close as I can make it."

Morani smiled. "Thank you, Zoe. This is very well done."

Alex watched Zoe swell with pride and almost forgave Morani for the predicament they were in. Almost.

"Batts," Morani turned to the agent standing at her elbow, "what would you say about this?"

Agent Batts straightened his shoulders. "Puzzles like this seem simple, but can actually be among the most difficult to decipher. It gives us four options, but very little information with which to choose."

"For my two cents worth, I'd vote not the death one," Jae butted in with a wink. "Or the pain one for that matter."

Agent Batts seemed taken aback. "That is hardly a properly informed decision."

Jae nodded sagely. "Through extensive research, I have come to the conclusion that neither death nor pain are advisable, and should be avoided whenever possible." He gave his most charming smile.

Morani laughed. "Any other revolutionary insights?" She looked around the group.

"What about these engravings?" Jani pointed to the decorative border that surrounded the flagstone. "I've seen images like them in some of the other rooms. Do you think they mean something?"

Everyone bent closer. Among the elaborate scrolling and abstract designs, each corner of the flagstone was adorned with the image of a fantastical looking monster.

"Look at that," Tyler gestured at a tentacled creature that had the face of a spider. "Now that's a freaky looking thing."

"Death and darkness," Zoe read the text beside the image. "I wonder if that's their name for it."

"If that's right, then this sea serpent with lots of fangs is 'ice and water', that makes sense, and this raging hulk kind of thing is ..."

"Pain and stone."

"Yeah. And *this* one is a dragon."

"Sky and fire," Zoe corrected.

"But it totally *is* a dragon, see? Scaly skin, flying, breathing fire, got to be a dragon."

"So which one do we pick?" Alex asked, unwilling to let the conversation get too off track.

"Dragons are the coolest," Tyler offered.

Agent Batts frowned. "This is not a popularity contest for mythological creatures."

Morani held up a hand for silence. "Go ahead, Tyler."

Grinning, Tyler grabbed the dial with both hands and spun it to face the image of the dragon. With a click, the flagstone disappeared. Once again there was nothing between their feet and the vast emptiness below.

Alex glanced around. No door, or walls. Just blackness. It shimmered around them.

"Um—" Tyler began, and stopped. Deep in the darkness beneath their feet, a red speck appeared.

As Alex knelt to look, the speck grew larger and brighter. Something was rapidly approaching, shooting upwards through the void beneath their feet. It was large, it glowed fiery red, it opened its eyes—

"It's a freaking dragon!" Tyler shouted.

Everyone threw themselves backwards as the dragon exploded past their feet in a burst of white-hot light.

Alex landed hard on his side, rolled, and got to one knee in time to see the creature unfurl its massive wings. Fiery light radiated off them, and every scale on its body glowed like a red-hot coal. Its thin, lithe body twisted in the air as it flapped its vast, leathery wings.

"Spread out!" Morani shouted. "Keep your heads down!"

The dragon turned, hearing her voice, and hovered for one moment, its wings beating the air. Red fire flickered in Morani's eyes. An instant later she flung herself to the side as the dragon dropped like an arrow, straight through the place where she had stood.

Alex watched as, far beneath him, the dragon pulled itself out of its dive, turned a somersault, blurred into a streak of red light, and divided.

"Look out!" he yelled as three dragons erupted from the depths.

Someone screamed.

A dragon wheeled above Alex's head, and he ran. Where to? There was nowhere to run, nothing to hide behind. Dragon light throbbed in the air, tearing the shadows apart.

Crack! Crack crack!

Alex threw himself to the ground as the echo of gunshots rang in his ears. Shadow descended again and he spun around to see the dragon wheel and turn away. Fiery light flickered across Agent Ventura, her handgun raised toward the sky.

Where was Zoe? Dark figures ducked and ran in the flicker of dragon fire. Another dragon wheeled, ready to dive, its eyes fixed on Jae. And his camera.

Alex ran. He dodged past Agent Ventura, barely missed someone cowering in the darkness, and barrelled into Jae at full speed.

White light exploded behind them. The air crackled with heat and the smell of singeing hair. Alex shielded his face with his arm until the furnace passed by. Distant gunshots punctuated the sudden silence.

"Ow," Jae moaned from somewhere underneath Alex.

Alex sat up gingerly and rubbed his head. "You have a death wish, don't you?"

Light flickered across Jae's face. He had a bloody nose.

Alex winced. "Sorry about that."

Jae shrugged. "At least the camera is okay."

Alex rolled his eyes.

Somewhere in the distance there was a flash of light and Tyler's best Tarzan yell. Alex struggled to his feet, his pack throwing him off balance. Flickering flames illuminated Tyler, brandishing an ice axe. A dragon circled and tipped into a dive straight towards him.

"Hey!" Alex yelled, "Hey lizard brains! Try and catch me!"

The dragon veered away from Tyler and, with a great sweep of its wings, plummeted towards Alex. Flames flickered along its sides.

Agent Ventura appeared beside Alex.

Crack crack crack!

The dragon swerved away, glowing fiercely.

"They are afraid of the guns!" Morani's voice rang out above the chaos. "Stay close to Batts and Ventura!"

A second dragon pinned its eyes on Morani and swooped toward her. Morani dodged to the side and something silver flashed in her hand. The dragon screamed and fell.

Dragonfire silhouetted Jae.

"Get out of there!" Alex yelled, "Stay close to Ventura!"

Another dragon wheeled. In the flickering light, Alex saw Fredrik. His face looked very white.

Alex started to run, but the dragon was faster. It dove toward its terrified victim, opened its mouth—

Fredrik fainted. His limp body was engulfed in dragonfire.

Alex reached Fredrik the same moment that Jani did. She stared at him with terrified eyes, a shadowy figure in the pulsing light of dragon wings.

Alex leaned carefully over Fredrick's motionless body. "I think he's still breathing!"

Jani had her pack off in an instant and pulled out her water and first aid kit.

Alex peered closely at Fredrik. It was hard to see properly in the undulating light, but he didn't want to draw extra attention by calling for one of the lanterns.

Carefully, he felt Fredrik's arm. He frowned. "His clothes are still cold."

"What?" Jani was beside him.

"His jacket. It should have been disintegrated. But it feels fine."

A brighter flash of light illuminated Fredrik's face. It was unharmed and peaceful.

Alex stared. "It didn't hurt him at all?" He felt Fredrik's skin. A little clammy, but notably lacking in burns.

Jani looked up. "They're not real."

"What?"

"The dragons aren't real. That's why the fire didn't hurt him."

"But I've felt it! That fire is hot!"

"You were expecting the fire to be hot. He was unconscious."

"So we all need to knock ourselves out?" Alex began, but Jani had already stood up.

"They're not real!" She yelled. "The dragons are not real!" Red light flickered across her face.

It is the way of the not, after all, a small voice spoke in Alex's mind. He surged to his feet. "It's a trick! It's not real!"

Tyler and Jae stared at them in surprise. Another dragon wheeled through the air, turned, and started to dive.

Agent Batts stood apart from the others, watching the oncoming dragon. He lifted his handgun. Just as the beast's mouth opened, he shot.

The dragon exploded. A wall of force knocked Alex over. Lights swam in his vision. He staggered to his feet and looked around. There was no sign of any dragons. Silence descended as everyone held their collective breath. The smell of gunpowder lingered in the air.

"Are they gone?" Tyler whispered.

"Perhaps." Morani straightened herself. "Or perhaps we now realize that they were never really here."

An indistinct humming drew Alex's attention. Beneath his feet, the floor turned stone grey. A few metres away a wall glimmered in the lantern light. In the wall was a door.

Morani nodded. "We passed the test. Tend to your wounds and have something to eat. We will rest before we move on."

Alex circled around to Zoe, who was watching her surroundings with a distrustful glare.

"You okay?" Alex asked.

"Yeah. You?"

"A little singed. And sore."

"You should probably stop throwing yourself at inanimate objects."

"I'll keep that in mind."

"The human body can only take so much, Alex."

She meant it. Alex gave her a reassuring smile. "Thanks, Zoe. I'll try to be more careful."

Zoe stared out into the darkness. "So, dragons, eh?"

Alex made a face. "Should have known they weren't real. Good job staying out of the way. That's what I wanted to do, but somehow I always end up in the middle of things."

"You just have to save everybody."

Alex shrugged sheepishly. "I guess so. I'd just never forgive myself if ..." He didn't need to finish the thought.

"So who is going to save you?"

Alex frowned. "What—" His brain caught up with what his eyes were seeing. Morani had moved a little apart from the group and was carefully trying to cut away her burnt sleeve. Alex's first aid training switched into gear and he hurried over.

"I know first aid, can I help you?"

Morani continued to wrestle with her sleeve. "If there are no other injuries to attend to, then you may."

"Okay, but don't try to cut that off by yourself. I'll be back soon."

Alex passed quickly through the group. Fredrik was mercifully burn free. Tyler had small first degree burns, which weren't bothering him. Alex sent him to check on Jae, who looked like he wasn't feeling great. Agent Ventura was surprisingly unscathed, and Jani was already patching up her own scrapes. Agent Batts was cleaning his gun. Alex decided to leave him alone.

When he returned to Morani, Zoe was helping her cut her sleeve off.

"Here, let me have a look at that." Alex carefully lifted Morani's arm. The sleeve was badly charred, and a large patch of skin underneath was burnt and blistering. Carefully, he lifted the sleeve as much as he could. It was stuck in the burn.

"We'll have to leave that in the wound," Alex showed Zoe. "Just cut the fabric as close to it as you can without pulling on it." Alex got out his first aid kit. He didn't have any burn cream, but he kept a couple cafeteria packets of honey that would work in a pinch. That and some long cloth bandages would be the best that he could do.

He turned back to Morani. "You're not going to like this, but with a burn that bad you should really get it looked at."

"That is why we have Doctor Nakano. It will be fine until she has a chance to look at it. Pass my bag over. There's burn cream in it."

Her expression remained constant, although Alex knew she must be in pain. He dressed the burn and wrapped it. "You should see Doctor Nakano as soon as possible."

"And if we go back to see our good doctor, what do you think we will find when we pass through this room again?"

Alex's heart sank. "We'd have to start all over again, wouldn't we? Except now we know that the dragons weren't real."

"Yes, it's a shame about that, isn't it?" Morani smiled thoughtfully. "Tell me Alex, when you left one of these rooms and entered it again, what happened?"

"It was different."

"Indeed it was. And the door that had been there was not there anymore." Morani stood, and the action demanded everyone's attention. "Ancient vaults like these only give you one chance. A door has been revealed. If we refuse it we will not receive the offer again. Batts, are you ready to proceed?"

Agent Batts slid his handgun into its holster. "Awaiting your word."

Morani gave a curt nod and strode towards the

door. Alex scrambled to reassemble his pack and follow.

By the time he caught up, Morani was poised motionless in front of the door, like a cat watching its prey. Swirling lights glimmered across the door.

Silently, Morani raised her forefinger.

Behind her right shoulder, Agent Batts spoke in a low voice. "Type three decorated door. Religious symbols. Quite possibly armed."

Morani didn't move her eyes from the door. Alex fought the urge to step closer or to step back. He'd seen swirling lights like that before.

Quick as lightning, Morani struck the side of the door, recoiled, made a circular motion with her arm, and tapped the door above, below, and then directly in the center.

Silently, the door swung open.

Agent Batts nodded. "The Stravinsky method. Good choice."

"Usually successful against type *fours*, I believe." A hint of a smile lingered on Morani's face.

Agent Batts glowered as Morani pulled a short copper pipe from her bag. She telescoped it, locked it into place, and expertly wedged the door. Her eyes gleamed as she stared into the darkness beyond.

"Everyone is ready to proceed, Commander," Agent Ventura reported.

"Good." Morani strode through the door.

Chapter 18

Alex followed right at Morani's heels. His brain caught up with him as soon as he stepped through the door. He didn't need to be up front. Why was he doing that? Stepping aside, he waited as everyone else filed through. Their steps echoed in the vast darkness around them. Agent Ventura came last and added her lantern to the small pool of light where everyone was waiting. They were waiting to be told what to do next, and Alex realized that they were looking from him to Morani.

Alex refused to say anything and stared pointedly at Morani. It didn't help. Morani continued to gaze into the darkness, as if sheer willpower would reveal its secrets to her.

Agent Batts advanced towards Alex. "Well, Mister Guide, aren't you going to find out what is in this room? You seemed eager enough a moment ago."

Alex took the lantern that was being thrust into his hands. Wasn't Morani going to say something? He didn't want to take orders from Agent Batts, but what could he say? That someone else should do the dangerous job of scouting?

With a resigned shrug, he stepped forward into the room. At least the floor was visible this time.

Moments later, blue fire blazed up on either side of him. Alex froze.

"Well done, Alex," Agent Batts spoke in his clear, even voice. "Now keep moving forward."

Alex glanced down. He was standing on a large flagstone, maybe two metres in diameter, and the blue flame was shooting up through the cracks on either side of it. He moved forward and stepped cautiously onto the flagstone in front of him. Blue flame shot up on either side of the new flagstone. He glanced back. The flame bordering the previous flagstone was starting to die down.

"Please do continue."

Alex shot a glare at Agent Batts and stepped forward. On the next flagstone, blue fire only appeared on one side. He moved on. The following flagstone once again had blue flame on both sides.

"And now back to the third flagstone," Agent Batts coached.

"I was already going to do that," Alex grumbled under his breath. He went through the opening in the line of blue fire, and another pathway appeared, once again lined with blue fire.

"A maze." Agent Batts' eyes flickered in the blue light of the flames. "You can come back now, Alex, thank you for your assistance." As Alex returned, Agent Batts continued, "Somewhere in this room is a door that will lead us closer to our objective. Our task is to find our way through the maze to that door. It will not be easy, for the ancients who made such places were very cunning and would suffer only the cleverest to pass. Lundqvist, you will follow me and take careful records of everything that I do. Even the smallest detail such as the way we walk and carry ourselves may affect our ability to pass. Come, Lundqvist."

Agent Batts took the lantern back from Alex and strode into the maze, followed by Fredrick.

"Well if it's a maze, the more people trying it out the better," Tyler grinned. "Come on, Zoe. Want to be team number two? I bet we can figure it out faster than old sour face."

Zoe gave him a smug grin. "Challenge accepted."

"Let's go!"

"Hey! Don't forget the photographer!" Jae called after them, brandishing his camera. Soon they were lost to view, except for the flaring blue lines of light.

Alex glanced at Morani. She was watching the proceedings with a pleased expression. "I eagerly await the outcome of this little competition. Perhaps I shall have a try." She stepped toward the flagstones, then stopped. "Ventura, be so good as to wait here by the door. If anyone runs into trouble they will know where to find you."

Alex watched her go. Other than Agent Ventura and himself, Jani was the only one left by the door. She turned to him. "I was thinking, Alex, that I'll stay here with Agent Ventura."

"Oh. Okay." It did make sense, Alex had to give her that. There was no point in everyone wandering blindly. But he knew he couldn't just wait by the door. He'd give the maze a try on his own.

It didn't take long for Alex to realize that this maze wasn't going to be as straightforward as the labyrinth he'd had to navigate before—was that three days ago? It felt like years. This maze kept changing, which made it nearly impossible to retrace your steps. Where was a magical ball of string when you needed one? He was sure he'd gone in a circle several times.

Finally, he ended up in one of the corners of the cavernous room. That seemed as good a place as any to take a rest. He leaned up against the wall and closed his eyes for a while. The first thing he was going to do when this was all over was take a week-long nap.

Slowly the blue fire that lined his most recent route faded and disappeared. The darkness was comforting after the unearthly light of the flames. By the distant door he could see Jani talking with Agent Ventura. There was a small patch of blue flame where he could just make out Morani's thin figure, and another patch of blue where Jae was absorbed in capturing a picture. Everyone else was in the center of the room, more or less. It appeared that Tyler and Zoe had met up with Agent Batts and Fredrik, and they were having a lively conversation. Probably discussing—or debating—their findings so far. He watched as they set out all together, followed a track of blue flame, and returned to the center. They set out again, retraced their steps several times, and ended up back at the center again. They set out again and again, but no matter what they did their track led them back to the center of the room.

Alex didn't have a good feeling about that. What was happening? Was this a trap?

An especially good trap for the clever ones, don't you think?

Startled, Alex looked around. There wasn't anyone nearby. No one was even looking in his direction. Had he just imagined it? But he hadn't imagined what was happening in the middle of the room. If it was a trap, he had to get Zoe out of there. He set out from his corner.

After a long journey of twists and turns and double backs, Alex ended up in another corner. No matter how much he had tried, he couldn't get to the center of the room.

Are you sure you want to go in there?

Alex shook himself. Why would he think like that? His sister was in there, and he had to get her out. Tyler was in there too, of course, but Alex didn't mind leaving him to save his own butt every now and then.

Once again, Alex set out for the center of the room, but again, the maze kept thwarting him. He ran faster as his frustration grew. Why wouldn't it let him through? There—something up ahead—

Another corner.

"You're playing with me!" Alex raged aloud, then checked himself. Who was he talking to? He wasn't about to go mad. Alex forced himself to stop and think. This was a puzzle he couldn't figure out, but he'd encountered puzzles in this vault that he couldn't figure out before. He looked across the room to where Jani still stood by the door. Maybe she would know.

Alex found his way back to the door remarkably quickly. He barrelled towards it just as Agent Ventura handed a small piece of paper to Jani. Alex looked at them in surprise.

"This is my daughter Sofía," Agent Ventura said with pride in her voice. "It is from her graduation this year."

Jani held out the picture to show Alex. It showed a young woman in the obligatory cap and gown.

"She wants to be a chemist," Agent Ventura continued. "And this is Matilde. She just turned fifteen." Another photograph was passed over. This one showed a girl hugging a cocker spaniel. "She wants to be a veterinarian."

Alex handed the photographs back to Agent Ventura, confusion clouding his mind. Agent Ventura was the pawn of a powerful organization with dubious intentions. It seemed strange that she had a family, and carried photos in her wallet. Of course, she was a person just like anyone else, but it gave him the distinct impression that she treated this like a normal job, as if she was going to swing by Timmies for a coffee after work before taking her kids to soccer practice. It was baffling. A job like this could consume you until there was nothing left of the person that you were, but Agent Ventura seemed fine. She even had a cocker spaniel. A small voice in the back of his mind wondered idly if the job offered a good pension plan—if you lived long enough to make it to retirement.

Alex pulled his thoughts back together. He needed to stay focused. "Jani, could I ask you something?" He pulled Jani aside. "When we were in the way of the holy, you figured out what to do when the rest of us couldn't. How did you do that?"

Jani looked puzzled. "I don't know ... it just made sense. In the murals we saw, the priests were always depicted as looking away from the artifact. Maybe it was a way of showing deference in their religion. And they cared a lot about completing circles. As I thought about it, it all just came together."

"So there weren't any strange voices in your head?"

Jani blinked. "No. There weren't any voices."

"Oh. Okay."

"Are you okay, Alex?"

"Yeah. Yeah, I'm fine." He couldn't look at her. "I'm just trying to figure this out," he offered by way of explanation.

He looked out across the maze to the puzzlers trapped in the center. He sighed. It was *not* a puzzle, for those who were *not* clever. Wasn't it?

Something laughed in his mind. *How clever of you.*

"Maybe I am clever, but how would I solve this if I *wasn't* clever?"

Now that would be telling, wouldn't it?

"Who are you?!"

"Alex?" Jani's forehead wrinkled in concern. "What's wrong?"

Alex shook himself. "It's fine. Really, Jani. I just need to think."

He strode off into the maze, not really paying attention to where he was going. He needed to be alone. He needed to think. This wasn't the first time strange things had happened that he couldn't explain, like the light that kept appearing and disappearing. The light—or something controlling the light—had seemed to understand him, maybe even enjoy messing with him. Now this voice in his head was clearly messing with him too. Could it be the same thing? He hadn't tried calling for the light ever since the Agency had found them. That was the last thing he wanted to try explaining to Morani.

Alex was hardly surprised when he ended up in a corner of the room again. Settling himself down on the floor, he did his best to think. Jani had found clues in the murals, but Alex couldn't think of anything he had seen that could help him. This vault was built to hold the artifact, that much seemed clear. And it was made to keep people away from the artifact, or at the very least only let the right kind of people in. Could there be some sort of guardian?

He shook his head. That didn't matter, as long as he could solve this puzzle, finish this job, and get his friends out of there. But how did the puzzle work?

No, there he was trying to be clever again. What was the opposite of being clever? Just doing something without thinking. Staring out across the room, Alex got his bearings. If the door they came in was *there*, the door toward the center of the vault should be roughly *there*. He closed his eyes and started to walk.

Several minutes later, the echo of his footsteps in front of him indicated the presence of a wall. He opened his eyes. In front of him was a large, ornately decorated door. He made it! Well, not quite. In front of the door was a wall of blue flame. A small hissing noise made him glance over his shoulder. The way behind him was completely barred by blue flame as well.

Okay, he couldn't go back, and he couldn't go forward. What *could* he do?

What are you going to burn?

Alex squinted around at the blue-lanced darkness. That damn voice again. He was inclined to ignore it, just out of spite, but something told him that wasn't the best idea.

What are you going to burn?

How about a campfire, a candle, and a few bridges for good measure. Something in his mind seemed to disapprove of his levity.

How badly do you want out of here?

"Pretty damn badly," Alex muttered to himself, but even if the vault offered a way out this minute, Morani would be an entirely different matter.

What had it meant, *burn*? He noticed now that in front of the door there was a small brazier among the blue flames. Was he supposed to put something in it?

Creeping closer, he saw that the blue flames were not just surrounding the brazier, they were flowing out of the brazier. What had the voice said? How badly did he want to get out? It probably had to be something valuable, whatever would be put in that brazier. He was tempted to try a toenail or something, but he didn't know if it would give him a second chance.

What could he give up? Going through his pack, Alex came up short. Everything was either of too little value to risk trying—water purification tablets, for example—or were things he really didn't want to give up. His rope, pitons, and climbing nuts had saved his life on several occasions now, and he didn't know what kind of challenges the next room might hold.

He shifted his pack and something clanged. Opening a small pocket, he found the two metal rings that Tyler had broken off the front door of the vault, so long ago. He really didn't want to lose them. If he ever made it out of this place it would be important to have something tangible to prove his tale. But if he was honest, the rings probably wouldn't affect his ability to make it out of the vault alive. That made them dispensable.

He reassembled his pack and returned one of the metal rings to the small pocket. Grudgingly, he approached the brazier and carefully set the other ring inside.

Really? The voice berated him.

"Hey, you know how much I didn't want to do that. Now open up."

The fire in the brazier flickered and went out. With a hiss, the flames around Alex disappeared, leaving him in darkness.

Alex spun around. The room was completely dark, except for the three small lantern-globes of light. The maze was gone.

"How did you do that?" Agent Batts demanded as he approached Alex. From across the room, everyone was hurrying to join him.

Alex shrugged. "I just figured out how to get to the door. After I got here the flames disappeared." Technically true, but Agent Batts glared at him.

"Are you *sure* there wasn't anything else? That maze was a trap, but it didn't seem to trap *you*."

"Closing my eyes helped."

Agent Batts snorted. "There is only one room left between us and the chamber where the artifact resides, and you want me to believe that there was a challenge so simple that it could be solved by closing one's eyes?"

"Maybe this way was made for those who are *not* so clever as you."

His words hung in the air.

"Well done, Alex. An astute observation." Morani stepped into the lantern light. She turned to Agent Batts and raised an eyebrow. "You were saying?"

Agent Batts lowered his eyes. "That it is high time we tried to open this door, Commander."

"Good. That is what I thought you were saying. You may proceed."

Alex moved out of the way. He wasn't interested in helping Agent Batts open the door, and he needed some space to think. Sitting by his pack, he rested his chin in his hands. Something was going on here, and he didn't like that he didn't understand it. The idea of a guardian of the vault didn't make much sense. The murals seemed clear enough that the artifact could take care of itself. In fact, it was depicted as having a sort of agency of its own. The people did what the artifact told them to do, then the artifact made them powerful. The artifact didn't need protection, it was the threat.

Did that mean that somehow the voice he heard was the artifact itself? That would be consistent with the story the murals told, but how was that possible? Besides, this vault was ancient. Nothing that existed back then would understand modern languages. Unless ... it was more powerful than that. Of course it was. It could make lights appear out of nothing and communicate directly into your mind. That was what waited at the center of the vault, and the Historical Acquisitions Agency wanted to find it.

What harm could an artifact like that do in the hands of an organization like this? What could it do in the hands of someone like Agent Batts?

Alex shivered. He had signed a piece of paper saying he'd help the Agency get to the center of the vault, it was true, and he would do that to the best of his ability.

He never said anything about letting them take the artifact.

The door opened. Alex wasn't sure who had figured it out or what they had done. He didn't bother asking, just grabbed his pack and followed the others through.

They halted just inside the doorway. The light from the lanterns reflected along the long corridor and illuminated the large, complex mechanisms at the far side.

Before anyone could move forward, Agent Batts announced that they were going to camp for the night.

Surprised, Alex checked the time. 8 o'clock. They had spent more than seven hours in the maze. It irked Alex that Agent Batts had made the call, but he had to acknowledge the logic in stopping for the night. Who knew how long the final challenge would take, and then they'd still have to get out of the vault. Better to rest now than be up all night.

Agent Batts got out a roll of reflective tape and methodically marked out the portion of the corridor they were not to move beyond.

Alex set his pack in the corner and had a look around. His friends were chatting and setting up their sleeping bags. Agent Ventura had set up a stove and was heating water. Agent Batts and Fredrik were sorting through papers and taking notes. Morani was examining the mechanisms at the far end of the corridor, from as close a vantage point as the taped-off area allowed.

Alex went over to have a look. It was an imposing sight. There were levers and pipes and a host of convoluted metal shapes all linked together. Someone would have fun figuring it out. Alex didn't have much heart for it. He looked at Morani. There was something about her that seemed to belong here, as if this world of darkness and mystery was more real to her than the world outside. She didn't acknowledge his presence.

Alex was about to turn away when Morani spoke. "Well, Alex, what do you think of this obstacle? A formidable challenge?"

Alex shrugged. "Maybe. It's probably easier than it looks."

Morani glanced at him, eyebrow raised.

"It would make sense," Alex continued. "Every challenge we've encountered today turned out to be a lot easier than we expected. Why would this be any different?"

"Even though this may be the door to the artifact itself?"

"If someone is smart enough, a simple solution can be nearly impossible."

The answer seemed to amuse Morani. She turned her gaze back to the contraption before them.

After a while Morani spoke, as if to herself. "I've learned that researchers are important, if a nuisance at times. I am beginning to see the use for guides as well. I will be sure to bring it to the Agency's attention when we assemble our new field division."

Alex gave a dry laugh. Guides? Important? Who would have thought.

He wanted to ask more about the Agency, what their business was, what they were trying to do, but Morani seemed to have forgotten his presence. Oh well. Hopefully this obstacle would be so simple it would stump everyone and then they could all go home. No. That's not how it would go. They would stand here forever banging their heads against a wall until they finally figured it out. They were determined, if nothing else.

Alex walked back toward the camping area, lost in thought. A sudden presence behind him demanded his attention.

"A moment, Mister Wieland."

Alex stopped.

Agent Batts moved closer and spoke into his ear. "Tomorrow is going to be a very important day, Mister Wieland, and you would do well not to overstep your position. I have been investigating this lead for years, and this is my moment. Don't ruin it."

Alex turned slowly and looked at Agent Batts. "I have only been following my orders, given by your commander, to guide this party to the best of my ability. There is no reason to think that I would do otherwise."

"Really. How admirable." Sarcasm dripped from his voice. "You want me to believe you just do as you're told, but it isn't obedience that draws Morani's attention. It's not every day she offers someone a job."

Alex glared at Batts. "We're only here because we were forced to be."

"And what do you think she was saying to you just now? Don't play stupid, Alex Wieland."

"She was just ..." Alex frowned. She was telling him about a new position for guides at the Agency. A job offer? Dammit, Morani. He turned on Batts. "Look, I have no interest in a job that might involve having to talk to you. Congratulations on single-handedly meeting your objective of keeping me out of the Historical Acquisitions Agency." There were many reasons he wouldn't work for the Agency, but Agent Batts was a lot of them.

Alex stormed back to his corner where he sat on his sleeping bag and glowered. He hated that he was trapped here, that he couldn't get away. He belonged up on the mountain in the free air. Even a natural cave would be better than this, where he could find a little nook and hole himself up for a while. But since he was trapped here, he was going to do everything in his power to keep the artifact out of the Agency's hands.

"Alex? Supper is ready."

Alex glanced up at Jani. "I'm not hungry."

Jani sat down beside him. "You haven't eaten since breakfast. Are you sure you're okay?"

"I'm as okay as I can be, given the circumstances. How's that?"

Jani made a face. "And if you don't eat, that will help you how?"

"I never said it would help, just that I'm not hungry."

Jani rolled her eyes. "And what would you be saying to me if I was on a mountain trip and I stopped eating?"

Alex sighed. "I know. I'll eat later."

"You're just like Morani. When she's on a mission she can't think about anything else. She doesn't eat, she doesn't sleep. Agent Ventura was telling me."

"I'm not like Morani."

Jani scrambled to her feet. "Then prove it."

Alex watched her go, then reluctantly followed. Jani, Tyler, Zoe, and Jae sat around the camp stove, sharing from whatever it was that Agent Ventura had prepared. Alex tried to eat, but the food seemed unbearably tasteless, and the conversation going on around him seemed equally so. They were all unbearably chatty. Even Zoe was more talkative than usual as they discussed the experiences of the day.

Alex made a pretense of writing in his logbook to avoid being included in it. It didn't hurt to record everything that had happened, anyway. You never knew when that might be useful.

When Alex looked up again, his friends had dispersed. Zoe had gone to bed. Jae was pestering Agent Batts. Jani and Tyler were sitting off to the side, having their own private conversation. Alex stood up slowly. He was very sore, and something twinged in his back. Maybe he should go to bed.

Silently, he slipped across the corridor to where his sleeping bag lay beside Zoe's. Making sure his candles, matches, and clock were close to hand, he crawled in.

Murmured conversations drifted through the air. Agent Batts' voice was raised for a moment, but Alex couldn't tell what he was saying. Instead of sleeping, his mind churned over the worries of the day. At this rate he'd never fall asleep.

"You awake, Zoe?"

"Somewhat."

Alex rolled over so his head was close to Zoe's. "Do you think ... have you wondered about what we'll find at the center of the vault?"

"The artifact this place was built for, probably. That seems to be what everyone is expecting."

"Have you thought about what the Agency will do with the artifact, once they take it?"

Zoe was silent for a moment. "Sell it, maybe. They don't seem to be the type that would donate it to a museum."

Alex frowned. "I wonder if I'm going crazy. I keep on ... I keep thinking that something really bad will happen. We don't know what this artifact is, or what it can do, but ..."

"The murals could be literal rather than figurative? I guess it's possible. Anything is possible in this stupid place." Zoe thought for a moment. "And you're not crazy. No more than usual, anyway."

Alex stared at the distant ceiling. He had his doubts. "It's just all so—"

"Yeah. It is. Just finish the job and get out of here. Right?"

"Yeah." But it wasn't going to be that simple. Alex knew that.

Far down the corridor, he could just see Morani in the shadowy light. She stood, unmoving, staring at the great obstacle before her.

The image burned itself in Alex's mind as he fell asleep.

Chapter 19

"Hey Tyler, how's that ankle of yours doing?"

Tyler looked up from packing his sleeping bag as Alex sat down beside him. It was early morning, and everyone was getting ready for the day. Tyler ran his hand absently along the brace. "It's not too bad."

"You were on it a lot yesterday. You think you'll manage today alright?"

"Yeah, should be okay. I am feeling it, but it's manageable. Nowhere near as bad as it was before."

Alex nodded. "I'm glad it's holding up. You doing okay otherwise?"

"Yeah." Tyler frowned and started shoving his sleeping bag into its stuff sack. He paused. "You know how I wanted to propose to Jani?"

"Yeah." Alex gave him a sympathetic smile. "The mountain kind of sabotaged that, didn't it?"

Tyler set his sleeping bag down and looked up at Alex. "I have the ring with me."

"Really?" Alex looked at him in surprise. "Tyler, I … I had no idea. I thought you—"

"You thought I forgot about it after we found the door."

Alex shrugged. "To be honest, yeah."

Tyler sighed. "I guess that's the kind of thing I would do, isn't it? But I didn't forget. I thought maybe I'd find just the perfect moment on this trip, but things didn't really go how I thought they would."

"That's for sure. None of us expected this." Alex glanced across the room at Morani who was having a private conversation with Agent Ventura.

Tyler looked down. His eyes were unnaturally thoughtful. "When we were trapped by the rockfall and I didn't know if we were going to make it out … I almost proposed to her then, in case there wasn't going to be a later. But I just couldn't."

Alex searched for words to say. He couldn't imagine what that would have been like, being trapped, waiting to see if any help would come.

A commotion further down the corridor drew his attention. Agent Batts was removing the reflective tape barrier that had marked out their camping area.

Alex put a hand on Tyler's shoulder and gave him an encouraging smile. "You'll find the right time." He hurried off to join the others who were gathering together.

Agent Batts watched him approach. "So, Mister Wieland, I suppose you are too clever to be of much help with our challenge for today? You'll leave us lowly-minded professionals to struggle our way through?"

"If you like." Alex wasn't going to take the bait. More than happy to stay out of the way, he hung back as Agent Batts and Morani strode towards the imposing mechanisms that filled the far end of the corridor.

Besides, he hadn't checked in with everyone yet. He wandered over to where Fredrik stood, clutching his notebook.

"How are you holding up?" Alex asked.

Fredrik looked around in confusion. "Who, me?"

"Yes. It's good for a guide to know how everyone in the party is doing." *Within reason*, he added to himself. No one was going to induce him to check on Agent Batts, but he had checked to see how Morani's arm was healing up.

"Oh." Fredrik seemed very uncomfortable.

Alex tried a reassuring smile. "Any pain or injuries I should know about?"

"Uh ... no?"

"There isn't a wrong answer. I just want to see if you're doing okay."

"You're new to the Agency aren't you?"

Alex looked at him sharply. "Why do you ask?"

"No one here has ever asked me how I'm doing before, till Jani yesterday and you today. And I'm almost done my five year internship now."

"You probably didn't know what you were in for when you signed up for this internship, did you?"

Fredrik stammered. "H-how did you know?"

"Just a lucky guess. What do you plan to do when you're done?"

Fredrik fiddled with his pencil. "I don't—don't know if I—I don't ..."

He didn't know if the Agency was going to let him go. Alex shook his head, thankful that he and Jae had so much control over the contract they had signed. He eyed Morani and Agent Batts across the room. "We're not a part of the Agency. We're only here because we were forced to be."

Fredrik nodded.

"So is there anything I can do to help you?"

Fredrik opened his mouth—

"Lundqvist!"

Fredrik cringed. "Coming, Mister Batts!" Hesitating, he pushed a slip of paper into Alex's hand. "For later," he whispered, then scurried off down the corridor.

"Take that lever there," Agent Batts ordered him. Tyler already had his hands on a lever on the opposite side, and Jae was holding another. Agent Batts himself took two levers.

Morani stood back a couple of steps, taking in the whole scene before her.

Alex slipped the paper from Fredrik into his pack and moved closer to the action.

"Lundqvist, push your lever," Agent Batts ordered. "Slowly!"

Alex tensed.

As the lever moved, the metal panels twisted and shifted, creating strange shapes.

Agent Batts pushed one of his levers. The panels tore apart, then congealed into new, even stranger shapes.

Morani beckoned Zoe to her side. She pointed to the symbols etched on the panels, speaking in a low voice.

Zoe shook her head.

Satisfied, Morani nodded for Batts to continue.

Alex sat down to watch. He tried to figure out which levers did what, but whatever algorithm controlled it was too complex and he soon lost track.

Jani hovered for a while, then also sat down to watch. Things were pretty crowded around the levers, which were tucked in close to the moving shapes, and even Agent Ventura stood back to watch the proceedings.

After a while, Morani dismissed Zoe, who came over to sit by Alex.

Alex nodded a greeting. "Any luck so far?"

"Not really. I've confirmed there's no text and that's about it."

Alex watched the shifting shapes for a while. "I don't know why they're trying so hard to figure it out. The entire point of the last room was that if you were trying to be too clever you'd be caught. Trying to puzzle their way through it isn't going to do anything."

Zoe thought for a moment. "But you're clever. Why didn't you get caught?"

"I'm not sure," Alex spoke slowly, "but I think that whatever it is ... behind that door ... I think it likes me."

Zoe looked at him with a deadpan expression. "Great. Now my brother has an alien girlfriend."

"What? No!" Alex sputtered.

Jani scootched closer. "What's going on?"

Alex glared at Zoe. "Just working out what clues we have so far."

"Can I help?"

"Sure."

Zoe looked thoughtful. "What I don't understand is if the last room was rigged against clever people, what about the first room? You had to *be* clever to figure out the dragons weren't real."

"Yeah, I guess so," Alex admitted.

"You think each room was rigged?" Jani leaned forward.

"Pretty sure."

"Well maybe the first room was rigged against something else, like strength."

Alex nodded. "Maybe."

"And if it was, this room might be rigged against the holy," Zoe finished the thought. "But what does that mean?"

They all stared up at the contraption.

"Those panels have symbols on them," Jani observed, "I didn't notice that before."

"Yeah, they appear and disappear depending on which way the panels are facing," Zoe confirmed.

"But they are all holy symbols. And there's a lot of them showing right now." Jani frowned. "In their religion you were supposed to look away from holy things."

Alex shrugged. "But this *is* the way for those who are not holy. Maybe that's what we are supposed to do."

"But then shouldn't we be trying to cover the holy symbols rather than showing them all?" Jani seemed agitated.

"Are you sure about that?"

Jani nodded.

"What do you think will happen?"

"I don't know, but Tyler is right there!"

To Alex's surprise, Zoe stood up and stormed over to Agent Batts.

"You're doing it wrong. You need to hide the holy symbols."

Batts frowned. "What are you talking about?"

"The first room was a trap for the strong: anyone who thought they could beat the monsters in a fight would never realize they weren't real. The second room was a trap for anyone clever enough to try to solve the maze. That means that this room is a trap for the holy, and you are currently covering this thing with holy symbols."

Agent Batts waved her away. "An interesting theory. We can try that one next."

"You should try it first."

"We are trying *my* way first."

Zoe pointed at Tyler and Jae. "My friends are right there, and they are the ones who are getting hurt if this goes wrong."

Agent Batts glared. "I am the head of research for this mission. Get out of my way!"

Jae was beside Zoe in an instant. "Hey Zoe, let's give him some space, okay? You're right, of course, but sometimes it takes people a little while to catch on." Carefully he steered Zoe over to Alex.

Jae leaned in close. "Hang in there. We'll be okay, just stay out of Agent Batts's way." He nipped back to his former position as Batts pulled another lever.

Jani stared as the shapes turned and merged. "It's making a picture!"

Alex stepped back and squinted at it. Yes, there were figures and shapes that resembled some kind of scene. "What's it a picture of?"

Jani's eyes widened. "I recognize it from the murals! It's a scene of a high priest being executed!"

Agent Batts pulled another lever. The images swirled and parted. Blindingly bright light shone through the gap.

Alex shielded his eyes.

"The way is open!" Agent Batts turned to Morani. "Commander, we await your leadership."

Morani stepped forward into the gap. Light streamed past her, reflecting and refracting on the images that still swirled around her.

"Careful!" Alex called out.

Morani glanced back for just a moment. Alex could see it—the wild look in her eyes. There was a way open in front of her. She wasn't going to stop now.

As Morani took her next step, the swirling images solidified into a picture again—the same picture—but Morani stood in the place where the high priest had been.

"Look out!" Jani yelled.

Morani dropped to the ground, just as a blade whizzed through the air, right where her head had been.

Everyone jumped back. Agent Batts clattered into some of the machinery and bumped a lever with his elbow.

The metal shapes began closing in.

"Morani! Get out of there!" Alex yelled, running forward.

Agent Ventura was faster.

Morani struggled to her feet, braced herself, then dodged as a metal panel smashed into the ground beside her.

"Shut it off!" Jani screamed and tore at Agent Batts who stood by, watching the scene.

Ventura dodged through the collapsing image as a twisted metal shape slammed into the back of Morani's head and she crumpled to the ground. A heavy beam fell. Ventura grabbed Morani and pulled her out of the way.

The mechanisms ground to a screeching halt.

A quick glance showed Jani hanging off the lever behind Agent Batts. Alex ran into the trap. "Careful! She might have a spinal injury!"

Agent Ventura carefully set Morani down as Jani rushed to join them. Alex was glad to note that Tyler guarded the offending lever.

Alex checked Morani's vitals. She was still breathing, but unconscious.

"We need to get her out of here," Agent Ventura said in a low voice. "She is not safe."

Footsteps approached.

"What an unfortunate injury." Agent Batts said in an even tone. "Agent Ventura, you will take the Commander to a safe place. The rest of us will press on."

"That blow could have injured her neck," Alex said to Ventura.

"There is a brace in my pack," Ventura replied. "Fredrick! Would you get it for me?"

Fredrick skittered off into the gloom and was back quickly with a neck brace that bore similarities to the brace on Tyler's ankle. Carefully, Alex wrapped it around Morani's neck.

When he was satisfied that he'd done the best he could, Ventura lifted Morani and carried her out of the trap.

"We will leave a lantern with you," Batts told her. "Lundqvist, make sure Agent Ventura has all that she needs, then follow us closely."

Agent Batts strode forward. Alex hurried to follow, weaving his way through the twisted metal shapes, and stepped beside Batts into a new room. This room was smaller than the others had been, and it was filled with a harsh white light. As his eyes adjusted, Alex saw a pedestal in the center of the room, ornately decorated. On top of the pedestal was a jewel. It was the largest gemstone Alex had ever seen, and the light radiated from it, casting harsh shadows over everything.

Jae, Jani, Tyler, and Zoe rushed into the room after him and stopped short.

"Whoa," Tyler breathed.

Agent Batts gestured for silence. "We have reached our objective. Spread out, but do not approach it." He eyed the jewel like a cat watching its prey.

Alex felt uneasy. "Agent Batts, I think there might be a trap."

"Oh there undoubtedly is a trap," Agent Batts smiled. "Don't worry. I have been trained for this."

Alex glanced at his friends as they spread around the perimeter of the room. Fredrik appeared at the door and froze.

Alex eyed Agent Batts cautiously. "Shouldn't you be waiting for your Commander?"

"Are you trying to stall me, Mister Wieland?"

"No, I'm trying to tell you that it is a bad idea to try taking the artifact. You could get us all killed."

"I am head of research and acting commander in case of Morani's absence. I know what I am doing."

"I am a guide, and it is the guide's job, first of all, to keep everybody safe."

"And it is *my* job to retrieve such artifacts. Stop getting in my way."

Alex's mind raced. Why didn't Jae say something? He was good with words. But Alex had never explained to him what was going on and how important this was. He hadn't told any of them, except Zoe. They were probably all wondering why he couldn't just let Agent Batts take it and go.

"I think," he spoke slowly, "that this artifact could cause a lot of harm in the wrong hands. It might be better to leave it alone and not remove it from its vault."

"That is none of your business." Agent Batts spoke firmly. "You are a guide. Nothing more."

"Without a guide, you would never have made it here, Batts." Alex was surprised by the force in his own voice.

"You were a fool then." Batts retorted. "I am here, and I am taking this artifact."

Alex stepped between Batts and the artifact. "I can't let you!"

"Can't?" Agent Batts gave a slow smile and pulled the handgun from his jacket. He pointed it at Alex. "Tell me more about this *can't*."

Alex froze. Behind Batts, he saw Fredrik's face turn white.

Click.

Everyone jumped and stared at Jae. He lowered his camera. "A dramatic moment, don't you think?"

Agent Batts stormed over to Jae. "What are you doing?"

"Just taking pictures," Jae grinned innocently. "That's what I'm supposed to do."

"Give me that camera," Agent Batts growled. "Now."

"But I'm the photographer!"

"You *were* the photographer. As the Commander's representative, I declare your responsibilities completed. Now turn over the pictures *as agreed*."

Jae's face fell. "I guess that means you want the rolls of film too."

"Jae!" Alex hissed, but it was too late.

"Yes, the film too," Agent Batts demanded. "Hand them over, now!"

Jae opened his pack, fished around, and produced four rolls of film, which Agent Batts snatched from him.

"The camera," Agent Batts prompted.

"Oh. Yeah." Jae slowly pulled his camera back out of his bag and handed it to Agent Batts.

"Very good." Agent Batts examined the camera for a moment, then smashed it against the ground.

Jae's mouth dropped open. Shocked silence filled the room.

Agent Batts examined his gun with an air of carelessness. "Any *other* objections?"

Alex looked from Jae's stricken face to the other terrified expressions around the room. Fredrik was gone.

Agent Batts straightened his shoulders. "Good. Now no interruptions."

Alex held his breath as Agent Batts stepped toward the pedestal. Deep beneath his feet, the ground trembled. Agent Batts moved slowly with his head cocked, as if listening intently. Twice he stepped to the side and approached the jewel from another angle. As he reached the pedestal and crouched to examine it, the deep rumbling grew stronger. Apparently satisfied, Agent Batts drew himself up to his full height and stretched out his hand above the jewel. The light flared, casting his shadow large across the room. For a long moment, Agent Batts waited, watching the jewel. His hand trembled.

With a quick movement, Agent Batts lowered his arm, grasped the jewel, and lifted it into the air. The deep rumbling grew stronger. The pedestal began to crack.

"Um, Batts, not to interrupt," Alex ventured, "but this is a bit concerning."

Batts examined the jewel. As it turned, beams of light shot around the room. The walls shuddered.

Something was wrong. Even beyond the shaking beneath his feet, Alex felt that something was going very wrong.

"Batts, you're being a fool."

Agent Batts seemed oblivious to his voice. The gemstone glittered.

"Batts—" Alex began again.

Agent Batts put the gem in his pocket and the room was plunged into darkness. Not complete darkness—Zoe carried their old lantern and Batts had left an Agency lantern by the door—but in the sudden absence of the jewel's light it was almost impossible to see.

Everyone edged toward the door, but Agent Batts was there first. As their eyes adjusted to the shadows, they saw that he was playing with his gun again.

"I thought I said no interruptions," he said softly, as if to himself. "Some people just don't know how to follow orders." In an instant, the gun was pointed at Alex again. "I know your type. You'll keep making trouble, even when this is all over. But I know how to deal with troublemakers."

Alex slowly stepped back as he glanced around the room. Batts had positioned himself in front of the door. There was no way to get out.

"Today is my day, Wieland, not yours." A thought struck Batts and he smiled to himself. "This isn't a day for any Wieland." He turned the gun toward Zoe.

Click.

Agent Ventura stepped into the light, her gun pointed at Agent Batts' head. "Drop your gun."

Surprise and anger flashed across Batts' face, settling into a glare of disapproval. "Agent Ventura, where is the Commander?"

"She is safe."

He drew himself up to his full height. "You abandoned your charge!"

Ventura's gun remained steady. "My job is to keep everyone safe, and that includes them." She nodded toward Alex and the others.

"I order you to lower your gun and return to the Commander!"

"My orders come from Morani, and you will not override them."

"You would kill your senior officer?"

"If that is what it takes to fulfill my duty."

"This will cost you your job!"

"Perhaps, but you will not harm these people. They are good people, and they are under my protection. Put your gun down. Now."

Batts' eyes darted around the room. Slowly he set his gun on the ground.

As Ventura collected it, the ground shook again. The metal that lined the doorway creaked and rattled.

Agent Batts scraped together his dignity. "We should proceed before the chamber collapses. Ventura, take the lantern, and—"

A shock wave passed through the entire room. Alex staggered and grabbed the wall to steady himself. A sickening crash reverberated in the distance.

"Agent Ventura!" Fredrik's panicked voice echoed through the doorway.

Ventura picked up the lantern and ran. Agent Batts dashed after her.

"Come on!" Alex yelled to the others.

Jae hurried through the door. With an ear-splitting squeal, the metal panels lining the way began to turn and collapse.

"Look out!" Alex yelled, barring Jani who was about to run through.

Jae yelled in pain.

"Get out of there!" Alex yelled, trying to see through the churning blackness.

Jae was bent double, trying to tug at something.

Alex dodged in through the collapsing panels. Jae's arm was caught under a metal beam. Together they managed to wrench it up. Alex grabbed Jae by his other arm and they staggered back into the artifact chamber. Behind them, the metal shapes folded and collapsed in on themselves, barring the door.

Alex sat Jae down to the side, then ran back to Tyler who was trying to force a way open. "Leave it, Tyler! We don't know what else is going to fall!"

"Ventura!" Jani yelled, "Ventura, we're trapped!"

The rumbling grew louder.

"Ventura!"

Zoe shoved a metal beam that protruded into the room. "She can't hear you."

"But won't she see that we didn't follow?"

"This whole place is falling apart. She's going to get Morani out first."

Jae got unsteadily to his feet. "I don't think this happened by itself. Batts darted off to the side once he was through the trap. I saw him. I wouldn't be surprised if he broke the lever right off."

Alex shook his head. He should have seen that coming.

"How are we going to get out?" Jani demanded.

"Shouldn't there be other doors?" Zoe asked.

"Maybe!" Tyler grabbed Jani's hand. "Come on, let's look!"

It was hard to see properly. The walls kept shaking, and their small propane lantern didn't cast as much light as they were used to.

Alex stared around the room. Well, the Agency was gone now. "Light?" he called.

Chapter 20

A globe of light appeared, hovering over the broken pedestal. It was filled with every colour imaginable, swirling and churning within its depths. Everyone froze in their tracks and stared.

Alex felt a presence in his mind again, and he knew. "It's the artifact."

"Whoa," Tyler gaped, "and I thought the other gem was impressive!"

This orb did not radiate light. It *was* light.

"But I thought—" Jani began.

"It was the way of the *not*, after all," Alex said quietly.

A hush fell over the room.

"What does it want?" Tyler whispered.

"I think," Alex said slowly, "that it's waiting to see what we do."

Zoe nudged him. "You talk to it. It likes you."

Alex stepped cautiously toward the light. "Hi, um, nice place you have here." The ground trembled beneath his feet. He lowered his eyes. "Thanks for your help. We really needed it."

Alex glanced around the room. The light had dazzled his eyes and it was hard to see.

"We need your help again," he continued, "the Agency trapped us here, and we just want to go home."

He looked at the light again. He couldn't help it. There was something about the light that drew him in. Deep within its coloured depths, a shape was forming. If he watched just a minute more, he would see what it was.

Voices called in the distance, but the light filled his mind, swirling and churning.

"Alex!"

Zoe's voice jolted through his body and tore his mind away.

Alex blinked and forced himself to turn his back to the shimmering orb. Dark blotches swirled in his vision. He could hardly see his friends in the shadowy darkness.

They were moving—no, he was moving. The floor had cracked open between him and his friends. The chasm surrounded the pedestal, cutting him off from the rest of the room. Without stopping to think, he jumped. It was farther than it looked. His feet barely made the crumbling edge and he slipped—

Tyler grabbed his arm.

As soon as his feet were underneath him again, Alex turned to face the globe of light. It hovered over its island in the center of the room, gleaming. *If you want me,* it seemed to say, *all you have to do is come and get me.*

"No," he said out loud, "if we take you it will be the death of us. Agent Batts is out there, and other people like him. I don't want a price on my head."

The globe of light flickered innocently. A low hum filled the room.

"I know that you can understand me," Alex retorted, "you've made that clear enough before. If my friends and I can get out of here alive, that is all I need. I don't want an artifact in my pocket."

The orb grew larger. Tendrils of light reached out in every direction.

"Just go away," Alex said desperately. "You weren't from this world in the beginning, we saw that in the murals. Go back where you came from, or find some-where else to go. This world is messed up. I don't want to give it one more thing to fight over."

The tendrils of light had almost reached him. He wanted to know what they felt like; the urge welled up in spite of himself. He wanted to see if he could pocket the real artifact with as much ease as Agent Batts had pocketed the fake one. He wanted to see the look on Morani's face—

Alex closed his eyes. "Just go away!"

Silence rang in his ears.

When he opened his eyes again, everyone was star-ing at him. The light and the pedestal had disap-peared, leaving a dark hole in the center of the room.

"Aww ..." Tyler began.

Jae sighed. "It's true, you know. The Agency would find out we had it, somehow, and they'd never leave us alone."

"But now what—?" Jani asked.

The room shook violently. Around the hole in the center of the room, the floor began to crumble away.

"—Oh."

"Stay back!" Alex gestured everyone away from the edge.

"Dang it, Alex," Zoe muttered, "I thought your magical girlfriend was going to help us."

"His *what*?" Jani demanded.

"Look out!" Tyler yelled.

Everyone scrambled away as the floor where they stood crumbled and fell into the vast darkness below. In alarm, Alex saw that they were cut off from the door.

"Alex ..." Zoe looked like she was going to freeze.

"Come on!" Jae urged. "There's got to be another way out!"

The friends scattered across the side of the room that still had a floor.

"There's cracks," Zoe ran her hands along the wall, "but I don't know what to do!"

"Just try something!" Jae stumbled backwards as more of the floor collapsed.

Alex's mind was completely blank. There wasn't time to solve another puzzle.

"Stay away from the edge!" Tyler pulled Zoe back.

The floor where she had been standing collapsed. The walls shook. Jae hammered at them with his fist.

"There has to be a way out!" Zoe scanned the room desperately.

"Should we rope up?" Jani tugged at Tyler's arm. "If we tie the rope to something we could—"

"Jani ..." Tyler held her close. "Jani, I don't—"

Zoe's eyes lit up. "Our ventilation shaft! Look! Look!"

High above their heads, barely visible in the gloom, was a metal grate they recognized instantly.

"Alex! Up on my back!" Tyler yelled, bracing himself against the wall.

Alex unslung his rope and scrambled up Tyler's back. He could just reach the grate. Quickly he looped the rope through it. "Everyone tie in!" Pulling his ice axe off his pack he jammed it behind the top edge of the grate. No time to be careful—he pushed all his weight onto the axe and jumped.

Crack!

Alex hit the ground hard. Shaking his head, he looked up. A corner of the grate was wrenched away from the wall. Zoe was already climbing up Tyler, her axe at the ready.

"Jani, get ready! You're up next!" Alex grabbed the end of the rope and quickly tied his prusik knots. Another loud crack told him Zoe had the second corner free. She grabbed the edge of the grate and dropped. It bent open under the pressure.

Jani dropped her pack and scrambled up Tyler's back, slithering head first through the hole. Her head poked back out. "Send up the packs!"

Alex hoisted the packs up to Zoe who was already back on top of Tyler. She fed them through the hole to Jani, then scrambled in after them.

"Jae, you're next!" Alex gave him a boost up and almost stepped backwards into thin air. Scrambling, he regained his balance. "Tyler?"

"You first."

"You secured?"

"Yup."

Alex climbed up and dove through the hole. Hitting the ground, he grabbed the rope and pulled it taut. Tyler slowly emerged, carrying the lantern.

In its light, Alex looked around. It was the same narrow passageway as before.

"Now what?" Zoe hissed.

"Wait, was that there before?" Jani pointed to a gaping hole in the ceiling above them. The passageway shook violently and more of the ceiling crumbled.

"Hey, look!" Tyler gestured to what looked like a rough chute stretching up into the darkness. "I bet we can climb that!"

"You're up, Tyler!" Alex grinned. "Packs on, we're climbing!"

Tyler clambered up to the start of the chute. "Good handholds," he reported, "steep, but should be safe enough without the rope."

"Good." Alex was already coiling it. "Take the lantern. We'll follow your lead."

Tyler clipped the lantern to his pack and started to climb.

Alex nodded at Jani. "You're up next. Then Zoe."

He turned to Jae as the light flickered into the distance. "Sorry that you're at the back with me, but I know you're not the most confident climber, and I want to be able to give you a hand. How's that arm of yours doing?"

"I'll manage."

Alex nodded. "Don't let me forget to check on it later."

Zoe disappeared up the chute.

"Okay, let's go."

Jae climbed up the pile of rubble and into the shaft above. Alex followed close behind.

Very little light trickled down to them from above. Alex had to feel for his handholds, and the shaking that still reverberated through the stone made it hard to hold on.

Progress was slow. Jae slipped twice, but managed to catch himself. They struggled on.

"You doing alright there, Jae?" Alex asked as Jae stopped climbing.

"There's a steep bit here. I can't find anywhere to grab on."

"Are your feet secure?"

"Kind of?"

"Okay. Stand up as tall as you can. I'll make sure you don't slip." Alex braced Jae's feet as he reached.

"Okay, I found something." Jae's legs were shaking. "Now what?"

Alex thought for a moment. "You know what? It's pretty narrow here. Lean your back against the wall and walk up it with your feet."

Jae inched higher.

"There you go. Take your time."

Finally the tunnel transitioned into an easier grade. The rumbling beneath them seemed further away.

The lantern was almost completely out of their sight, but they soon caught up. Zoe had noticed they'd fallen behind and called for the others to wait.

Jae was still shaky, so Alex suggested a rest. It wasn't a long one. The stone around them was bitterly cold and soon they were forced to keep moving.

The tunnel wound on and on, higher and higher. Alex wanted to check the time, but that would have meant stopping to light a candle, or shouting the question up to Tyler. He didn't have enough energy for either option.

After another long steep section, the group stopped again.

"There's something up here!" Tyler called. "Just a sec!"

Alex leaned back against the rock wall. If this was a dead end ...

Jae sank to the ground and stared at him with tired eyes. "Thanks, Alex. I couldn't make it up without your help."

Alex gave him a tired smile. "No problem, Jae. I'm glad you're with us." It was true. The group wouldn't be the same without Jae. He sighed. "Sorry that I haven't always been the easiest to get along with."

Jae shrugged. "It's okay. I know I'm not the easiest to get along with either. I've never had many friends."

Alex looked at him in surprise. "But you're so—"

"Outgoing? Yeah. I'm good at getting attention, but that isn't the same as people actually caring about me."

"Well, we care about you."

"Yeah, I know. Thanks."

A flurry of excitement echoed past them.

"The tunnel's filled up with snow!" Tyler called. "Hold tight, I'm going to try knocking a hole through!"

Alex jumped to his feet. Blue light reflected on the walls around the lantern's orange glow. Thudding and stamping echoed down the tunnel. Chunks of snow and ice tumbled down toward them. Should he go help?

Sudden light filled the tunnel, followed by a rush of cold, clean air.

Alex ran. He scrambled and climbed, past rock, ice, snow, and into the open air. The sun shone down, glistening on the white snow beneath his feet. Blue sky stretched as far as he could see. The fresh, icy wind filled his lungs and tingled down his spine. They were free!

Jani laughed. Tyler jumped up and down. Jae flung his arms to the sky, spinning in circles. Zoe flopped to the ground, almost disappearing in a poof of snow.

Alex took in the sight around him. They were on a high dome of snow. Below them in every direction was a carpet of clouds. He gasped. "We're—we're on top of the mountain!"

Everyone stared in amazement.

"No way!" Tyler laughed.

"How is that possible?" Zoe demanded.

"We did climb up for a long time." Alex grinned. "How's that for getting lost in the right direction!"

Jae laughed. "We made it to the top of the mountain after all!"

Dropping their packs into the snow, they stared all around them. In the distance, other peaks pierced the sky, like islands in a sea of cloud. The sun cast their long shadows onto the glittering snow behind them. A lively breeze blew stray wisps of cloud into the brilliantly blue sky.

Jani gave a long sigh. "It's so beautiful!"

Tyler stepped beside her.

Alex and Zoe exchanged glances and slowly stepped away.

Tyler took a deep breath. "Jani, there's something that I've been wanting to tell you. I wanted to tell you before, the day we were supposed to summit this mountain, but, well, that didn't happen, and so many crazy things have happened since then, but ... I love you. And over these past few days, watching you grow in confidence and treat everyone with so much kindness, even when things were dangerous, it made me love you even more than I thought was possible. You're not my obsession. Obsessions come and go, but when I'm with you I feel like I'm home. I want to put you first, before everything else, and I am sorry for every time that I made you feel like you weren't important. Because you are important to me, Jani, you're more important than anything else, and I want to spend the rest of my life with you. Jani—" Tyler knelt in the sun-dazzled snow, "—will you marry me?"

Tears glistened on Jani's cheeks and she threw her arms around Tyler. "Yes! Yes, of course!" She laughed, and Alex cheered. Zoe clapped her hands.

Tyler and Jani held each other close, their voices drifting away on the mountain breeze. Sunlight glinted on the ring as Tyler slipped it onto Jani's finger.

Alex smiled. They both looked so happy, and they certainly deserved it.

Moments later, Jani rushed over to Zoe, bubbling with excitement. "Look, Zoe, look! Isn't it beautiful?" She held out her hand for Zoe to see the ring.

Zoe nodded.

Jani smiled, almost shyly. "Tyler and I both want you to know that we will make the wedding however small it needs to be so that you can be there, Zoe."

Zoe's eyes widened. "Really?"

"Of course! You're one of my best friends!"

Zoe's face lit up with surprise and delight.

Alex smiled. Striding over to Tyler's side, he gave him a big hug. "Congrats, Tyler."

"Thanks!" Tyler was beaming.

Alex looked up at the sky. "You couldn't have asked for a better setting. I just wish we could have gotten pictures for you."

"But I did!" Jae called from behind him.

Alex turned. Jae waved his camera in the air.

"What—" Alex gasped, "how—"

Jae grinned. "I had two cameras with me of course. Come on guys, let me get a group photo."

Everyone gathered together.

"Wait!" Jani called. "Jae, you have to be in it too!"

"Alright!" Jae bounded over to the group and held the camera aloft. "Smile!"

After the click, Alex turned to Jae. "If you had two cameras, does that mean—"

"I still have the picture of Agent Batts pointing a gun at your face? Yup. I have all the important pictures. The rolls of film I gave him were duds. I wondered if something like that would happen, so I took some extras." He looked thoughtful. "I hope he likes my roll of selfies."

Alex shook his head and laughed. "You did promise them the pictures, you know."

"Sure. I imagine they'll come by sometime to pick them up, but by then we'll have our own copies."

"Nice one, Jae." Zoe punched him on the arm.

Jae fell to the ground. "Ow!"

Zoe looked worried. "That was your hurt arm, wasn't it? Sorry."

"All good!" Jae gave her a thumbs up. "When my arm is better, I'll punch you back."

Zoe grinned. "Deal."

Beneath their feet the mountain rumbled. Alex exchanged a glance with Tyler, and one by one everyone stopped and listened. The rumbling grew louder.

"Oh come on!" Jae protested.

Alex grabbed his pack. "Sounds like it's time to go."

"But it's completely socked in down there." Tyler

frowned. "We don't have a map or anything."

"Last trip we had maps with, right?" Jae asked.

"Yeah, and we have maps this time too, but only for one side of the mountain. I'm not too keen on going that way."

"But I brought our trip plan from before." Jae pulled it out of his pack and offered it to Tyler.

"What? Why did you bring that?"

"I thought it might be useful."

"It sure is!" Tyler turned the pages until he found the map. "See? There's the route we had planned, all marked out. Now if only our GPS would work." He pulled it out of his pocket and tried it. Nothing. The mountain trembled under their feet.

"But a map is better than nothing, right?" Jani gave him an encouraging grin.

Tyler squeezed her hand. "Sure is! And just look around—the sun's there and we know it's ..." he checked the time, "two in the afternoon. And there's that ridge of mountains to the east. We'll get ourselves heading the right direction."

Zoe uncoiled the rope. "What are we waiting for?"

Jae raised a hand. "I'm just putting it out there that I should not go first."

Chapter 21

The friends roped up as quickly as they could in preparation for their descent. Alex took up his place in the rear and tied in. Tyler, map in hand, was in the lead.

"Ready?" he called over the rising wind.

"Ready!" Jani called.

"Ready!" Zoe called.

Jae raised a thumbs up. "Born ready!"

Alex stared at the dark, seething mass of clouds before them. The mountain shook beneath their feet.

"Alex?" Tyler called.

The shaking grew stronger.

"Alex?" Tyler's voice was strained. "We should go!"

The wind gusted stronger, whipping snow into their eyes. Something was happening. Alex felt it—a sudden absence. The ground shook violently. The clouds to the west billowed up into the sky, covering the mountaintop in shadow.

"We need to go! Now!" Tyler turned and took his first step. Beneath him, the snow gave way.

Alex threw himself back into the snow, the point of his ice axe buried deeply with the force of his fall. The ground shook. With a jerk the rope went taught, but the axe held firm. In the distance he could hear the rumble of the avalanche gaining speed down the side of the mountain.

"Is everyone okay?" he yelled.

The replies were muffled by the snow. Raising his head, Alex saw Jae and Zoe, also in self-arrest positions. Beyond them, the rope cut through the crown where the snow had fallen away.

"I've got this," Zoe called. "Alex, make an anchor."

"Sure thing!" Getting to his knees, Alex set up a snow anchor and clipped in.

Zoe called down to Tyler and Jani while Jae kept hugging the ground. "They're going to climb up," she reported.

"Good." Alex nodded. "Do they need a boost?"

"Jani says they're fine, as long as we're good and secure."

Alex watched Jani's head appear over the crown. She clambered up, both hands firmly on the rope. Tyler followed.

"Would it be bad taste to say I swept her off her feet?" Tyler asked with a wry grin.

Zoe rolled her eyes.

Alex gestured them further up. "Better get away from there. Don't want to get caught again." The rumbling hadn't stopped. Dark clouds billowed toward them.

"Do we have a plan B?" Jae asked as they stumbled back toward the summit.

Alex watched the sky grow dark. They couldn't go south, it was too unstable. They couldn't go west——that was where the door was. As he watched, another avalanche let go to the east. He turned to Tyler. "The north face."

"The north face?" Tyler protested, "are you nuts?"

"There's no other option, and we can't stay here." The wind gusted so strong they had to shout to be heard. The mountain shook violently beneath their feet.

"What's happening?" Jani crouched low to keep her balance.

"The mountain's falling apart!" Tyler yelled.

"What? Mountains don't just collapse!"

Alex stared into the billowing clouds. "They might if something inside them just disappeared."

Everyone stared.

"It's gone, isn't it?" Jae said quietly.

Alex nodded. "You saw how it was falling apart. I don't expect there's anything left."

"You mean the whole vault is just ... gone?" Jani's eyes widened. "But the Agency is still there!"

"I imagine that they are."

"But what if they don't get out in time?"

Alex put his hands on Jani's shoulders. "We can't save them. But we can do our best to save ourselves, and when we get down we'll tell Search and Rescue where they are."

Jani nodded. "Okay. Let's go."

Still roped up, they staggered north.

"I was looking at the map," Tyler yelled over the wind. "It looks like there is a bit of a cliff to the north, but if we rappel down we'll find a ridge we can follow."

"Sounds good," Alex called back.

"A bit of a cliff?" Zoe eyed Tyler suspiciously. "Just how big is—?"

A few paces in front of them the snow ended. Beyond, all they could see was blowing snow and cloud.

"I dunno," Tyler grinned. "Let's find out!"

"Or, you know, you could count the contour lines," Zoe retorted.

"Go for it." Tyler shoved the trip plan into Zoe's arms, then lay flat on his stomach and crawled toward the cliff.

Zoe scanned the map, then showed it to Alex. "A hundred metres?"

Alex nodded. "Should be able to do that in three or four rappels. How does it look, Tyler?"

"Looks good, as far as I can see."

Alex sighed. The visibility was rapidly dropping. "Okay, let's do this!"

"Whoa, whoa, wait a sec," Jae interjected, "just to confirm what I'm hearing, we are going to climb down a cliff on a mountain that is actively deconstructing, while the rope we are tied off to is attached to said crumbling mountain?"

Alex nodded. "That about sums it up."

"Damn." Jae thought for a moment. "Can I at least take pictures?"

Alex laughed. "Knock yourself out. Just don't drop the camera this time."

Working with Zoe, Alex set up three snow anchors: two with the weight equalized between them and the third for backup. Everyone clipped themselves into the anchor, then the rope was threaded through and the knotted ends tossed over the edge. Tyler sorted through his climbing rack and set up his belay device for the rappel.

"Got everything you need?" Jani asked him.

"Yup. Good to go!"

"Okay. Careful down there."

Tyler nodded and gave her a quick kiss, then stepped backwards and disappeared over the edge. Alex leaned over and watched the rope move in and out with Tyler's bounding steps. Finally it went still. He would be finding a place to set up their next anchor now.

After several minutes, the rope jiggled and Tyler's voice could just be heard over the howling wind.

"Okay," Alex turned to the others, "who's next?"

"I'll go," Jani volunteered. She set herself up for the rappel and hesitated only a moment before stepping backwards off the cliff.

Alex waited in silence until a yell from below told him that Jani was secured at the next anchor.

"Okay Jae, you're up. Least experienced climber in the middle."

"Hey," Jae protested, "I've rappelled at least three times now."

"You remember what to do?"

Jae nodded, but Alex double-checked before he let him go.

Then Zoe rappelled, and Alex was alone on top of the mountain. He stood up into the wind. Blinding snow stung his face. The sound of crumbling stone and ice filled his ears.

Another call on the wind. Alex set up his rappel. They would be leaving their anchors on top of the mountain, there was nothing he could do about that. Leaning back, he stepped over the edge.

Alex lowered himself quickly down the rockface and came to a stop beside his waiting friends. Tyler had found a small ledge, and there he had set up another three-point anchor, this time with climbing nuts jammed into cracks in the rock. They were all clipped into it and were standing or sitting on the narrow ledge. Alex clipped in too. He could feel the trembling, deep within the rock. Further along the cliff, a chunk of stone shook itself free and plunged into the depths.

After confirming that everyone was secure, Alex pulled the rope down from the anchor far above and fed it through the new anchor. He shifted out of the way. "Carry on, Tyler."

As Tyler rappelled down the next stretch, Alex had a look around. They were sheltered from much of the wind here, though beyond the lee of the cliff the wind still blew the snow in whirling gusts. He could just see what might have been snow, far below them, but in every other direction was only the dark, vertical rock face, blurring into grey obscurity.

After Tyler called up that the next anchor was ready, Jani rappelled down, then Jae, then Zoe. Usually Alex would have pulled out two of the climbing nuts, leaving only one for his rappel, but the shaking beneath his hands made him pause. Could he trust one climbing nut to hold? It wasn't worth it. He'd pay Tyler back for the nuts he left behind.

Lowering himself, he stopped beside the next anchor. Tyler hadn't been able to find a ledge this time. Jani and Jae were wedged into a large crack. Tyler and Zoe hung out from the cliff face on long leashes.

Alex clipped in. The ground below them was clearly visible now.

"Think we can do it in one more rappel?" he asked Tyler.

"We'll see," Tyler grinned. He pulled the rope down from the previous anchor and fed it through the new one. The rope made it down to the snow below with a couple of metres to spare.

"Perfect." Tyler nodded. "Down we go!"

It took longer to set up the rappels, without the security of a ledge beneath their feet, but at last Zoe called up that everyone was secured at the bottom, and Alex prepared for his descent. He glanced down. Why had they stayed clustered together, right at the foot of the climb? Beneath his feet, a chunk of rock shifted and fell.

"Rock!" Alex yelled.

Everyone scattered as the rock crashed to the ground between them, tumbled down the steep incline, and disappeared over the edge of another cliff.

Was the shaking beneath his feet growing stronger? Not waiting to find out, Alex lowered himself quickly, sliding to a stop as he reached his friends.

The icy snow was steep. Alex almost lost his balance as he tried to stand.

"Here, clip in," Tyler called. "Then you can get your crampons out."

Alex nodded and clipped into the anchor that Tyler had made. As Zoe pulled the rope down, Alex sat to snap his crampons onto his boots. "So, Tyler, where's this ridge you mentioned?"

Tyler gestured. "Down there, I think."

A spur of rock was barely visible in the blowing snow.

"Check the map?" Zoe suggested.

Another rock tumbled down, not far away.

Alex shook his head. "No time. We'll just have to feel our way."

They roped up. Even with their crampons, the steep incline felt slick and treacherous. The trembling beneath their feet made it difficult to keep their footing.

"We still have a couple snow anchors," Tyler suggested.

"Good plan." Alex unclipped his last snow anchor from his pack and pounded it in.

As soon as the rope was secured, Tyler moved cautiously down the slope. One by one the others followed.

While he waited, Alex cleaned the climbing nuts Tyler had used to build the anchor at the base of the cliff. The rock crumbled under his fingers.

As soon as the rope was stretched out to its full length, Tyler planted another snow anchor and clipped the rope in. Alex pulled his anchor out of the snow and followed. Tyler had done his best to kick some rough steps into the icy slope, but even so Alex stepped carefully. He didn't want to fall.

The spur of rock stretched out below them. As they approached, it did appear to be the start of a ridge, jutting out into the billowing clouds. Occasional patches of snow clung to the jagged rocks, a narrow spine with steep sides dropping into the grey-obscured depths below.

With their feet on rock once again, they paused to remove their crampons and shorten their rope. Behind them another rock fell, tumbled, and plunged into the unseen depths.

Tyler eyed the ridge of rock stretching before them. As it shook, small pebbles and stones slid off, falling into grey obscurity. "Will it be solid enough, do you think?"

Zoe gave him a sidelong glance. "Do we have any other options at this point?"

Tyler made a face. "No, not really."

"Then why ask?"

"Fair." Tyler pushed himself onto his feet. "Onward, then?"

Alex knew that they were pushing hard. By rights they should have taken a rest and eaten something, but he didn't want to stop where there was a risk of the ground crumbling beneath his feet, and he knew the others felt the same way. Better to press on now and rest once things were safer. The ridge was narrow, though never dangerously so, but the fierce, icy wind made every step a challenge.

After a while, their pace began to slow. The rock beneath their feet still trembled, but not as violently as before.

Out of the driving snow, dark rock loomed before them. Alex's heart sank. The mountain had a subpeak. It stretched up into the gloom as far as they could see. On either side, cliffs dropped off as steeply as ever. There was no way around it—they would have to climb the subpeak to get any further down the mountain.

"Damn," Tyler groaned. He sounded tired.

With nowhere else to go, they approached the pinnacle of rock, gathering in a cluster at its foot. When Tyler touched it, bits of rock flaked off in his hands. "This isn't stable, Alex. I don't think we can climb it."

Alex looked around. There was no other way down.

"Hey Alex." Jani gestured around the side of the rock. A deep gully stretched up as far as they could see. It was filled with ice, formed by snowmelt from the heights above. "Think we could climb it?"

Alex nodded. "Looks thick enough. In this cold it will be more solid than this rock seems to be."

"Then you're up, Alex," Tyler eased himself down onto a boulder. "Ice climbing is your gig."

"You good to belay me?"

"If you give me a minute."

Alex looked back the way they had come. Snow obscured any sight of the mountain summit behind them. The wind tore along the ridge, chilling him right through his down jacket. This was no place to stay for long.

"I can belay," Zoe offered.

Alex clipped his crampons back onto his boots and made sure that his ice screws and other equipment were clipped into his harness where he wanted them. Most mountaineers only took one axe for glacier travel. Alex was thankful he'd brought two.

When Zoe was ready, Alex tied in to the rope and Zoe checked the knot. She nodded. Alex draped the rope over his shoulder where it would be out of the way until he placed his first piece of protection.

He had to scramble around the rock to get to the ice. Scree slid out from beneath his feet, plunging down into the depths below.

Alex placed his axes on the ice. "Climbing?"

"Climb on," Zoe called.

Alex lifted his foot and kicked the point of his crampons into the ice. Putting his weight on them, Alex stood up and jammed the pick of an axe into the ice above his head. Making sure that his footing was secure, Alex unclipped an ice screw and twisted it into the ice. Pulling the rope off his shoulder, he clipped it into the carabiner. "On belay?"

"Belay on!"

Alex let out his breath. As long as he didn't let himself get too strung out, he wouldn't have to be worried about a big fall. "Climbing!"

He continued to climb. As soon as he was above his last screw, he placed another one. The ice creaked beneath him. Normally he'd relish the chance to lead a climb like this, but today he just hoped that the route wouldn't be too long. Gradually the ice thinned into mixed climbing. He set the blade of his axe gently on the rocks to avoid breaking off the ice.

A call from Zoe warned him that he was running out of rope. He looked up. Just a few more steps and the rock levelled out significantly. Even if it wasn't the top of the spur, it would be a good place for an anchor.

Alex stretched himself up and climbed slowly. Almost there ...

"That's it!" Zoe's voice echoed from far below. "Stop, Alex!"

So close. Alex reached as far as he could, his arms stretched over the rim of rock. That crack felt promising. Carefully he reached behind his back, unclipped a climbing nut, and brought it up over his head, feeling around to find the crack and slide the nut into place. A jerk on its tether showed it to be secure. He felt around for another crack, placing two more pieces of protection in the same way. Using long leashes, he finished building the anchor and clipped in.

"Secure!" he yelled down to Zoe.

"Off belay!" she called back. "What's the plan?"

"Give me a minute and I'll belay the next person from up here." Alex untied the rope from his harness, knotted the end, and fed it through his belay device. "Ready when you are!"

A couple of minutes later Tyler's voice called, "On belay?"

Alex tightened the rope. "Belay on!"

Tyler appeared around the corner, an axe in each hand. He scrambled across the rocks, then stared up the pillar of ice. "How's the climb?"

"Not bad," Alex called back. "Just take your time."

When Tyler reached the first ice screw he wedged himself securely, unclipped the rope from the screw's carabiner, and pulled the screw out of the ice. After clipping it to his harness, he continued climbing, stopping to do the same at every piece of protection. Now that the rope was anchored at the top, they were not needed anymore.

Alex continued to pull in the slack as Tyler approached. He was moving slower than Alex expected. "How's it going, Tyler?"

Tyler stopped to catch his breath. "It's fine, just putting more strain on my ankle than I expected."

"I guess that brace isn't rated for ice climbing, eh?"

"Yeah, probably not." Tyler's voice broke, betraying how much pain he was in.

Alex tightened the rope. "Sit back for a minute, Tyler. There's no rush."

"No rush?" Tyler glanced at the wind-driven snow streaming past the spur of rock.

"Better a minute now than an hour later."

"True." Tyler sank back into his harness and lifted his foot.

Alex shook his head. It was bad if Tyler was convinced that easily.

"You sure didn't skimp on the protection," Tyler commented, eyeing the number of pieces he still had to remove. He glanced down at the clouds blowing by far below. "I don't blame you though."

Tyler pulled himself closer to the ice and got his feet under him again. "Climbing."

"Climb on."

Alex breathed a sigh of relief when Tyler stepped beside him and scrambled over the ledge of rock.

"Secured," Tyler called a moment later.

"Good. Off belay." Alex stretched. "Could you pass me down those axes?"

"Sure." Tyler handed them down.

Deftly, Alex tied all four axes to the end of the rope, then lowered them down the ice.

"I've sent down the axes," he called to Zoe. "Now you should have enough down there for everyone."

"Alright. Who's next?" Zoe called back.

"Better send Jani up."

"You said that for me, didn't you?" Tyler asked from behind his head.

"Yup. And for Jani. You complaining?"

"... No."

A hiking pole appeared around the corner, hooked the end of the rope, and pulled it out of sight.

"On belay?" Jani called a few moments later.

"Belay on!" Alex replied.

"Climbing!"

"Climb on!"

Jani's climb went well, and soon she joined Tyler on the ledge above Alex.

"Ready for Jae!" Alex called down.

"Um, Alex?" Zoe called back, "You do realize that Jae has never ice climbed before."

Remembrance hit Alex like a ton of bricks. "Shoot. Right. Well there's a first time for everything."

"And his arm is hurting."

"Yeah, yeah I know. Just show him the ropes and give him a pep talk will you? I can coach him once he gets around the corner."

"You realize I am the worst person in the world for that job?"

"I believe in you, Zoe!"

Alex didn't have to see Zoe to feel her glare.

Several minutes later, Jae's voice called, "On belay?"

Alex pulled the rope tight. "Belay on!"

"Climbing?"

"Climb on!"

Slowly, Jae scrambled into view. When he reached the ice he stopped and looked back. Zoe's head popped around the corner. She gestured up the ice, but her words were lost to the wind before they reached Alex.

Jae nodded and started to climb. Alex kept the rope as tight as possible, but even so, Jae seemed quite anxious.

"I've got you!" Alex called down. "You won't slip."

"Yeah," Jae called back, "that's what Zoe said."

Alex could see that Jae was using his arm with extreme care. He looked up. "Hey Jani, mind lending a hand? With some extra weight behind me we could pull Jae most of the way up."

Tyler sat up. "Assisted dyno! Come on, Alex!"

Alex laughed. "No, Tyler. You're staying off your feet for as long as you can. Doctor's orders." He leaned down. "Alright, Jae! We're going to do our best to pull you up. Just kick your crampons in and help lift yourself up with your legs. You don't have to use your arm at all."

"Okay."

It took a while, but with Alex and Jani pulling together, Jae finally reached the top of the climb and scrambled up to join Tyler.

Zoe made quick work of the climb, and Alex followed her up onto the ledge where the others waited. It wasn't the top of the subpeak, but the ledge gave them a way to skirt it without having to climb any higher.

They roped up again. Although the snow-covered scramble looked easy enough, the consequence of a fall was too great. Everyone was tired after the climb. Alex could see it in their eyes, and they stumbled as they walked. It took a lot longer than Alex hoped before they finally circled the far side and saw the ridge stretching out below them once again.

After a little more scrambling they found an alcove, somewhat sheltered from the wind. Wordlessly they huddled together, pressed tight against the cold, bare rock.

Alex closed his eyes, exhaustion pulling at his limbs. They couldn't make it down like this. Already the grey light surrounding them was growing darker. If the storm didn't clear up they'd only have another hour or so of daylight. Maybe two if they were lucky.

Willing himself to keep going, Alex sat up and turned to Jae. "How's that arm doing? Sorry I never got a chance to look at it."

Jae rubbed his arm gingerly. "It's sore. Thankfully I can manage without it." He glanced at Tyler who sat with his head bowed over his knees.

Alex nodded. "Do you want it in a sling?"

Jae frowned. "I don't know. I think I'd be worried about falling and not being able to catch myself."

"Okay, but let me know once you do want it in a sling and I'll hook you up. Alright?"

Jae nodded.

Alex turned to Tyler. He didn't know what to say because he already knew the answer. "It's bad, isn't it?"

Jani nodded. Tyler didn't move.

"Tyler?"

The wind whistled past, whirling snow into their faces.

Alex shifted. "I hate suggesting this, but Doctor Nakano gave you pain medication, right? That might help get you off the mountain."

Jani looked at Alex with pain in her eyes. "He already took some. When you started climbing the ice."

Alex's heart sank. This was Tyler's pain level *with* meds. He glanced around the group. Discouragement and exhaustion were etched on every face. They needed something, but what could he do? A hot meal wouldn't work. Even though they were somewhat sheltered, the wind was still strong enough to wreak havoc with a stove. Wait ... there was that one pocket on his pack that he hadn't used in days, because it held his electronics and those had been no good to him. But it also held something else.

Alex reached into his pack and pulled out a small plastic bag. "Hey Tyler ... want some candy?"

Tyler turned to look at him, slow recognition spreading over his face. "Alex ... what ..." he blinked. "You raided my sock drawer!"

Alex jiggled the bag tantalizingly. "You want it?"

"Hey! Gimme that!" Tyler snatched the bag and yanked it open. "How'd you find it?"

Alex laughed. "Honestly, you were not nearly careful or clever enough."

"But it's all still here!"

"I completely forgot about it until this moment, to be honest."

"Good thing!" Tyler grinned, a tired but heartfelt grin. "Here, everyone, dig in!"

That was better. Zoe smiled and Jae laughed. Jani's eyes were sparkling again.

"Oh right." Zoe reached into her pack. "Here's your camera, Jae."

Alex looked at her in surprise.

"What?" Zoe turned the look right back at him. "Someone had to get a picture of his first ice climb."

"To be honest though," Jae mumbled through a mouth full of candy, "I was mostly pulled all the way up."

Alex patted him on the back. "It still counts. Next time come with us and we'll introduce you to ice climbing properly."

Tyler nodded at the camera in Jae's hands. "I'm glad you have that with you. If the door really is gone forever, at least we have pictures."

Alex nodded, then glanced down at his pack. If the door was gone forever ... could it be ...

He pulled out his SPOT. It turned on.

"Alex—" Zoe gasped.

Everyone else turned to look. With a trembling hand, Alex pushed the help button. The light started to flash.

"Wait," Tyler stammered, "does that mean—" he pulled the GPS out again. "It's working!"

Everyone scrambled to open their packs and pull out their electronics. The radios worked. Their watches worked. The headlamps worked.

Jae laughed. "I have never been so excited about a headlamp in all my life!"

Alex reached back into his pack to pull out his radio and felt a piece of paper. Pulling it out, he recognized it as the slip of paper Fredrik had given to him. He opened it.

"What's that?" Zoe asked.

"It's ... a list. Of names and numbers." His eyes widened. "It's contact information for the Agency. Look, there are phone numbers, even an address!"

"Where'd you get that from?"

"Fredrik gave it to me. I asked him how I could help ..."

Zoe raised an eyebrow. "And he wants you to bust the Agency?"

"Perfect." Jae grabbed the paper out of Alex's hand. "My dad is going to love this."

"Your dad?"

Jae carefully slipped the paper into a folder in his pack. "Didn't I ever tell you? My dad is an international lawyer."

Zoe blinked. "Well that explains a lot."

"What's that supposed to mean?" Jae sputtered.

"Will he take us on, do you think?" Alex asked quickly.

"Oh I *know* he'll take us on. Once I get him a copy of our pictures and the contract we were forced to sign, he's going to be on their case within the day."

Alex looked down at his SPOT. The light had stopped flashing. "It sent."

Jani's eyes lit up. "Does that mean help is coming?"

"Yes and no. Search and Rescue has been on the alert since Tuesday morning, I learned that much from Morani, but the weather was keeping them off the mountain." He stared out at the blowing snow. "I don't know if they will try risking it yet, but at least I've sent our coordinates to Mac now, and the SPOT is set to track us. As soon as SAR can get up the mountain, they'll know right where we are."

Tyler stared down from their alcove high on the spur. "This isn't a very accessible spot."

Alex gave him a sidelong glance. "It really isn't."

"If we get down the mountain as far as we can, SAR will get to us sooner."

"It's true. But Tyler, your ankle—"

"—Won't be bothering me too much if I die of exposure on the side of the mountain."

Alex shook his head, but he couldn't help laughing. "It's your call, Tyler."

"Oh, well then I'd definitely go for not dying on the mountain. Onward?"

Zoe nodded.

Jae cheered.

Jani leaned close to Tyler and whispered something in his ear. His face flushed.

Alex laughed.

As the others reassembled their packs, Alex turned his radio on to scan. Maybe it would catch a signal if SAR was already in the area. He strapped his headlamp to his helmet and put his watch back on his wrist.

Tyler shoved the GPS Alex's direction. "Look at this. If we follow the ridge down a little further, we should be able to drop down to that glacier and follow it out."

Alex nodded. "Glacier travel would be faster than scrambling across these rocks, as long as there aren't too many crevasses. Everyone up for that?"

There was general assent. Some scouting by Zoe showed the descent to be a class four scramble, so they didn't bother roping up.

The energy in the group was infectious as they made their way down toward the glacier. Alex was glad to see that when using both of his arms for the scramble, Tyler was able to keep his injured foot up without much trouble.

Before long, they reached the surface of the glacier. "Same marching order as before?" Alex asked as they roped up yet again. He was glad to have Tyler up front. As the injured party, he could set the pace. Tyler nodded and got out his hiking poles.

They set off at an eager pace, but were soon forced to slow down. The glacier was steep. For every step forward, Alex slid another two. As they moved away from the protection of the ridge, the wind picked up again, but the snow didn't sting quite as much as it had before.

On and on they trudged. They passed a couple of crevasses, giving them wide berths, and gradually the glacier eased into a gentler slope. Alex started to wish he had checked to see how far they still had to go, but Tyler had the GPS and Zoe had the map. He didn't want to shout up to them.

Snow continued to fall, but the wind had slowed to a normal sort of gusting flurry. They walked on, and the snow grew deeper.

After a while, Alex noticed that he was catching up to the others. Tyler had stopped, and as Alex drew closer he saw that his face was quite pale.

"It's acting up again," Tyler said, gesturing to his ankle. "I know we can't stop here, but I was thinking, if I wasn't breaking trail ..."

"Of course, Tyler," Alex reassured him, mentally kicking himself. "I should have thought of that."

Jani laid a hand on his arm. "We all should have thought of that."

"I'll go first," Alex offered. "If you come last we'll have a good path stamped out for you."

Tyler agreed, and they reversed their marching order.

It was a slog, breaking the trail. Alex had been managing to ignore his exhaustion for the most part, but it soon flooded over him again with even greater intensity. He couldn't stop now. Tyler had kept going for ages, and with a busted ankle. He'd take his fair turn before handing it off to someone else.

The grey light around them slowly faded as they tramped on and on. Alex put one foot in front of the other without thinking.

A small voice in the back of his mind told him he was too tired, that he wasn't paying attention, but he didn't have the strength to listen. Just keep moving. He had to make it down. If he just kept on—

The world dropped out from beneath him. He fell in a shower of snow and ice. With a jerk, the rope halted his tumble and slammed him into an icy wall. Darkness swam in his vision and pounded behind his eyes. Finally he oriented himself—the ice wall he clung to—the band of grey sky above him, rimmed by dark walls of ice. A crevasse.

Jae's head came into view. "You okay down there?"

"Yeah … I think so."

The head disappeared, then reappeared.

"You going to be able to climb out of there?"

"Give me a minute."

Alex leaned his head against the crevasse wall. His arms were shaking and his heart rate was way too fast. He tried to pull himself together, but he couldn't find any strength left to give.

"Actually … I don't think I can."

Jae disappeared, then reappeared. "We're going to pull you out. You ready?"

Alex nodded, then remembered to speak. "Yes."

Slowly the rope pulled him up. He did his best to walk up the wall and balance himself, but his legs didn't want to move.

The edge of the crevasse was within reach now. The rope pulled him closer, scraping his face against the ice. He should be able to pull himself up, but he couldn't. Someone grabbed him under the arms, dragged him up, over the edge, onto his hands and knees.

Alex sank down into the snow and rolled onto his side. Jae's face looked down at him. Strange. Jae didn't often look worried.

"He's secure!" someone yelled.

Zoe knelt over him. "Let's get you away from that edge." Her voice sounded far away, but Alex let her pull him to his feet and walk him away from the crevasse.

He tried to think clearly, but only managed to mumble, "We've got to get off the glacier."

Zoe sat him down and looked at him intently. "You've done a lot to take care of us. Now let us take care of you."

Alex nodded, just enough self-awareness left to know that he was not doing well.

"Shock?" someone asked behind him.

"Or just sheer exhaustion," Zoe's voice replied. "Either way, we can't camp for the night here. Is the water hot, Tyler?"

Zoe left Alex's field of vision. A little while later, someone removed his pack and a cup of hot chocolate was thrust into his hands. He was so tired, he just wanted to sleep, but someone made him drink it and his head started to clear.

Zoe sat beside him again. "You think you can walk for a while now?"

"Sure," Alex replied without really thinking. He could always walk a little further.

"Okay." Zoe helped him to his feet.

"Aren't we roping up?"

"We're at the edge of the glacier now. We're in for a scramble, but we shouldn't be too far from the tree line. If we make it there, we can hunker down and wait for SAR to find us."

Alex climbed, and Zoe stayed beside him. As his body got moving, his mind slowly caught up. After a while, the grade levelled out and they clambered their way across a snow-covered boulder field. Even with the light of their headlamps it was hard to find their footing.

"How's Tyler?" Alex asked after a while.

"He's doing alright." Zoe glanced over her shoulder. "A Jani under one arm and a Jae under the other."

In front of them, the ground stopped abruptly. Alex and Zoe stopped abruptly too. At their feet the ground dropped into a steep slope, curving away to either side of them like a large, snow-filled bowl. Alex felt his heart sink. It would be so far to walk all the way around and down. At the bottom Alex could see the shadowy forms of trees standing out against the lighter snow. They were almost there. A faint glow in the clouds overhead indicated the presence of the moon, even if it remained unseen. Snowflakes still drifted down, but the night air was calm and peaceful at last.

The harsh light of headlamps approached them from behind. Tyler gave a low whistle as he looked down the slope.

"We're almost there," Jani whispered.

They stared down at the long, smooth slope below them.

"That's snow pack," Tyler said after a while.

"Yup." Alex gave Tyler a sidelong glance.

"Looks run out at the bottom too."

"Yup."

Everyone looked at Alex. He sighed. "Okay, let's do it."

"Yes!" Tyler grinned.

"Do what?" Jae asked.

"This!" Tyler pulled a plastic bag out of his pack and sat on it. Gripping his axe in front of him, he pushed himself over the edge. With a whoop of delight he slid down the slope, disappearing in a spray of snow.

"Hey! Wait!" Jae shouted. "I should go first, so I can take pictures!"

He sat down and scooted after him.

Jani shook her head. "Trust you guys to get a glissade in whenever you can."

Alex gave her a tired smile. "Did you want to walk all the way around?"

"No, not really." Jani settled herself squarely on a plastic bag, gripped her axe, and started her slide. Alex watched the trail of snow streaming behind her.

Zoe gave Alex a sidelong glance. "Race you to the bottom."

Alex grinned. "You're on."

Without waiting to get out a bag, Zoe grabbed her axe and skidded down the slope.

"Hey!" Alex yelled and propelled himself off the edge. Wind rushed past him and snow pummelled his face. He gripped his axe tight as the bottom of the bowl rushed toward him, but it wasn't needed. Skidding to stop, he was engulfed in a heap of snow.

As he wiped the tingling flakes off his face, Zoe crawled out of the drift beside him, laughing harder than she had in days.

Alex struggled to his feet. "Who won?"

Jae cocked his head. "A photo finish, I'd say!"

A figure stepped out from the shadow of the trees. "How's the powder?"

Alex turned and his jaw dropped. "Mac! Of all people, am I glad to see you!"

Mac's broad face spread in a big grin and he engulfed Alex in a bear hug. "And I'm glad to see you! All present and accounted for?"

"Sure are. You know Tyler and Jani. This is my sister Zoe and our friend Jae."

"There was quite the stir in the SAR camp when we got your ping that you were taking the north route. Where'd you disappear to for so long?"

Alex glanced around at the others. "That is a really long story."

"Would it have something to do with the whole south-west corner of the mountain caving in?"

"It might. We'll tell you all about it, don't worry. But honestly right now we just want to get off the mountain and get some sleep. Oh and maybe have a shower."

More members of Search and Rescue emerged from the trees. Mac pulled out his radio. "I.C. this is Alpha One."

The radio crackled. "This is I.C. Go ahead, Alpha One."

"We found the whole party. Minor injuries. Walking them out. Over."

"Copy that, Alpha One. Glad to hear it. Bring them home."

"Alpha One out."

"Oh," Alex gestured to Mac, "there's also a group of about twenty people right in the area of the cave-in. They might be in a bit of trouble."

"Twenty?!" Mac stared. "What are so many people doing on this mountain?"

"That's a part of the long story. Some of them have handguns, so be careful."

Mac put a hand on Alex's shoulder. "We'll take care of this now, Alex."

Alex glanced around. Two members of the SAR team talked to Tyler about his ankle. Jani stood beside him, showing her ring to a member of the team that she knew from first year. Someone else was putting Jae's arm in a sling. They were in good hands now.

Mac followed his gaze. "You got them off the mountain. Well done." He nodded and walked away.

Alex let out a long breath. Zoe looked at him and they exchanged an understanding glance. For the first time in days, Alex felt a weight lift off his chest. They were safe. It didn't matter how long the walk out was going to be. They were on their way home.

Chapter 22

Alex wandered through his empty apartment. Five days had passed since they made it off the mountain; five busy days of phone calls and meetings that he found just as exhausting as the mountain had been. All the appropriate people had to be told about their experiences, everyone who had been worried about them had to be assured of their safety, and there were endless questions from the authorities and law enforcement officers. Finally, today, things seemed to be settling down.

He wasn't quite sure what to do with himself.

When they had returned to Monksford, Jani had gone straight home. Her family had been beside themselves since her disappearance, and she knew that they needed her. After some x-rays at the hospital, Tyler went to join her, and there was great excitement over their engagement. Alex hadn't seen much of them; they were busy getting ready for their trip to India that was coming up in just a few days. The apartment felt quiet and empty without them.

Zoe had decided to fly home to Ontario. The story of their dramatic rescue from the mountain was getting a lot of attention from the news, even if the details of what they had found on the mountain were being kept secret for the time being. The attention was more than she could take, and their parents were more than happy to have her home.

Alex had stayed in Monksford. His name was on the contract, after all, and he wanted to be at the apartment when the Agency turned up. He knew they would eventually.

He spent quite a bit of time with Jae and his dad, answering questions and offering his guesses on how the Agency might respond to the legal proceedings. Some high powers were not happy at all with what was going on, it seemed, and several levels of government were getting involved. Jae was having the time of his life offering exclusive interviews and dropping sensational photographs.

There was a knock on the door. Alex stopped his pacing. That was what he'd been waiting for. Briskly, he walked over to the door and opened it.

Morani stood outside.

Alex watched her for a moment. "I was expecting you at least two days ago."

She raised an eyebrow and waited for what else he might say.

Alex didn't oblige.

"May I?" Morani asked after a few moments of silence.

Alex nodded and stepped aside.

Morani strode into the living room. Alex shut the door behind her and followed. Her arm was in a sling, he noticed, but otherwise she did not look any different than when he had first met her in the corridors deep under the mountain. Within her poise she carried the dark mystery of that hidden place with her, spilling it out into the everyday world.

She scrutinized the room with a keen eye. Reaching over to the mantel, she turned off the video camera. A moment's pause, and she stepped over to the coffee table. Lifting a textbook, she uncovered the cell phone hidden beneath it, which Alex had set to record. She handed it back to him. "You are very prepared."

Alex stared at her intently and waited. A flicker of doubt crossed Morani's eyes and she looked around the room again. Walking over to the counter she picked up the voice recording pen Jae's dad had lent him. She gave Alex an incredulous look.

Alex shrugged. "To be honest, I didn't expect you to be by yourself."

This satisfied Morani and she nodded. "I am not the official delegation. That will be coming shortly: the head of the Agency himself, I hear, along with his lawyers. You've certainly made an impression."

"What do they want from me?"

"They want you to drop your charges."

Alex snorted. "Do they expect me to cooperate?"

"Probably not. I told them about you."

Alex gave Morani a shrewd glance. "Why are you here?"

"For answers."

"And you expect answers from me?"

"I do."

Morani's keen stare was fixed on him. She waited.

"Where is Batts?"

Morani gave a nod of approval. "Detained. As we were evacuating the vault, he was found to have departed from the site without authorization in an attempt to make contact with certain diplomats. Unfortunately for him, our helicopter arrived first. He was most displeased, but not as displeased as the board of directors was when they heard about it. He is facing serious repercussions." She thought for a moment. "Ironically, all they found in his pocket was a piece of common quartz. Strange, since type two vaults only collapse when their artifact is removed."

Her eyes rested on Alex, but he refused to flinch under their unspoken question.

"Can he hurt anyone?" Alex asked.

"No. He is currently detained and under guard. Ventura was very insistent on that."

"What will happen to him?"

"I do not know, but there are several powerful governments, including the government of Canada, that are very upset that he was selling secrets behind their backs. He will not be getting off lightly."

"Are we safe from him?"

"I am an expedition commander. I have no authority in the current proceedings. You will need to speak to the delegation about that."

Alex nodded.

Morani gave a small smile. "Sadly, Batts never got to see the masterpiece that was the collection of photographs Jae left with us. Out of curiosity, what have you done with the other ones?"

"A copy to our lawyer and a copy to the police. The originals are hidden. We have a set put aside to deliver to the Agency, as agreed."

"Good. Speaking of agreements," she pulled an envelope out of her pocket, "your wages, as agreed upon." She set the envelope on the coffee table.

Alex eyed it but did not pick it up. He gestured to a folder on the counter. "Do you want the pictures?"

"No. You will need them when the lawyers arrive. Make sure they fulfill all their contract obligations before you hand them over." She fixed her piercing gaze on Alex. "There is only one thing I want to see, and you do not have it in that envelope."

Alex returned Morani's stare. "I didn't take it."

"You want me to believe that?"

"It's the truth."

Morani held his gaze, as if her eyes could bore deep inside him.

Alex didn't flinch. "I would have been a fool to take it. Do you think Batts or anyone else would ever leave me alone if I had something like that in my possession? Life would have been hell."

"But you saw it?"

Alex gave Morani a cold stare. "Yes, I saw it."

"And you touched it?"

"No. I did not touch it."

"But it was within your reach?"

"Yes, it was."

"And when it lay before you, glimmering, you wanted to reach out to it." Morani watched him closely.

"It wanted me to reach out to it."

Morani raised an eyebrow.

"It's alive, you know. A living thing."

"And you know this …?" Morani's eyes glittered.

"Because of what I saw in the vault. The murals were very clear."

Morani looked at him thoughtfully. "You did have uncanny insights."

"I gained those on my own merit, and through my friends."

"And why did it speak to you?"

"Maybe because I didn't want it."

Silence hung in the air, and Alex refused to break it. Finally Morani was forced to speak.

"You didn't want it."

"I wanted my friends to live. You understand single-minded focus. Mine just had a different target than yours."

Morani continued to read him. This time Alex conceded. "You did see the murals, right? That vault wasn't made to protect the artifact from the world. It was made to protect the world from the artifact. Why would I want it?"

"You freely left behind something powerful enough to save all of humanity."

"Batts wasn't trying to save all of humanity."

"True. But you are not Batts."

"If it wasn't him, it would be someone else like him. Power doesn't fix humanity. It only amplifies what is already there."

"And you don't think you're a good enough person."

"I know I'm not a good enough person. I don't want to save the whole world."

"No one could turn down a prize like that."

"I left the mountain with a better prize."

"Alex, the type two vault collapsed. The artifact is gone. What did you do with it?"

"I told it to leave."

Morani stared. "What?"

"I told it that humanity would always try to misuse its power, and for the survival of humanity it needed to leave. Forever."

"And it did?"

"It disappeared. And the vault collapsed."

"But somehow you still managed to save your friends."

"We almost died."

"How did you get out?"

"We climbed, and we got very lucky."

Morani gave him a long, thoughtful stare. Had he convinced her? Alex wasn't sure, but she seemed to be ready to let it rest. For now.

Morani looked away. "You can tell Jani that everyone made it out. Knowing it was a type two vault, my crew was prepared for an evacuation. There were very few injuries."

After a moment of silence, Morani strode over to the window. "That contract of yours has caused a lot of trouble. Now the board is saying that all future expeditions must include a member of the legal team." She turned to look at Alex. "How is that for a legacy?"

"Sounds miserable."

An amused gleam flickered in Morani's eyes. "They know what I think of it. Thankfully, I have other options."

Something caught Morani's eye. Too late, Alex remembered the broken metal ring that he had carried with him off the mountain. Reaching up, Morani took it down from the place where Alex had set it, high on a shelf. She turned it over gently in her hands. "The last remaining piece of an ancient legacy." She spoke, as if to herself. "It is strange that so often it is only the broken piece that survives to tell the tale." She held it up to the light. "It was a beautiful door."

She knew, so Alex saw no point in denying it. He shrugged. "I used the other one to disarm the maze."

Morani nodded. "I wondered what you had used." She set the ring down on the counter with delicate precision. "You're good at what you do, Alex, and so are your friends."

"All I was trying to do was bring them home."

"And you did."

She gave him a long appraising look.

An unobtrusive beeping broke the silence. Morani glanced at the device on her wrist. "They are coming. I should go before they arrive." Her eyes met Alex's questioning glance. "Officially I am in our medical centre's sick bay, under strict orders not to leave. It would be a shame if I was found breaking orders, don't you think?"

She strode over to the door, then stopped and looked back. "They aren't dangerous. Just don't let them boss you around." A smile flicked across her face, as if she couldn't imagine Alex letting someone boss him around.

Alex nodded. "Thank you."

That seemed to surprise Morani. She stared at him with her piercing gaze until a thought occurred to her. "Ventura and Fredrik send their greetings. Fredrik leaves the Agency tomorrow for a new job opportunity. He seems to be very excited about it."

Alex smiled. "I am happy for him."

"As am I." Morani straightened. "Good afternoon, Alex."

Morani let herself out of the door and closed it behind her. Alex listened to her footsteps recede into the distance.

He shook himself. If a delegation from the Agency was on its way, he should get ready. Going back to the living room, Alex restarted his recording devices. He set up a couple of chairs and put the kettle on for tea.

His mind ran over his conversation with Morani. Was that all she had wanted to know? Probably not, but she had looked satisfied as she left. That was a concerning thought.

Alex picked up the metal ring. It hummed gently under his fingers, the same hum that he had felt in the vault itself. Had Morani felt it? Of course she had, but she hadn't said anything. Not yet, anyways.

Alex set the ring carefully back in its spot on the shelf. He had a feeling he hadn't seen the last of

Morani, sick bay or not. He picked up the envelope from the coffee table. There was money inside. He counted it: the full amount owed to him and his friends, plus some extra. He put the envelope in his pocket and looked down. Where the envelope had been there was a newspaper clipping. It told of a series of unexplained tremors in the Caucasus Mountains. Alex picked it up.

Underneath the clipping was an employment contract.

The doorbell rang. Alex quickly shoved the papers under a couch cushion where they joined the fragmented remains of Tyler's class syllabi.

Giving one last glance around the room, Alex went to the door. Apparently he had already made an impression. He might as well keep it up. Putting on his most stoic, unimpressed face, he opened the door.

"You're late."

Leane Winger is the wife of an avid mountaineer and has heard countless stories about the highs and lows of her husband's many mountaineering, rock climbing, and ice climbing trips. A lover of the great outdoors herself, Leane joins her husband on his adventures whenever she can, and together they share their love of nature and story with their two exuberant children who keep pestering their mom for "the next chapter of the story".

Leane is an author, poet, and playwright who is praised for her engaging and authentic writing. Learn more about her upcoming projects on her website: leanewinger.com.

Thank You

Along with the giver of story himself, there are so many to thank for the success of this book:

Thank you to Paul Kane, Janae Mercier, and David Song for lending their perspective and expertise.

Thank you to my patrons for their support and to Adria Baker, Vince Bennallack, Rachel Blenkin, Jacob Harada, and Julie Woloschuck for test-reading.

A huge thanks to Angela Winger, Charlotte Winger, and Caitlin Winger for being my first audience. Your encouragement meant so much to me.

And thank you to my wonderful husband, who answered countless "what would you do if..." questions. Your support and belief in me made this book possible.